VINDICATED

Also by M. G. Reyes
EMANCIPATED
INCRIMINATED

VINDI

CATED

M. G. REYES

KATHERINE TEGEN BOOKS
An Imprint of HarperCollins Publishers

Katherine Tegen Books is an imprint of HarperCollins Publishers.

Vindicated
Copyright © 2017 by Reynolds Applegate, Inc.
All rights reserved. Printed in the United States of America.
No part of this book may be used or reproduced in any manner
whatsoever without written permission except in the case of brief
quotations embodied in critical articles and reviews. For information address HarperCollins
Children's Books, a division of HarperCollins Publishers, 195 Broadway, New York, NY
10007.
www.epicreads.com

ISBN 978-0-06-228901-8

Typography by Carla Weise
17 18 19 20 21   PC/LSCH   10 9 8 7 6 5 4 3 2 1
❖
First Edition

For Junior,

who was there with us, all along.

GRACE

Grace was used to avoiding the eyes of the men in the state prison. She knew how to keep her gaze focused ahead, to ignore the open curiosity of the other condemned men.

Her father, Alex Vesper, had been a model prisoner for most of the past decade—mainly for the pleasure of seeing his daughter without a thick glass barrier between them. Her visits meant everything to him—she knew that.

To think I almost didn't come today.

At the table, her father's welcoming smile greeted her. He raised his cuffed hands in a gesture of solidarity, and she leaned in for a hug, pressing him close as he placed a gentle kiss on her cheek. Grace took a seat and smiled.

"Sweetheart," he said. He placed his hands on the table between them, palms facing up, the handcuffs scraping the tabletop. Grace brought her hands to rest on top of his. Her eyes brimmed with instant tears—they always did.

"Where's Cousin Alice? It's so good of her to give up her Fourth of July to come see me."

Alex Vesper always asked after his twenty-eight-year-old niece from San Francisco. Alice was Grace's only other relative within hundreds of miles. She accompanied Grace on her prison visits, but she always gave Grace and her father a little time alone before joining them.

"She's in the waiting area. She'll come visit with you after I'm gone, Dad." Grace held her breath for an instant. "I almost didn't come because I thought Alice was going to be busy."

Alex Vesper looked relieved. "Wow. Yeah, that's lucky. One day Alice is going to find herself a boyfriend, and I guess it'll be trickier then. On the other hand, if this execution date is the one that sticks . . ." He smiled weakly.

"Daddy," Grace said, squeezing his hands, "don't say that! You think I'm going to let you stay in here any longer?"

This seemed to make her father uncomfortable. He changed the subject. "You've got a ride back home?"

"Yeah, with my friend Paolo. I told you about him."

Her father's smile fell away. "The tennis coach? The one who screws around?"

Grace lowered her eyes, flustered. She'd been an idiot to tell her dad the gossip about Paolo. It had been in one of their earliest phone calls, back when she'd been trying very hard to persuade herself that Paolo was off-limits as a certified skeeze.

Now it was Grace's turn to change the subject. "Dad,

please, I need to talk to you about something serious. You're going to get out of here. I mean it. You were right—there was a witness that night at the party. Someone who may be able to prove you didn't kill Tyson Drew."

Grace told him about her housemate Lucy's decision to come forward, about her memory regression hypnotherapy and what she'd remembered seeing that night at the party in Hollywood; she told him about Lucy's attempt to talk to the police the day before.

When she'd finished, her dad simply stared, stunned into silence.

"Daddy? Are you okay?"

His eyes snapped back to hers. His voice was faint, his hands slack. "Uh . . . sure, honey. It's a lot to take in."

Grace risked a nervous smile. "But it's good news, isn't it?"

"Anything new is good. So your friend saw a *woman* holding Tyson under? Who could it be?"

"Well, Dana Alexander," Grace said. "Obviously."

He frowned. "Why 'obviously'? Dana Alexander is not the kind of person you'd ever imagine doing anything physical. She's not a big woman. Skinny, too. Back then, she was riding high from starring in that Macbeth movie. She was like a princess, royalty. On the Hollywood A-list right next to Meryl Streep."

"You can't think of any reason Dana Alexander might have wanted Tyson Drew dead?"

"Baby, I've had three appeals. If there'd been any hint of a case against anyone else . . ."

"But it was her!" Grace's voice grew loud enough to attract stares. She bowed her head, stared at the table as she and her dad linked hands again.

"Okay, honey, maybe there's something there. Maybe, I dunno, what if he was blackmailing her?"

"Why?"

"Who knows? She's rich, and she's famous. Blackmailers tend to prefer people like that."

She nodded hopefully. "So maybe Dana has a secret?"

"Maybe. But if she does, Drew took it with him to the grave. And nine years later, Dana is still smelling of roses, so it doesn't look like anyone else knows."

Grace took a deep breath. "All I'm telling you is what Lucy remembers seeing. A woman drowned Tyson Drew. And it looks like Dana Alexander has been stalking Lucy for *years*. What reason could she have *other* than keeping Lucy quiet?"

Alex Vesper held her gaze for a moment, searching his daughter's eyes. "You only just found out about this?"

Grace leaned forward. "I found out last week. Dana Alexander blackmailed one of the housemates," she said. "Do you remember Maya, my friend who makes apps for smartphones?"

Alex nodded.

"Well, Maya's mom works for Dana; she's her driver," Grace went on. "There's something wrong with her mom's immigration documents or something. Whatever it is, Dana has been holding it over Maya, forcing her to spy on us all in the house we share."

"Huh." He shifted in his chair. "That's a pretty rough gig for a teenager."

She looked in her dad's eyes to make sure he was following what she was saying. "Then Lucy realized that a friend—someone she's trusted for years—has probably been spying on her, too. And to top it all, Dana's been sending us threatening messages."

Her father leaned forward. It was clear he was paying close attention now. "What kind of messages? Honey, are you in danger?"

"Like, 'O judgment! thou art fled to brutish beasts,'" Grace quoted.

Vesper relaxed a little. "Doesn't sound all that blood-curdling."

"It's from the play *Julius Caesar.* And it's a kind of warning that we've lost our minds; we're making terrible mistakes and now we're gonna pay," Grace explained. "The point is—it's Shakespeare. And you can imagine how obsessed Dana Alexander is with Shakespeare, since his play made her a star."

"I see." He leaned back in his chair. With his left hand, Vesper began to rake his fingertips through the short whiskers of his beard. "Grace, I gotta say, I did not expect any of this. I was mentally preparing for, well, more of a good-bye visit."

Tears clouded Grace's vision. "A good-bye visit?"

He shrugged and tried to smile. "Well, y'know. They've set the date. . . ."

"Daddy!" The tears rolled down her face. "I asked you not to talk like that!"

Then she was crying and he was comforting her, and the other condemned prisoners were nodding seriously to each other and agreeing with the prison guards: it was a shame when a father with young kids was booked in for an execution; it really got you in the heart.

JOHN-MICHAEL
PARKING LOT, SAN QUENTIN STATE PRISON, SATURDAY, JULY 4

"Okay if I smoke?" asked John-Michael, his lips clenched around an unlit cigarette.

Maya didn't react. It wasn't clear she'd heard him—she was miles away. Probably thinking about last night, he guessed. His own thoughts hadn't strayed too far from it, either. It wasn't every day a hit man walked into your home, tried to kill your friend, took a blow to the head, and ended up having a convulsive fit. So the guy was dead—he had no one to blame but himself.

John-Michael fervently wished he'd been able to persuade the would-be assassin to let them call an ambulance before he'd started having convulsions, shooting off his revolver at random.

What a night; what a mess you could get into when fear and panic took over. John-Michael had tried to do the right thing. But in the end, he'd suffocated the man under a sofa cushion rather than risk his friends' lives.

His friends—they'd been a godsend to him. Since his dad had died, John-Michael had been on his own—and before that, he'd been living on the street. Then he'd heard about this house where a bunch of kids who'd been emancipated were living on their own—a place on Venice Beach. It was perfect. He'd met Paolo, brought in his own friend, Lucy, then met Grace, Candace, and Maya. In just a few months, the six had become like a family.

And just like a real family, each had their secrets. Grace's dad was on death row for a crime he hadn't committed. As a young girl, Lucy had witnessed the crime, but hadn't remembered who the killer was. Paolo had gotten pulled into a scheme to scam a rich kid out of his car. And Maya? She'd been blackmailed into spying on everyone in the house. Candace—well, she was the only one without a secret.

John-Michael's secret was the biggest of all. He'd assisted his dad's suicide. And now he'd committed another crime. Well, *crimes*, plural.

All John-Michael wanted was to be calm, organized, thoughtful. Like Maya.

He lit the cigarette with the car's lighter and took a drag—the first he'd had in days. "Okay, what now?" he asked Maya.

When Grace and Paolo had suddenly taken off after breakfast without letting anyone know, Maya and John-Michael had jumped into Candace's Prius to find them. John-Michael had guessed that San Quentin State Prison was their destination. Last time he'd driven her there, Grace had applied to visit her father on July fourth.

They managed to follow Paolo and Grace all the way to San Quentin without being noticed. Now Paolo's Chevy Malibu was parked two cars ahead of them. It was empty.

"So what now?" John-Michael said.

"Wait for Grace and Paolo, make sure they don't go anywhere but the prison," Maya replied.

"You think she's gonna tell her daddy what went down yesterday?"

"Yeah, I do." Maya ran one hand through her sleek, mahogany hair. "Maybe it's a good thing," she said slowly. "Maybe her dad can help with an escape plan."

"Escape? From who—Dana Alexander's people?"

"From the police, John-Michael. From the law."

John-Michael sucked on his cigarette. He had put that idea at the back of his mind. The law was a much lesser threat than Dana Alexander's goons, who might try again to kill Lucy—and possibly the rest of them, too. They'd gotten rid of the first two assassins—would that buy some time? It might take a little while for Alexander to find out what had happened to them. But she certainly would.

Then Maya spoke up again. "Taking that bag of money was a mistake."

"Huh. Don't recall you objecting at the time."

Maya took the cigarette from between his fingers. "You don't? Pretty sure I did."

"Maybe. A lot of things happened last night." He leaned

back, watching as she clumsily placed the cigarette between her lips. When she choked on the first lungful, he reached over, took the cigarette from her mouth. "It only reduces stress if you're used to it. Better you don't start."

"I could use a stress-reducer," she said, but with such calm assurance that John-Michael found himself scrutinizing her.

"You don't *seem* stressed."

Maya coughed twice. Her eyes began to water. "Not everyone goes bat-shit crazy. Some of us like to think things over."

"Maybe it's better if you don't," John-Michael suggested.

Things had a way of coming back to you whether you thought about them or not, but Maya didn't need to know that. Not yet. She didn't need to know that after the initial memory faded, doubts and uncertainties would build up until you were totally confused.

There was a very long silence. He could see Maya glancing at him, a sidelong look she probably hoped he wouldn't notice.

"Did you kill your father?" Maya asked, bluntly. When he didn't answer right away, she said, "I'm not judging, John-Michael. I just need to know. How deep is all this going to go if it starts to fall apart?"

He placed an elbow on the open window and tapped off the cigarette's ash. "Oh, if things start to fall apart, I'm going to have a lot of problems. And not just me."

She blinked. "Who else? Lucy? Paolo?"

John-Michael nodded, a little reluctantly. He hadn't intended to betray Paolo's secret. As far as he knew, he was the only housemate who had any clue about Paolo's affair with Meredith Eriksson, or that he'd been with the woman when a hit-and-run driver had killed her in Malibu Canyon.

"Paolo and Lucy are the only ones who really know for sure what happened to the first hit man," Maya mused. "To Mr. Shooter. What if it wasn't really self-defense?"

"You mean, what if it was intentional?" John-Michael shook his head. "Paolo didn't have any other reason to kill that guy."

"That's your opinion; it's not proof. If the cops come calling, they'll ask. We won't be able to say for sure what happened before we got home."

"You think they embellished?"

"When they told us what happened?" she asked impatiently.

"Yeah—Lucy and Paolo—you think they made stuff up about the guy who came looking for Lucy, stuff that maybe didn't happen exactly the way they said?"

"I know what 'embellished' means," Maya said sharply. "Look, I'm just asking you to consider another theory. They had time to make something up."

"No—before you talk to the cops, believe me, you need to spend a lot of time constructing a watertight story." John-Michael was beginning to lose his patience, too. "I don't think they're lying. That would be insane." He shook his head again and then carefully mashed the cigarette stub against the edge of the window.

But Maya wasn't done. "Don't you find it interesting that Paolo came up with that plan to make it look like the hit man was the victim of a hit-and-run?"

John-Michael swallowed. This was getting uncomfortably close to something he could never reveal—the fact that he knew exactly what had inspired Paolo's idea for how to dispose of the first hit man's body. "No," he lied. "He had time to come up with something before we got home."

"Paolo had time," she agreed. "But why would he even try, if it really was self-defense?"

"What's your point?" he asked, a little too aggressively.

"Oh, you know. . . ." Maya drifted off.

John-Michael couldn't bear to let her wander off on this line of thought. He had to know—was Maya going to cause trouble for Paolo? "No, I *don't* know. What?"

"Just, who knows?" Maya shrugged. "Maybe Paolo has seen a hit-and-run before? Maybe he actually *did* one?"

"Maybe he saw it on TV?" John-Michael said, exasperated. "Who knows where he got the idea?"

"If he saw it on TV, he'd have said so. Like, 'Oh, I saw it on *Law and Order*.' But if he was actually involved, then he'd never tell. Maybe that's what Paolo is hiding? If the cops start to ask questions, it could come out. Which would explain why he seems so nervous."

The fact that Maya had almost nailed Paolo's secret on

her second guess was so unnerving that John-Michael lit another cigarette. He was desperate to distract her. "You think he's nervous?" he asked, trying to sound casual.

Maya looked at him. "Everyone's kind of jittery these past two days."

"Except you."

"Trust me; I'm mostly jitter." Maya leaned across and tried to take the cigarette from him. "Let me have another try."

John-Michael held the burning cigarette out of her reach. "Forget it. I've already implicated you in criminal activity. Don't make me guilty of lung cancer thirty years down the line."

Maya withdrew her hand, which shook slightly, he noticed. "People drink booze when they feel like this, don't they? Or they smoke pot. Do you have any pot?"

Smoke erupted from his mouth when he laughed. "Yeah—I brought weed to smoke in a prison parking lot. Listen, I know you're coming up with a plan of action somewhere in that beautiful brain o' yours. How about you clue me in?"

"I'm still thinking. There's a lot to consider. And we're going to need an endgame strategy."

"Endgame?" John-Michael asked, raising an eyebrow.

"Like in chess."

"You mean like 'sacrifice the queen'?"

"Something like that." Sighing, she folded her arms across her chest. "There may be something we can do.

It's not fully formed. I'm still moving things around in my head."

"You make it sound like something neat and tidy, like one of your computer projects. But life gets messy."

Maya shook her head skeptically. "We'll see."

John-Michael bit his lip. Real life never worked out in such a predictable fashion, not in his experience. If his father had organized a tidy suicide in a Swiss clinic or something, things would have been much simpler. After his dad had thrown him out, there wasn't much love left between them.

There were things that you could count on from your family—at least that's what his dad claimed. Yet when it came to actually helping Chuck Weller to die, it hadn't been easy. He'd agreed to supply the heroin, but watching his father prepare his arm for the syringe, John-Michael had second thoughts. When his father had started choking on his own vomit, the poor man had begged so pathetically to end it.

That's what had moved John-Michael to finish him off. It wasn't a rational decision made in the cold light of day. It was pity. Pity had moved John-Michael to kill his father—not hate or resentment: *pity*. Who knew that violence could result from an uncontrolled surge of compassion?

There was no logic to how you felt in the heat of the moment. Feelings were unreliable. Better to let go of them, to drift away, like a balloon slipping through a child's fingers—tied up one minute and then gone. *Free*.

John-Michael smiled bitterly at the mental image.

Because nothing could be further from the truth.

Parents could give you the illusion of freedom. They protected you from the worst consequences of mistakes. But emancipation? Every duty of the law-abiding citizen weighed directly on you.

It kind of sucked.

GRACE
SAN QUENTIN STATE PRISON, SATURDAY, JULY 4

After Grace's outburst of grief, one of the guards brought her a plastic cup of hot cocoa from the vending machine. She cradled it in both hands, blowing across the top to cool the frothy liquid. When she was feeling calm again, she continued.

"Dad, there's more. Something happened last night, something bad." She described how she and Candace had returned to the empty house in Venice to find the rug missing, the blood, and her housemates gone out, their phones left behind. They hadn't returned for hours, and when they had, they were obviously shaken. They'd insisted everyone leave the house immediately.

"I see," he repeated. He sat up a little straighter.

"Dad," Grace said, her voice low. "What are you thinking?"

"Your friends may have gotten into something heavy," he said pensively. "My guess is that it was someone sent by Dana Alexander—probably to deliver a message. The blood suggests things got out of hand. There was probably more of it on the rug. But none of your friends got hurt, right?"

Grace pressed her lips together, hard. She'd noticed John-Michael wincing now and then since, as though he were in pain. He limped a little, too. Her guess was that he *had* been hurt. None of the others were willing to talk about their mysterious evening, however, so she couldn't be certain.

"I'm not sure," she said, hedging.

"You'd notice if one of them got a serious wound, right?"

Timidly she said, "There wasn't a lot of blood."

"Not after they cleaned it up, maybe. That they left any at all makes me think that yeah, there *was* a lot of blood."

"Oh," she murmured. "Candace and I didn't think about that."

"Your housemates don't seem like violent types, so it probably means that whoever spilled blood in your house is still out there. Biding their time, probably." Vesper paused briefly, and then covered his mouth with one hand.

Grace tried to resist the impulse to glance at the security camera he was avoiding, but her eyes skipped over it quickly.

"That'd account for the jumpiness. Unless I'm wrong," her dad went on, speaking beneath his palm. "If they actually *killed* whoever came a-callin', well, that could be even more dangerous. Because people in that line of business tend to be connected."

Grace gasped. She hadn't really thought about that

possibility, but now that she did, it seemed so obvious. The rug had been removed. The bloodstain on the floor. Could her friends have *killed* someone?

"Grace, sweetie, listen very carefully. All things considered, I'd prefer it if you had some security right now."

"Security . . . ? But nobody knows where we are," Grace said. "One of Maya's investors lent us her house in Napa. We're staying there for a few days. Just until we figure things out . . ." Her voice trailed off.

Vesper nodded grimly. "I know guys who track people down for a living. You would not want to get on the wrong side of someone like that. No; if Alexander's got a beef with Lucy or with any of the rest of you, and blood has already been spilled, then it's pretty obvious to me. You need a bodyguard. Do you have a pen and paper?"

Dazed, Grace shook her head.

"That's okay, honey. I'm going to ask you to memorize a telephone number," her dad continued. "There's a man named Peter Martens. He's white, around forty-five years old, short brown hair that's mostly turned gray, no beard, eyes gray, narrow, like almonds. The password he'll use to identify himself will be 'Kingfisher.' Now, Grace, repeat that back to me."

In a shaky voice, Grace did as he asked. They spent the next few minutes testing her memory of the phone number.

"Pete is a good friend," Vesper told her. His manner had changed. Once he'd started to give instructions, he sat taller, his eyes filled with intense concern. "He'll take care of you."

"Is . . . is he someone you know from here?"

"Pete did five years for manslaughter," her dad replied. He said it as though it were nothing.

"Oh . . . okay," Grace said, setting down the half-empty cup. She wasn't sure how to feel about this. Her dad was in prison, but wrongfully. Could she really trust a person who'd killed someone to protect her?

"He's former armed services, Grace. It can be difficult for those guys to adjust to civilian life. One minute they're in an environment where you shoot your enemies. The next, they're expected to deal with trash talk, petty violence, all without blinking an eye." Her father shrugged. "Sometimes they misjudge the situation, overreact. But I know Pete Martens; I trust him. With my own kid's life. With *your* life," he said, taking her hands in his.

"Thanks, Daddy," Grace said quietly. She had no clue how she was going to broach this subject with her housemates. Her stepsister, Candace, was in denial about just how serious the situation was.

Now that Grace was seeing things more clearly, she wondered if she should call ahead to warn Candace. Then she remembered they'd agreed not to use their usual phones to make calls, and she'd left her burner phone at the house.

"When should I call him?" Grace asked.

"Right away. Find a public phone. Call that number.

It's his cell. Now, I don't know where he's at right now, so it might take him a day or so to get back to you. But he will, you can count on that. If Pete doesn't answer, don't leave a message; keep trying, but always from a public phone. You got that, sweetheart?"

"Okay, Dad. Thank you," Grace mumbled.

"Now," he announced, folding his arms. "I want to hear more about this boy you seem to like so much."

"Paolo?" Grace said, laughing uncertainly.

"Mmm." He nodded, gravely. There was a glint of severity in his eyes. "How was it you described him: a *ladies' man*? Yeah, that's what you said. Well. He's not the guy for you."

"I don't know what it is about him," she confessed. "But Dad, I really, really like him."

"Oh, I believe you," he said. "I see it here all the time. You wouldn't believe some of the women these guys have waiting for them back home. A lot of them are as sweet and honest as the day is long. You can see it in their eyes when they visit. *Shame.* That's how you look when you visit me, baby. Ashamed." Her dad paused and looked her right in the eye. "Sweetie, it's bad enough you've had to feel ashamed of me. God forbid you should end up with a boy who makes you feel that way about him. I want you to be with a *good* guy. A decent guy, a law-abiding type."

Grace felt her lips tremble. She wanted to deny that she felt any shame at visiting her father in prison, but she couldn't.

Vesper watched for a moment, impassive, and then nod-ded. "That's okay, baby. I've gotten used to it. It's shaming, to be in here. That's the part that's hardest to take."

"But you're not guilty," she whispered, unable to look at him.

Her father's shrug barely reached his shoulders. "We'll see."

PAOLO
NOVATO, SATURDAY, JULY 4

Grace was the first to spot them. "What the hell . . . is that Candace's car following us?"

Paolo checked his rearview mirror, flushing with embarrassment that he hadn't noticed. Grace was right—Candace's car was two cars behind them. He couldn't quite read the license plate, but he recognized a red parking sticker from Hearst Academy, the school the Deering sisters attended.

"You want me to pull over? It's kind of dumb to just let them follow us."

"I can't believe they did this," Grace fumed. "What business of theirs is it if I go visit my father?"

Paolo didn't respond—he didn't want to make Grace angry. But he'd wondered if it was wise to visit Grace's dad, given that they were supposed to be in hiding. Only when Grace had mentioned that she'd booked the visit long ago did he realize that it might be better not to change any long-standing plans, in case people got suspicious.

He slowed his car to a crawl. Behind them, frustrated drivers began to sound their car horns, so he pulled over. Behind them, the car pulled over, too.

Grace opened her door. "Let's go." She sounded furious.

Maya opened the Prius's passenger door. She and John-Michael stepped out of the Prius and waited, leaning against the side of the car.

"Following us? Guess you're still spying, right, Maya?" Grace spat. "And you've dragged John-Michael along, too. Find out anything interesting?"

"Grace," began Paolo, touching her hand gently. But Grace shook him off. "Were you in on this, JM?"

"No, he wasn't—it was my idea," Maya said. "I needed John-Michael to drive since I don't have my license. Grace, I'm sorry. But we can't risk not knowing where you're at." She looked at Paolo. "Did you talk about last night?"

"I said I wouldn't, and I haven't," Paolo said hotly.

Grace was unmoved. "Maya, please, you need to calm down. I wanted to talk to my dad because if *you're* in trouble with the police, then I do *not* know anyone who could help us."

"So you *did* say something to Grace?" Maya said to Paolo. A tiny inclination of her head was the only sign of her mounting anger.

"When?" he replied. "Up till now, I haven't been alone with Grace since we got to Napa."

John-Michael opened his mouth to reply, but Grace cut him off. "Hey—give me some credit, Maya. It's not all that difficult to put together a scenario. A scenario where maybe Dana Alexander sent someone with a message for Lucy? And you guys got into a fight?"

There was a long pause during which the only sound came from the steady stream of cars passing them.

"My dad thinks you hurt someone. Is he right? Tell me!" Grace insisted.

Again, silence.

"Now you're afraid Alexander will send the cops to visit. That's why we had to leave Venice Beach. *Isn't it?*" Grace demanded.

Paolo and John-Michael looked at Maya, waiting.

"It's not a million miles from that," Paolo admitted.

"My dad wants to help," Grace said. "In fact, he insists. He gave me the number of a bodyguard–Peter Martens."

A look of sudden understanding spread across Maya's features. "You made a call when you guys stopped at that Wendy's?"

"Shoulda told us you were following," Grace said sourly. "No reason you had to drive back hungry."

"Maybe we should get back in the cars and all go some-place where we can talk?" Paolo said. He threw a nervous look in the direction of the road. His hands hovered an inch from Grace's arms and waist, as if he wanted to touch her for reassurance.

Maya ignored him. "Grace, did you call this Martens guy?"

Grace sucked in her lower lip. "It's safe, talking to him.

My dad got him to use a password and everything."

"Is someone coming to the house?" There was a definite edge to her question, and it ended with pure steel. "Is one of your father's *prison* friends coming to Alexa Nyborg's *house*?"

Paolo shuffled anxiously, his fingers searching for Grace's. "Hey, girls, c'mon . . ."

Grace withdrew her hand from his touch. She allowed a supermarket truck to pass them before answering Maya's question. "I called, but Martens didn't pick up. Dad said he might not right away."

"Did you leave a message?"

"Maya, I'm not an idiot."

"So no one is coming to the house?" Maya asked again.

"No—I already said that."

Maya shook her head. "You *said* you hadn't talked to Martens—yet."

Grace went back on the offensive. "Look, my dad thinks you've done something to get us into trouble. I don't hear anyone denying it." She waited for two seconds, eyeing John-Michael and Paolo. "My dad's doing what he can to keep us safe. I thought you'd be grateful."

"Paolo's right. We need to get back in the cars and talk about this at the house," John-Michael said.

Paolo took Grace's hand. "Exactly." He walked her back to his car, and then made a quick excuse and ran back to the Prius.

Maya and John-Michael were taking their seats when

Paolo caught up. Stonily, they glared at him.

"Look," Paolo explained. "I'm sorry. Okay? Grace needed me. I won't let her do those prison visits alone."

"You understand that this changes everything?" Maya said indignantly. "We're gonna have to find somewhere to hide the cash."

"Maya's right," John-Michael said. "I don't think whoever Grace's father sends can be trusted."

"To protect us? He's probably fine. To not take the money? Who knows? It's not like Grace could tell her dad about that," Paolo agreed.

John-Michael nodded slowly, his eyes on the road. "It's a lot of money. We could just share it with him."

"Assuming he wants to share. I'm guessing he has a gun. Which makes sharing anything with us pretty optional."

"What were you planning to do with the cash, anyhow?" John-Michael's tone was flat.

"You really have changed your tune," Maya told him. "I said from the beginning that we should have left that cash where we found it. But now that we've got it, it's our only bargaining chip. We can't afford to let it go."

Paolo glanced over his shoulder. "Look, guys, I'd better get back to Gracie."

"Whatever," said John-Michael. His hand went to his top pocket, fingers seeking out a cigarette, but Maya snatched his lighter from his hand.

"Just go," she told Paolo fiercely.

He turned and walked back, shaking his head. This

was tearing him apart, keeping so many secrets from Grace. She deserved better, someone honest.

Maybe it was smarter not to even start anything with her. They hadn't really done anything yet, anyhow. They hadn't even kissed.

But he wanted to. He wanted it really, really badly. And he could tell that Grace wanted it, too. It was in the regretful tilt of her head every time she looked away when he caught her gazing at him.

It was bound to happen naturally once they had some quality alone time. Paolo wondered if he could avoid being alone with her.

He doubted it. It went against every impulse in his body.

LUCY

After Lucy had completed a brief stroll around the guesthouse—known as the *casita*—and the pool, she returned to the kitchen. Maya, John-Michael, and Paolo were back from their trip to San Quentin and more food shopping. Now Maya and JM were getting ready to bake.

Squint, and another person could pretend this was a vacation. Just a regular July fourth. But not Lucy.

"Candace is showing Grace around the estate," John-Michael said. "I'm guessing we have ten minutes before they get back."

"We should start by deciding what to do about the money," Lucy said, with more conviction than she felt.

Maya was working her way through a heap of shiny green apples with a peeler. "I stashed the duffel bag in the bedroom cupboard, behind some spare pillows," she said, not looking up.

Lucy snorted. "Well, I guess at least our *half a mil in cash* is secure."

Maya looked up. The peeler stuck up from her tight fist like a dagger. "There's really nowhere else."

"At least whoever comes looking for it won't have to torture any of us to give up the location," Lucy said derisively.

The other three laughed uneasily. They sounded as worried about that possibility as Lucy felt. As crazy as it sounded, they couldn't rule out something like that. Things had gone from bad to incomprehensibly worse last night in Malibu Canyon. Who was to say it wouldn't happen again?

If she hadn't been so scared, Lucy would have had a lot more to say. But she didn't dare let her friends suspect how angry and resentful she was. If one person in the group turned on the others, the whole scene might fall apart. And then what? Last night at the beach house, she'd seen how a disagreement could spiral out of control.

If walking away from any of this was a realistic option, Lucy would have taken it. But it was too late now. Everything and everyone were all tangled up. People's business all up in her face, and no obvious way to extricate herself.

Paolo tried to diffuse the situation. "How much longer do you think we can keep Grace and Candace out of the loop?"

"Until I get a chance to talk to the cops," Lucy replied. Going to the police station in Venice hadn't been easy. She didn't relish another visit, this time to a completely different precinct, where they'd want to go through the basics all over again. What if she found herself confessing everything—telling the cops what had happened last night?

"Well," Paolo said brusquely. "You'd better step up. Grace needs your help."

His tone bummed Lucy out. "You're not the one who has to be interviewed by cops."

"I know, hon." Paolo gave her an uneasy grin. "Didn't mean to sound like a jerk. You should be totally straight with us if you're feeling bad."

"It's too soon to process everything," Lucy said.

Maya shrugged. "Not everyone takes nine years to process their reactions to violence, Lucy."

Lucy had to stop herself from shredding the younger girl right there and then. But the silence from John-Michael and Paolo stalled her.

"You're seriously gonna put this on me?" Even as Lucy said the words, she realized she felt the same way Maya did. None of this would have happened if she'd confronted that dark memory of the Hollywood party years ago. Instead, she'd *refused* to think about it, buried the memory as deep as it would go.

"No one's putting this on you, Luce," Paolo said mildly. "You're the only one of us who didn't want to go up to Malibu Canyon to get rid of a corpse. You're the one who wanted to bring the cops in from the beginning."

Lucy turned away so that her friends wouldn't see the mounting desperation in her eyes. What Paolo said was true. But in the end, so what? If she'd spoken up earlier, none of it would have happened.

She took a breath. "What are we going to say? Not to Grace and Candace, but to the cops?"

"How's this," suggested Maya. "We went to watch the sunset on a beach—El Matador. We took the rug from the house to have something to sit on. It got damaged by a barbecue fire, so we threw it out."

"Works for me," Paolo said.

"What did we do there, what did we talk about?" demanded Lucy. "They're going to want some evidence that went up there."

"If anyone asks, we say that Maya explained her new app to us," John-Michael replied. "And if we don't remember details, we'll just be all like '*jeez, dude, it was all so techie, I can hardly remember.*'"

"They might buy that," agreed Paolo. "It's probably time you actually *did* explain Promisr to us. What's so great that Alexa Nyborg wants to be your buddy?"

While Maya talked, Lucy's thoughts drifted. Her former friend Ariana had told Dana Alexander that Lucy was ready to go the cops. Ariana was a spy for Dana, and Lucy had allowed her into their lives. Part of what had happened was on her.

Grace and Candace were returning to the house. The sound of their laughter pulled Lucy out her reverie.

"Maya's telling us all about Promisr," John-Michael said as they walked in. He offered Candace a platter of sliced bell peppers, carrots, radishes, and cucumber. She took a handful and began to nibble on a radish.

"Good! 'Cause I didn't understand a thing you said about it so far," Candace replied.

"Well, you know how hard it is to get anything done, right? Like, a project, but not something you really want to do. Something you have to do, like schoolwork or a diet or whatever," Maya said.

Listening closely, Lucy took a handful of raw veggies. "So, Promisr is a way to tag friends and other people to help you do difficult stuff."

"Why would anyone agree to be tagged?" asked Candace.

"It's like, you scratch my back, I scratch yours. You learn Spanish, I bake you a pie. Now I've racked up some credit. I cash in that credit against another, future promise."

"Sounds truly dumb," pronounced Candace dismissively. "If I don't learn my lines, I lose my job. That's all the motivation I need."

Normally, Maya would have snapped back at Candace. But the remark just seemed to roll right off her, like Maya was Teflon-coated.

This post–Malibu Canyon Maya was going to take some getting used to.

"This whole industry is run on optimism," Maya admitted.

Lucy sniffed. "I could use some of that." There were

expectant looks from the housemates at this, but not from Maya.

Optimism, yeah, right. Maybe if we all just stop thinking about Malibu Canyon, we can just wish the whole thing away.

MAYA

Maya was the first one up the next morning, still on a code-lagged sleep schedule. She dressed quickly and headed out for a hike. It'd be good to be by herself for a while, away from the unspoken tension simmering between her friends.

She had experienced worse July fourths, but never in a place as beautiful as Flor de Canela, Alexa Nyborg's home-away-from-home in the Napa Valley. Even the guesthouse where they were staying, the *casita*, was more luxurious than their place in Venice, and the beach house in Venice was *great*.

At first, the housemates had tried to act like normal rich kids enjoying their parents' luxury home: putting just the right music on the poolside sound system, pretending to know which of the wines that Nyborg had thoughtfully left in the fridge went best with the food John-Michael had prepared. They'd eaten zingy ceviche made from delicate tilapia, followed by grilled chicken and snapper fillets with crunchy salads.

But what Candace referred to as the "Secret Thing" was ruining everything. The four who'd been in Malibu Canyon needed to talk about what happened there, which they couldn't do—not with Candace and Grace around. By the time they'd moved on to dessert, they'd given up.

Now all Maya wanted to do was to take a look at the main house. She'd caught glimpses through the windows. It was magnificent: arched ceilings of white adobe, as pristine as a monastery, heavy oak floors polished to a hard sheen. The furniture was mission-style, and the walls and mantels were decorated with *artesanía* that could have come straight from a Mexican market.

Maya's grandmother had probably worked in a house like this. She remembered stories of the grand house in Mexico City's Polanco district, where Abuelita had worked as a cook—and where Maya's mother had been raised, sharing a tiny room in the basement with her own mother. A house where even the regular main meal consisted of five courses—soup, salad, fish, meat, and dessert.

Maya's mother had told her stories about that house, noting proudly how much better she'd been able to provide for her own daughter. The house in Polanco didn't exist anymore. It had been turned to rubble, making way for Mexico City's ring road. Maya's mom spoke with pride that she'd lived in such a place. It didn't seem to rankle that her mother had been a servant there.

Maya peered into the kitchen of Nyborg's home, looking for the telltale door leading to the basement. Did it lead to tiny, bare quarters that a maid would share with the laundry machines, with giant pink bars of carbolic soap and drying racks, as Abuelita had often described? Maya doubted it. To a wine cellar, more likely. Americans were less comfortable with the idea of humiliating their servants in their own homes. The help would arrive by day and leave at nightfall for some distant apartment; the wealthy didn't have to lay eyes on the miserable living conditions of their domestic help.

Maya decided then and there—she wouldn't decorate her own luxury home in such a foolishly romantic style as Flor de Canela. She'd go for something in white concrete and glass—clean, sterile, minimalist. Not something that would remind her in any way of her humble past. She'd build her house by the sea, with an infinity pool. Any servants would live in immaculately clean apartments on the same estate.

Maya's phone buzzed. She checked it quickly and returned it to her back pocket. Jack Cato—again. She'd managed to avoid talking to him on the Fourth of July, but he hadn't given up.

Jack was the nicest, smartest guy she'd ever known. An amazing kisser. And she was longing to hear his voice. But speaking to Jack right now would put six people's lives at risk—and it could drag him into a world of legal trouble, too.

Every day apart from Jack made her appreciate him even more. The guy was adorable and brilliant. If he was here, Maya would feel safer and stronger, too. But he wasn't. And it wasn't fair to ask him to risk his own neck. She'd have to keep ignoring his calls.

One day she'd explain everything. When they were both rich.

Maya left the estate, following a trail that began close to the rear garden, which backed onto the lower reaches of the Robert Louis Stevenson State Park.

An hour later, wisps of cloud threaded across the hiking trail before her. Beyond, a mountain caught the midmorning light, a bright emerald contrasting with the mist-shrouded shadows of distant peaks. The sky was clearing and the rolling landscape opened before her. Vineyards striped the plain and climbed the lower slopes.

Last night, Grace and Lucy had seemed especially disturbed by the brittle atmosphere. Paolo seemed anxious, Candace was irritable, and John-Michael . . . ? As she strolled along a hiking trail at the top of a low ridge, Maya thought for a moment about John-Michael's methodical silence as he'd prepared the evening meal. He didn't show a lot, but then he never had.

As the evening had turned into night, the housemates' gloom had only increased. In the kitchen, Maya had heard Candace say to Grace, "Honestly, wouldn't you rather we were yelling and screaming at each other, like yesterday?"

Of the two sisters, Grace probably had the better grasp of how serious things really were, especially after the visit with her father in prison. The hollowness of her gaze, the drawn quality of her features . . . it all suggested that she knew something was fundamentally wrong.

Maya was fairly certain that Paolo, Lucy, and John-Michael had not yet leaked the truth, but you never could tell. People seemed unable to stop themselves from blabbing at the most inconvenient times. If only everyone had managed to keep quiet, none of this would have happened. Of course, Maya reflected, she was equally guilty. She'd accidentally let slip that Dana Alexander's driver wasn't really her aunt, but her mother. The news had gone down like a ton of bricks.

She turned and looked back down the slopes she'd just climbed, at the bright pink spots of bougainvillea dotted around Alexa Nyborg's estate. What a place. It felt unreal.

Then again, Venice didn't feel like a real place either, not to Maya. It was nothing like the cramped, fifth-floor apartment in the "Spanish" part of downtown LA, where she'd grown up. When all was said and done, Venice Beach had felt about as real as the swanky private school she'd been attending. It wasn't easy to be around all those rich girls. People like Lucasta Jordan-Long, who took being rich for granted. Maya didn't begrudge her housemates their comfortable upbringings, but when John-Michael talked quietly of his year living on the streets, she knew instantly that the two of them shared a bond the other four would never understand.

Last night in Venice Beach, when it had come to defending his friend, and later in Malibu Canyon, John-Michael had barely flinched. He'd turned into a killer.

Maya had *talked* about being the one to shoot the second hit man, but would she have actually done it?

Yes—she could have done it. It had come down to a question of *us* or *them*. For Maya, that wasn't a question. She had to make good on her parents' sacrifices, their hard work to ensure that their daughter, their only child, made a success of living in America.

So how would things unravel now? It was impossible to predict. Too many variables, like multiple software bugs that might cancel each other out when you ran the compiled code.

It was crucial to keep their location a secret. Not easy, now that Grace was so eager to invite a convicted criminal into their midst. This Peter Martens guy was supposed to protect them, but the whole thing made Maya nervous.

As for the bag full money, she'd have to find a better hiding place. Anyone who suspected they had something to hide would find it in minutes.

What would they do with the money? Every physical interaction with cash could put them in danger. If only it could exist as pure credit, floating in the ether, accessible at the touch of a button. Like Bitcoin, she thought. If only there were some way, quickly, to get ahold of that much Bitcoin.

Her phone buzzed again—an email from her mother. She read it swiftly, eyes widening in shock.

Why? Why did her mother choose *today* to deliver that kind of news?

JOHN-MICHAEL

GARDENS, FLOR DE CANELA, SUNDAY, JULY 5

I'm where I said I'd be, John-Michael texted Maya on her burner phone. Where are you?

"Right behind you," she said, approaching from behind a tangerine tree.

"Okay, what's up?" John-Michael probably sounded impatient, but Maya liked it when you cut to the chase. "You shouldn't just go off like that, by the way. Grace and Candace were asking about you."

"Were they worried?" Maya seemed a little surprised.

"Yeah, they were. They're totally edgy right now. Haven't you noticed?"

"Okay. Sorry."

"All right. What's this news from your mom?"

Maya showed him the email on her phone.

I'm done with trying to reach you by phone, Maya.
Obviously you're avoiding me. But I have to tell you why
I did what I did because you're not taking it seriously. I

would have preferred to tell you face-to-face, but in the end it's more important that you know right away. And maybe it's better like this—you can have time to think before you respond.

Hija, you need to know the truth. The reason I'm so afraid of Dana Alexander is that she has seen our documents. Your birth certificate—the real one. The one that shows that you were born in Mexico. We lived there for over a year after your birth, and then we moved to the USA. Maya, I had another baby girl, but she died. Your sister was born in a little hospital in San Ysidro, but she died suddenly, in her cot, five months later. We were still illegals at the time. She would have been fifteen at your last birthday. After she died, we didn't report her death because we realized we could pass you off as your sister, and you would be registered as a US citizen.

John-Michael broke off. "Wait . . . you're older than fifteen?"

"Close to seventeen, probably. I've been thinking about it. A few things are beginning to make sense. Like, Mexico. Technically, I've never been there. And yet I have these faint memories. I thought it was from TV, but I guess not."

"Is Maya even your real name?"

"Nope; keep reading. Apparently it's Julia. Maya was my little sister."

He rubbed his forehead. "This is pretty crazy. You're not really 'Maya'?"

"Well, *now* I am."

"You were born in Mexico."

Maya nodded. "My mom has my real birth certificate."

"How come Dana Alexander knows?"

"Mom doesn't say. But nothing would surprise me about that woman. She's super-paranoid. I bet she had my mother investigated."

"Jeez. Why's your mom telling you now?"

Maya shrugged. "Maybe because I'm getting older? Maybe she feels guilty?"

"What are you going to do?"

"What is there to do? *Nothing.* I'm not going to change my identity again. The official birth certificate is what validates my passport. And that says that I'm Maya Soto Padilla, born October 12, 1999. Not Julia."

John-Michael thought for a couple of seconds. "Kind of handy though. A spare birth certificate, if you ever need it."

"To switch identities? Yes," Maya agreed. "Yeah. I could do that. There are people who have spare birth certificates from relatives who die. They sell them to undocumented people who can use them to apply for passports. Or to take on another identity if they need to stay off the grid."

"Sounds like you're considering a new line of business," John-Michael said, grinning.

"Oh, John-Michael. What are we going to do?" Maya asked, flopping down next to him.

"About you actually being 'Julia' and being sixteen years old? Nothing. Probably. Although, it does give Alexander more leverage. All she has to do is to tell immigration she found your *real* documents."

There was determination in Maya's voice. "I'm not going back to Mexico."

"Would you have to?" Maya grimaced, and John-Michael nodded. "I guess you would. But do you think Dana would really want to talk to the cops at a time like this? She must have guessed by now that something sketchy happened."

"Who knows?" Maya said. "But what I meant to say, really, was—what are we going to do about the *money*? I'm starting to think it was a mistake to take it."

"Lucy did warn us."

"It's done now," Maya replied tartly. "Not a lot of point thinking about *what-if* and *why-did-we*."

"I guess we should hide the cash," he said. "I already checked for places in the *casita*, but there's not much space."

"Somewhere outside might be good," Maya said. "That's why I went hiking. You can see a long way once you get up onto the hills. This estate is pretty isolated. There's a huge vineyard starting on just the other side of the road. That's Nyborg's closest neighbor. It goes on for miles."

"Think we should bury the money somewhere on the estate?"

"No," Maya said. "I may never get another invitation to stay here. No; I've started to think about something safer. Some kind of safe haven, no physical presence. Online."

"I think someone at the local bank might notice if you

deposited half a mil in cash."

"If we find the right guy, there won't be any questions."

John-Michael found her attitude weirdly cryptic. "Huh? What 'right guy'?"

She shrugged. "I was thinking about Bitcoin. I have an account; I have the app on my phone and on my laptop. I just need to find a miner—one who'll sell for cash."

"Bitcoin—the virtual currency? Isn't that what drug dealers and criminals use?"

Maya laughed. "Maya Soto, accomplice to murder. Pleased to meet you."

John-Michael looked across to where two olive trees met to form an archway, the entrance to the garden. It was all very well for Maya to smile about it, but he had the blood of three men on his hands; his father and the two hit men. He hadn't wanted to kill any of them, and yet he had, because it had become necessary.

"Isn't it strange?" Maya murmured softly. She closed her eyes as she relaxed into the warm, dusty grass. "Two days ago, we did something terrible. And already I'm starting to forget."

CANDACE

"You're not going to believe this, but there's a car in the driveway."

A tremor of guilt flared within Candace, but she hid it behind a careless toss of her head. "It's just Yoandy. I figured we could use some excitement after yesterday's snoozefest."

She hadn't expected anyone to actually be pleased, but even so, her housemates' response was something of a surprise.

"Are you a moron?" thundered John-Michael. "I mean, in all seriousness, Candace, are you suffering from some kind of head injury? Because what part of 'we can't tell anyone where we are' don't you understand?"

Candace pouted. "Uh–overreacting much? Like anyone else is sticking to not talking."

Candace could tell John-Michael was furious. Okay, she knew that some of them wouldn't be all that happy that she'd broken their little rule. But it was only Yoandy. She knew she could trust him. It wasn't like she'd told her mom.

"I'm sticking to it," Paolo said. "I told my mom I was in Yellowstone."

"I'm not even taking calls," Maya added.

Yoandy's red BMW was now parked neatly alongside Candace's Prius. He stepped out and waved, and then removed a black rolling suitcase from the trunk and sauntered toward the six housemates, who stood on the patio around the pool as if they were planted to the spot.

It was this, finally, that began to ring the faint alarm bells inside Candace. It wasn't just John-Michael being a jerk. They were all shocked and actually kind of upset.

It was too late to do anything about that, but Candace felt a stab of misgiving. This whole isolation thing— evidently they'd meant it. Even Grace seemed horrified.

It crossed Candace's mind that Grace might know more than she was letting on. She was turning out to be quite the secretive one. After all, she'd kept the truth about having a death-row dad from Candace for years. On Friday, Candace had been prepared to believe that her stepsister didn't have any more secrets. But maybe she was just being naïve.

Yoandy joined them on the patio. He kissed Maya on the cheek, murmuring, *"Hola, mucho gusto, soy Yoandy."* Then he shook hands with the boys and kissed the girls in turn.

He turned to her last, opening his arms with a quizzical grin. *"Bueno,* Candace, here I am." When they embraced, Candace's lips brushed the warm skin of his throat, felt the smoothness of his chin against her cheek and smelled the heady aroma of citrus and sandalwood.

Yoandy released her and clapped his hands together, looking around. "So. What's going on? You having a secret party out here?"

"Yes," Maya said bluntly. "We weren't expecting any guests."

"But I insisted," Candace broke in, improvising. "Because last night was just plain dull."

"I brought pork steaks from my mom's kitchen. I got beans, plantains, tomatoes, cucumbers, *limón*. How about I treat you all to a typical Cuban dinner—*lechón asado*? You have rum? I brought mint leaves, too, for mojitos."

"We have wine," John-Michael said. "Not rum."

"Then it's good I brought rum, too," Yoandy said, grinning. He pulled a bottle of Havana Club from an outside pocket of his suitcase.

Without a word, John-Michael led Yoandy toward the kitchen. He showed him the cupboard where bottles of spices, salts, and dried chilies were neatly arranged.

Yoandy plucked out garlic powder, cumin, and oregano. "You have oranges?" he asked John-Michael.

"I'll show you," said Candace, joining them in the kitchen.

She led Yoandy toward the tangerine tree in the estate's rear garden. As soon as they were alone, he took her hand in his. His palm felt smooth, warm, and bone dry. "What's the matter, *chula*?" he said mildly. "You don't seem very happy to see me. And your friends, they seem kind of mad."

"They are," she said, sighing. "I wasn't supposed to tell anyone we were here. But, Yoandy, I was so bored."

He squeezed her fingers affectionately. "Okay, I'm relieved to hear that. I thought you'd changed your mind about seeing me."

"I wouldn't have let you drive all the way up here if I didn't want to see you," she murmured. She maneuvered herself in front of him and he stepped into her embrace.

He kissed her hair. "I'd drive even farther to spend time with you, *nena linda.*"

"Ugh. You don't want to know how depressing it got yesterday. John-Michael made all this delicious food and *still* no one was in a good mood. They didn't want to light fireworks. On July fourth, can you believe it? In the end we just watched frikkin' *Game of Thrones.*"

"I wanted to be in that show," he mused. "But my agent said that you pretty much have to be able to do a British accent."

"Yoandy!" She tugged at his forearms, watching a teasing grin appear. "Come on! I need to know you're with me on this. You saw their faces. That's too much doom and gloom for one person to combat alone."

Yoandy drew her against him. "Oh, Candace, I cannot believe how much I missed you. Did you put a *bilongo* on me, woman, did you put something in my food? I feel like an addict. Just your smell is making my heart beat faster."

Candace pinched his neck, good and tight, until he let

out a yelp. "Hey. I didn't put anything in your food—yet. But if you don't help me perk up my friends, then, well, I can't promise that I won't."

With the fingers of one hand, Yoandy lightly traced the contours of her face. "You got it, *nena*. Satisfaction guaranteed. We're gonna make a real *guaracha* tonight. Great food, great music. Your buddies are going to be dancing and singing, I promise you."

"Good," she said, emphatically. "Because God knows they need a laugh."

"Why, did something bad happen?"

Candace turned away then. Something bad? Uh, *yeah*. On Friday, she'd assumed that they were exaggerating, with all the panicky talk about getting away from the house. She'd thought they'd lighten up once they got to Napa, but the somber mood had only gotten worse.

"I guess maybe Maya wasn't really supposed to invite so many people to the *casita*," she said, offering Yoandy a plump tangerine. "She asked us not to tell. You know how people can be: one moment you're telling someone something super-personal; next thing you know, it's gone viral."

Yoandy turned the tangerine over in his hand. "Let's go put on some music—I noticed there's a poolside sound system. I'll make everyone a mojito. It'll be the best you ever had."

"It'll also be the *first*," she said.

"Well, I'll be the one to teach you how they *should* taste.

Then I'll prepare the *lechón*. You ever eat Cuban pork steaks with fried plantains and *moros y cristianos*?"

"I don't even know what that is," confessed Candace.

"Beans and rice," he told her, beaming. "My mother's recipe. Your buddies are gonna love it."

LUCY
PATIO, FLOR DE CANELA, SUNDAY, JULY 5

Around seven, they sat down to eat the Cuban food that Yoandy had prepared. The night before, they'd eaten in relative silence. This time, the quiet was punctuated by sighs of pleasure.

"Seriously, Yoandy," Lucy asked. "How can this be so incredible?" A combination of rustic flavors combined with the smoky tang of carbonized meat, black beans rich with garlic, and the crispy sweetness of fried plantain.

Lucy watched her housemates, saw their faces flicker in the light of candles laid out over the three pinewood tables they'd pushed together. The air smelled delicious—a combination of the deep, musky perfume of jasmine flowers and Cuban cuisine. Over the poolside music system, a woman sang in Spanish—some kind of romantic music from Yoandy's iPod. It sounded hopeful and yearning, with a soft, syncopated rhythm.

Yoandy wasn't at all what she'd expected from watching his Reggaeton videos. In those, he tended to dress in very tight jeans and revealing T-shirts with chunky gold necklaces. After he'd finished cooking, Yoandy had dressed for dinner–a fitted dress shirt, black with white-and-silver vertical stripes, white linen pants. Lucy and Candace had given low whistles of appreciation when they'd seen him. And Paolo had grumbled, "Hey! We didn't agree to dress fancy."

Yoandy was surprisingly formal, too. Fancy manners, lots of hand kissing. An interesting combination of tough and tender. It was funny, Lucy thought, because Paolo had been the group's peacock. Yet in Yoandy's presence, who even looked at Paolo?

Yoandy's presence actually seemed to set Paolo at ease. His jokes and smiles were more relaxed, as if he was happy to be out of the limelight. *Yep*, she thought, *that figures.*

"I think your hostess really loves Latin culture," Yoandy told Maya. He had to repeat himself before Maya noticed he was speaking to her.

Lucy was fascinated by Maya's apparent distraction. That girl was interesting–not at all what she appeared to be.

"Alexa Nyborg? I guess so," Maya agreed flatly. "At least Spain and Mexico."

"And Peru," Yoandy said. "The name of her house–*Flor de Canela*–the cinnamon's flower!"

"Is the cinnamon flower native to Peru?" asked Lucy.

Yoandy looked surprised. "You don't know the song?"

Candace and Grace shook their heads. "Maya, how about you? You know the song 'La Flor de la Canela,' don't you? Come on! Every Latina has to know this song."

Maya shrugged, blinking. "Eh. I dunno. Maybe if I heard it . . . ?"

Yoandy rose to his feet. "Okay, let's do it. Lucy, did you bring your guitar? Maybe I could borrow it?"

She grunted. "The acoustic? Yeah. But seriously, you're going to sing? Now?"

"Sure, and then you," he offered.

For once, she wasn't really in the mood to play. Music was definitely a mood thing. And tonight, Lucy wasn't feeling it.

Everyone except Lucy joined in with halfhearted cheers for Yoandy to sing. "And then Lucy," Candace insisted. She was really getting into the spirit of the moment. Which was a little odd, because rallying the housemates was more of a Grace thing.

Lucy leaned across to Grace. "What's gotten into your sister? Is *she* handling the pep talks now?"

Grace only smiled, eyes closed. "Candace can be that way. It's hard to tell sometimes, but she really cares about the people around her. It's like she has a flashlight inside her, and once in a blue moon, she turns on the high beams."

Lucy nodded. "She's even trying to put the spotlight on me."

"You don't feel like playing?"

"Nah. But I'll do it anyway, after Yoandy." Lucy grinned. "Since you asked so nice."

When Yoandy began to sing, the sweetness of his tenor

voice silenced the housemates' chatter. The song was achingly soulful. Lucy's knowledge of Spanish wasn't fantastic, but she heard snatches that sounded elegant, old-fashioned, from an era long gone. "Jasmines in her hair, roses in her face, lightly walked the cinnamon flower." Nice.

She imagined Yoandy singing it to an audience of swooning fans at one of his concerts. Lucy would give anything for that kind of success. If she could only put this whole Tyson Drew murder and Alex Vesper death row scene behind her, maybe she could finally move on with her music career.

It sucked to be reminded of all that. Lucy picked up her mojito and drained it. Then she poured out more from the pitcher. Rum helped; it helped a lot. She glanced at Candace. It was obvious she had no clue what they were hiding. *Lucky girl.* How great would that be? She only had eyes for Yoandy. You could totally tell that she was smitten.

The alcohol hit Lucy's bloodstream like sinking into a warm bath. Lazily, she smiled and raised her glass to Yoandy. "Yeah!" she called out. "Man, you rock."

John-Michael joined in. "Dude, you can really sing that romantic stuff!"

"Thanks, man," said Yoandy. "It's just songs I learn with my family. But the world's already got one Romeo Santos. So I figured I'd specialize in *Reggaeton romántico.*"

"JM, didn't you have a poster of Romeo Santos in your room at band camp?" Lucy drawled.

"Oh," he replied, breathlessly. "Romeo! Don't *even.*"

Lucy caught Yoandy's eye, and they both laughed. He started another song, this time singing directly to Candace. This one was even more heartfelt and sentimental, with a slight rhythm he emphasized with an occasional tap on the side of the guitar. Before long, Candace was dragging Maya to her feet in a ballroom-style hold. "C'mon, Maya. Show me how to dance!"

"Me?" Maya mumbled, but she didn't pull away. "Eh, what even is this? A bachata . . . ? You want me to lead?"

After the first verse, John-Michael grabbed Lucy's hand, leading her in the same dance as Maya and Candace. The steps looked easy, but they weren't. Lucy dissolved into giggles.

When he'd finished, Yoandy was beaming at the sight of their clumsy dancing. "That was a Juan Luis Guerra— 'Mi Bendición.' A blessing for a beautiful girl who put a spell on me." He glanced at Candace meaningfully.

"How about 'México Lindo y Querido,' Maya?" Yoandy continued. "Will you sing with me?"

"Are you kidding? I don't know how to sing those songs," Maya said. But this time, there was a trace of a smile on her face.

Yoandy swung the guitar off his knees and handed it to Lucy. "Okay, if Maya won't sing, then it's time to hear Lucy."

"Yes, sing something from the Piglet movie, like you did at the Amnesty benefit!" pleaded Candace.

"Great idea!" Grace added. "It was so cool to see a punk

rocker doing something so cute."

The other housemates cheered in approval. Lucy gave them a coy smile. "I guess I'm just about drunk enough to sing a ditty for y'all." She began strumming Carly Simon's "With a Few Good Friends." After the second verse, most of the housemates joined in. When she moved on to "The More I Look Inside," they grew quiet again, listening.

"God, that's beautiful, Lucy. But stop it, you're making us cry!" Candace said. "Someone, quick, think of something *fun*, for the love of Gandhi."

"I could show everyone how to dance the Madison," John-Michael suggested.

"The line dance from *Hairspray*?" Candace said. "I know it; *way* too complicated."

But John-Michael was adamant. "Wrong! The original Madison is super-simple. It's from a black-and-white French movie called *Bande à part. Band of Outsiders.* I saw it inside the *casita*. Nyborg has a big stack of DVDs in there."

"Omigod I swear I've seen that movie," Maya said. "In French class. Where the three friends try to rip off some cash in a house where the girl is staying? And they wind up running off to South America or something? I remember a line dance in a coffee shop."

"So basically," Candace said, rolling her eyes, "it's hipster bullshit?"

"Quentin Tarantino named his production company after that movie," John-Michael said. "I bet you'd die to appear in one of his movies for a single minute."

"Stop arguing," Lucy said, laughing. She couldn't tell whether Candace was just pretending to be irked, but it was still funny. "John-Michael, on your feet."

"Yeah," grumbled Candace. "Let's see this super-simple Madison."

Yoandy was beside her, grinning. "And then maybe I can teach you some salsa?"

Singing those songs for her friends had lightened Lucy's mood more than she had guessed was possible. She sat down and took the chair next to Grace.

"You happy, hon?" Lucy asked, taking Grace's hand. "You should be. Monday morning, we're gonna go down to that police station. You and me. And we're gonna take care of that business with your dad. Then he's going to come home to you and it'll all be fine, okay? You'll get your dad back. And Dana Alexander? She'll find out what it's like to be arrested for murder."

Grace gazed at her, a warm smile coloring her entire face. "Oh, Lucy. I hope so."

"Honey, count on it."

GRACE

Watching her housemates singing and dancing on the patio, Grace wondered if everyone but her had forgotten that they were in danger. Lucy's speech had been unexpected and kind of affirming. But she suspected that it was partly the booze talking. She looked longingly at the pitcher of mojito cocktail. Maybe she should have a drink, too.

Despite the party atmosphere, Grace was scared. She didn't even know just how scared to be, since the others were determined to "protect" her and Candace from the truth. She had to reach Pete Martens. Her own father suspected that they needed protection. How could she forget or ignore that?

Every instinct warned her: *pay attention.*

In the meantime, she and Paolo sat quietly at the table. The shadows from the candles played across his features, giving him a mysterious look. She thought again about John-Michael's bruised torso. He'd been careful to wear a T-shirt by the pool today. She'd caught him flinching in pain earlier. One of Paolo's hands was bruised, too, but he wouldn't say why.

Grace didn't associate Paolo with violence. He really didn't seem like a fighter. Surely guys like Paolo could get what they wanted with a smile? He was a born heart-breaker.

It was already too late. Grace looked down into her own plate, feeling tears sting her eyes. Watching Paolo's face in the wavering candlelight, Grace knew that the heart that would be broken was hers. What was it that kept him so quiet tonight?

What had happened to the others on Friday night? She knew that it had affected Paolo in some dramatic way—more than just a few bruises, too. He simply wasn't the same person. Even the way he looked at her had changed. There was sorrow in his eyes—an unspoken apology.

Yoandy was telling the housemates a long, funny story. When Paolo's attention shifted from Yoandy to her, Grace felt her heart fluttering. Her quiet smile disappeared as their eyes locked. Paolo was able to hold her gaze for under two seconds.

It was this, finally, that made Grace's eyes overflow. Tears fell into her food, thankfully unnoticed by anyone else. Hurriedly, she reached for her glass of Coke Zero and gulped down a mouthful to cover up her sniffles.

She'd tried to resist, but it was no use. Grace was in love with Paolo. And there was nothing she could do about it.

Everyone else was dancing. Would Paolo ask her to

dance? He probably didn't know how. He met her gaze and reached for her hand under the table. He held it tightly, caressing her palm with the tip of his thumb. Grace felt slightly woozy as her fingers closed around his. It hardly felt real. But she couldn't let it go on. Not until she knew.

"What happened on Friday? The truth, Paolo."

He looked torn, sorrowful. "Baby," he whispered. "I can't. We all *agreed*."

Grace pushed his hand away. The sudden movement jarred the table. But the others were so happy with their singing and their dancing, they didn't notice.

Only Candace seemed aware of her sister's quiet distress. "Hey, sis," she said, leaning over. "What's up?"

Grace pulled Candace away to the farthest end of the pool with as little fuss as she could manage. Paolo was watching them, but he didn't react. Yoandy was dancing with John-Michael and Maya, leading both in fancy salsa steps while Lucy drank and looked on. They were oblivious to what was going on with Grace.

When she'd gotten Candace far enough away, Grace whispered, "We need to find out what happened on Friday."

"Yeah, but they don't wanna say," Candace said. "That's what we get for hanging out with a bunch of petty criminals."

"It's not petty crime, Candace," Grace snapped. "And it's not just the cops who are looking for them."

Candace's eyes narrowed. "What do you know?"

"I don't *know* anything," Grace stammered. "I suspect. I *strongly* suspect."

"No; that's *really* not how you sounded, just now. Sounded like you *knew*. What made you say that it's not the cops who're looking for them?"

"I think the cops *are* looking for us. Or rather, for *them*," Grace replied, tipping her head in the direction of Lucy, Maya, and John-Michael. They seemed to be politely oblivious, but it was almost certainly an act.

Candace beckoned to Paolo. He got up slowly and walked across to the sisters. "Who else is after us, Paolo?" Candace hissed. "Apart from the cops?"

Paolo clamped his jaw shut.

Candace's mouth fell open. "Omigod, you're not denying it."

"Grace, Candace," he pleaded. "Trust me; we *cannot* have this conversation with Yoandy here."

Candace stared at him. "So that's it—you're clamming up?"

"Ask Yoandy to get something for you, from the car," Grace suggested. "Because I really, really need to talk about this right now."

Candace did even better—she asked him to prepare more mojitos. He disappeared into the kitchen, grinning with pride.

"Okay," Candace said briskly, loud enough for the other four housemates to hear. "Confession time. What's been going on? Why did I just send Yoandy away?"

No one answered.

Grace fumed. "I guess we were right."

"About what?" Candace asked.

"About them hurting someone." Grace shifted her eyes from one housemate to the next.

Candace turned to Paolo. "So it's true?" she asked.

He paused. "Yeah." Paolo's voice broke a little. "Someone came to the house."

"Stop right there, Paolo," warned Maya.

"Someone came to the house," echoed Grace, her impatience mounting. "Someone with a message from Dana Alexander. Yes? For Lucy. And you hurt him—I'm guessing it was a him. How am I doing? Right so far?"

Paolo exhaled nervously. "Pretty good."

"How badly did you hurt this person?"

Another silence. As the implications of this sunk in, Grace's next words became almost a whisper. "Did . . . did you *kill* someone?"

Grace's eyes met Candace's. Her sister's face was raw with uncomprehending fear.

"Is this a joke?" Candace whispered.

"It's not a joke," Grace said. "My dad was right."

"How did your dad know?" Maya asked.

"He worked it out," said Grace.

"We could have worked it out, too," Candace said. "Except that, *oh yeah*, we weren't aware that anyone we know would actually *do* a thing like that!"

Grace broke the brief silence that followed. "Who did it?"

More silence.

"I want to know, too," insisted Candace.

"I did it," John-Michael said after a few seconds. "The guy was going to kill us all."

Grace stared at him, and then turned to Paolo.

"John-Michael was protecting us," Paolo confirmed.

"Why didn't you just call the cops?" Grace asked. "It's not against the law to defend yourself against a home invader."

"It's not that simple," Paolo told her. "John-Michael kind of, well, I guess you'd have to say that he finished the job. But, Gracie, I'm the one that hit first. The guy fired a handgun, and then I hit him with a shovel, and then things got kind of crazy. Then he turned the gun on all of us, and John-Michael jumped him."

Candace gasped, almost a laugh. "'Jumped him'?"

"I smothered him," John-Michael said calmly. All eyes turned to him. "He was having some kind of seizure. Epilepsy or something. He was firing his gun every which way. I finished it. It was the only way to keep us safe."

Candace looked baffled. "Okay but . . . that's still basically self-defense, like Grace said."

"Yeah, except . . . smothering?" Lucy didn't seem to want to complete the sentence.

Grace understood where Lucy's thoughts were headed. John-Michael had smothered his father—and the cops suspected as much. All they needed now was some kind of proof. It wouldn't look good if he did the same thing to someone else—even a home invader.

Candace still seemed to be struggling to make sense of what John-Michael had said. "But he fired his gun, is that what you said?"

"He shot a blank at Lucy. After that, the bullets were real and . . ."

Grace interrupted. "Wait a minute—the first shot was a blank?"

"I guess he was trying to scare her."

"Then it *was* a message, a warning?"

"But things got way out of hand," agreed Paolo.

"That's exactly what my dad said," Grace breathed.

"Well," Paolo said calmly, "your dad was right."

CANDACE
PATIO, FLOR DE CANELA, SUNDAY, JULY 5

Candace couldn't speak. She was still reeling from the news.

"All right," Grace said, with a quick glance at her sister. "You killed him. Then what?"

"Then, well," Paolo said, this time reluctantly, "we took his body up to the hills."

Candace found words now, but barely. Her tongue felt thick and dry in her throat. "You dumped the body?"

"Yeah," Paolo said. "Yeah. We did."

Candace felt her anger beginning to surge. "Of *course* you did. Why *wouldn't* you hide the body?"

"Right," agreed Paolo. He didn't seem to have picked up on Candace's ironic tone.

No one else seemed all that eager to speak now. They were all watching Paolo.

"And then what?"

Grace's question seemed to freeze Paolo. "What do you mean?" he asked nervously.

"And what happened next?" Candace said firmly.

"And then," Paolo said, more hesitantly still, "and then, well, another guy came looking for his buddy. Another guy with a gun."

"Another *hit man* came to my *mother's house?*" pronounced Candace.

Paolo nodded. No one else moved—they barely breathed. They all waited for him to speak again.

When he didn't, Grace squeaked, "And then *what?*"

"We killed him, too," admitted Paolo.

John-Michael shot him a wary look. "*I* killed him."

"JM was kind of badass," Maya said dryly. "He swiped the guy clean off the side of a cliff."

Candace shook her head. "So what you're actually telling us right now is that you killed *two* people?"

"They weren't Jehovah's Witnesses, Candace," Paolo said in a tired voice. "These were hired, professional killers."

"We also took a bag of money they were carrying," Lucy said. It had been a little while since she'd said anything, and there was an unmistakable hint of anger in her voice.

"They came to threaten Lucy, but we outsmarted them," Maya said briskly. "Now they're dead, we've got their money, and we're all hiding out here to stay out of trouble. Okay, now that we're all up to speed, can I suggest we get back to our vacation or *whatever* this is and get some rest?"

Grace gasped. "Are you out of your mind?"

"Yeah, why did you have to drag us into this?" Candace demanded. "Grace and me—we didn't have anything to do with it. Now we're implicated. Gracie, we should just leave."

Maya threw both hands out in front of her in desperation. "If it's blame you're looking for, there is a *lot* to go around. *Everyone* is implicated. *Lucy* started this entire thing by freaking out and not telling anyone what she saw that night at the Hollywood party. *Grace* should have said something when she realized that Lucy was gonna be sharing a house with us. Plus, Grace kept a secret from you for years!"

Candace looked at Grace, who gasped again.

"*Candace* ignored all our advice and chose a boyfriend who would totally piss off Dana Alexander," Maya plowed on. "Paolo . . . *Paolo*! What the hell made you come up with that idea to hide the hit man's body? And *John-Michael* . . . ?"

Maya didn't say it. None of them would. Yet it was blatantly obvious. John-Michael must have killed his own father—and apparently two more men on Friday night.

John-Michael rubbed his forehead. "Thanks for reminding me."

This was too much for Lucy. "Maya—you do *not* get to play down your own part in this. You spied on all of us."

"You think I can ever, ever forget it? I was *blackmailed*, Lucy."

"You didn't give a damn about any of us," Lucy shot back.

John-Michael held up one hand to stop them. "At least we're safe, and we have time to plan. Maya's been thinking about that."

But Lucy just oozed cynicism. "Maya? Of course. What a schemer you turned out to be."

"If you've got any better suggestions," Maya replied tartly, "then let's hear them. All I'm doing is thinking of a way to keep us alive—and out of jail."

Candace had stopped listening. Her insides felt like they'd been tied into knots. She gulped down a chunk of air, and then another.

After a moment, Paolo spoke. His words were barely a ripple in the air. "Say something, Grace."

Candace forced herself to watch as Grace responded. "I don't know what to say." She took a deep breath. "I'm calling my dad's friend Pete Martens."

"Don't you need to call from a public phone?"

"Candace can drive me to one. Or you can."

"If you're sure?"

Maya must have heard the quiet exchange, because she interrupted. *"No."*

"Why the hell not?" Paolo fired back.

"It's too late for us to go out. It's safer to stay on the property. After all, that's why we're here."

Maya's suggestion was sensible. Yet Candace didn't want to be sensible, didn't want to play safe. She wanted to forget everything she'd heard, starting about six minutes ago. She wanted Yoandy to come back to the patio with fresh, mint-stuffed mojitos and for it all to have been some idiotic prank.

She wanted the tight pain in her guts to recede, to feel her breath slow down, to quell the unsteady hammering of her heart.

PAOLO

CASITA, FLOR DE CANELA, SUNDAY, JULY 5

Paolo and Grace agreed to wash the dishes, which seemed only fair since neither had done anything to prepare the food. Candace hadn't done much either, but when she stormed out to show Yoandy around the estate, Paolo had kept his mouth shut, waiting to see Grace's reaction.

It was quite a payload they'd just dropped on her and her sister. You couldn't predict how anyone would react after a thing like that.

He wasn't the only one to notice Candace and Yoandy sliding off into the shadows at the edge of the patio and into the rear garden. "I guess that's one way to handle stress," John-Michael noted slyly.

Grace looked uncomfortable. "Candace can take care of herself."

"She seemed pretty upset," said John-Michael. "It's a beautiful evening. Moon and stars and whatnot. Plus, the horrible news."

"Yeah, okay, horrible," Maya said, "but, one—it didn't

happen to her, not exactly, and two—am I the only one icked out by the fact that one of us might stumble on them?"

"Can we please stop talking about my sister that way?" Grace pleaded.

"I'm never having sex," Lucy declared, shaking her head. "Just the thought that y'all might discuss me is enough to put me off."

"Don't worry, there's a curse on our house," John-Michael said. "Didn't you notice? Ever since we moved in together, none of us has gotten any action."

Paolo noticed Grace's eyes on him as John-Michael said this. He nodded along with everyone else, but his heart sank a little. Grace knew he'd seen women from the tennis club. She probably suspected he was some kind of sex addict. No wonder she was wary.

"I kind of hope they are doing it," Maya said. "The alternative is worse."

Grace seemed puzzled. "What alternative?"

"That she's telling Yoandy about . . . everything."

The housemates fell silent.

"That's no good," Paolo said. "Lucy, you want to go break it up? Maybe go with Maya?"

Maya sighed. She tugged at John-Michael's elbow, then Lucy's. "You're coming, too. I don't want to be grossed out all by myself."

The moment Paolo and Grace were alone, she started to blush. When he stepped a little closer, she could barely look at him.

He cleared his throat. "You okay?"

Grace shivered and wrapped her arms around herself. "Not really. But I will be."

"Your dad . . . I've been wondering about him," Paolo admitted. "You booked yesterday's visit a while ago. Isn't that true? John-Michael told me. I wish I'd known about his . . . situation . . . earlier."

His words seemed to upset her; she wrung out the dishcloth, discarding it into the sink. "I thought about telling you."

Paolo pressed on. "But you were going to cancel on him, last minute. Grace, I don't think you would do anything to hurt your dad, and canceling on him would have done that. So the only reason you would have considered canceling . . . is if it was too painful to see him."

Grace nodded and looked down for a few seconds before facing him again. "It *was* painful. His execution is booked for nine days from now, Paolo." Tears sprang to her eyes and she inhaled shakily. "Hard to believe, isn't it? And now all this other stuff, too."

Paolo stepped toward her, uncertain. She looked so vulnerable, he could only think of holding her. To his relief, she let him. He bent his head to kiss her temple. "I'm glad you changed your mind. I bet it meant a *lot* to your dad."

Another nod. "It really did. I told him that Lucy and I are going together to the police station in Napa tomorrow morning." Grace looked up at him and blushed. She quickly turned to the sink and picked up another plate.

Paolo smiled. Her obvious nervousness made him suddenly feel shy. Slowly, he placed the empty glass on the countertop. He came up behind Grace and placed both hands on her waist. She glanced over her shoulder and nodded almost imperceptibly. When he leaned forward and placed a kiss on her cheek, they both crumpled with nervous laughter.

He drew her closer until he could feel the heat of her against his chest. His hands went gently to hers. He took the dishcloth and dinner plate from her fingers and placed them on the drainboard. Her breath caught as his palms returned to her waist.

A cough from the outside door brought them to their senses. Grace turned quickly, pushing Paolo aside.

Lucy stood framed in the doorway, one eyebrow arched. "Hey there, you two crazy kids. Need any help with the dishes?"

CANDACE

Candace and Yoandy found a relatively private spot at one end of the patio, next to the jasmine bush that surrounded the rear garden. The flowers' perfume was almost over-powering this close up: sweet, dense, and sweaty.

"Eww," Candace said as her lungs filled with the cloy-ing scent. "We should go for a walk."

Yoandy took her hand in his. "Anything you say, *mi amor.*"

Anything to get away from the drama inside the *casita.* Another minute and she'd have let rip for sure. Yoandy would have seen a side of Candace that she wasn't prepared to show someone she wanted to be her boyfriend—at least, not before they were serious.

Grace's prophecies of doom had been right all along. Candace couldn't even begin to deal with it. Better to pre-tend it wasn't happening. Maybe it wasn't? It did have the feel of a hideous dream. "You can't say '*mi amor,*'" Candace grumbled, leading him away. But she was quietly enjoying the feel of his muscular arm against her own as they began walking. She already felt calmer. "We've only known each other a few weeks."

"Why not? I've been thinking of you that way since that first day."

"When I kicked your ass in a stage fight?"

He chuckled. "Exactly."

"Yoandy, pay attention." Candace turned to face him. "You can't use words like that if you don't mean them. Not with me." She hesitated. Even in her head, the next thing she planned to say sounded too stern. Yet sometimes, Candace knew, you had to be prepared to draw a line.

Yoandy's eyes filled with concern. "What is it?"

"I really like you. And I know it seems like I'm confident around boys."

"You?" He grinned. "Nah."

Candace shook her head, deciding to change tack. "I wouldn't like to think that you were playing me."

"Playing?"

Again she hesitated. "Tricking me into falling in love with you. I think you'd be good at that."

He looked surprised, but Candace wasn't convinced. Easy enough to play innocent—not so easy to own up to being a *player*. But she needed to know now, needed to have some idea of how much to trust him. After the news she'd just heard from the housemates, her feelings were jumbled and she needed an anchor. Yoandy, maybe?

"All the sentimental stuff," she said, wrinkling her nose. "Is it for real?"

This time, he seemed genuinely shocked. "You think I'm acting?"

"I . . . I don't know," she said. "You're kind of . . . *high volume.* At least, compared to boys I've hooked up with. And I know it's not a Latin thing because I dated a Mexican boy once."

"Candace, you never dated *me* before," he said, very simply.

"Are you like this with all girls?"

"You keep asking me about other girls. It's not very . . ." He seemed to be searching for the right word.

"Attractive?" Candace jumped in.

"It doesn't make me feel very confident."

A shard of anger sliced across her face. "Is it my job to make you feel confident?"

"Why not?" Yoandy asked. "I try to do that for all my friends. I tried to do that for you and your friends tonight. And it worked. It worked so well that when I left you to make mojitos, you all got sad." He knocked her shoulder teasingly. "See? Everyone needs a little Yoandy in their life."

Candace felt her heart rate subside. "Yes, you calmed us all down. It was amazing, actually." She leaned against the wall of the rear garden, her forehead lightly grazing the rough bricks. With a deft touch, he turned her around, drew her close, took both her hands in his and raised them to his lips. He kissed her fingers gently and then her mouth, as soft as a caress.

Candace felt as though she were on the edge of a

precipice. When she felt the first touch of his tongue against hers, it was like being borne high by a rising wave. She grabbed his shirt and pulled him against her. "Don't stop."

They kissed frantically. His hands were in her hair, her fingers fumbled with the buttons of his shirt as she pressed him against the brick wall, dizzy with a passion that felt almost violent. It was definitely not like anything she'd experienced before.

Candace heard her own breathing, but it sounded like someone else's. Her thoughts and imagination were racing ahead—far ahead of the tiny voice of reason that was saying, hopefully, *"Um, hi there . . . could we take a minute and think this over?"*

Yoandy took over the kiss. He lowered her slowly to the ground. She felt the prickle of dry grass through the thin cotton of her blouse and on the bare skin of her legs below the line of her skirt. Candace clung to him. The little voice was gone for good.

After a moment, he broke away to look at her. She panted slightly, trying to get her breathing under control.

Yoandy pulled away, first up onto his knees. He tugged at her hands until Candace was kneeling in front of him, and then he rested his forehead on her shoulder. "Maybe we should take it easy, Candace."

"Because I'm not eighteen?" She put her arms around his neck, focused on the warmth between them.

"I . . . I talked to my, ah, priest about you. My *santero*. He said I need to be careful. With *you*."

"Omigod, don't tell me you're one of those abstinence people," Candace groaned.

Yoandy laughed. "Nothing like that. Homero says that you are important. To my future. Homero says I have to take care of you, that there is danger ahead."

Candace drew a quick breath. Right now, *danger* sounded a little too close to the truth. But she made a show of rolling her eyes. "Trust me to pick a guy who believes in fortune-tellers."

Yoandy squeezed her shoulder. "Candace," he said earnestly. "I'm being serious. I try to consult the orishas before important decisions. They always guide me well."

She said nothing at first; it seemed less risky. Orishas? "I'm an important decision?" she asked timidly.

"Of course! I don't give just any girl the necklace of Our Lady of Charity, of Oshun. I don't take just any girl to meet my parents. We'd be there now, remember?"

Candace reached up to touch the necklace of yellow-and-ocher beads he'd given her. She smiled, unable to resist a further tease. Or maybe it was a test? "Did you ever take Kay Alexander? When you 'weren't' dating her, I mean."

"When I wasn't . . . ?" His puzzled expression quickly turned to a grin. "*Ay, niña*, don't be bad! Again with asking me about other girls, *no, no, no*! Kay was just a friend. Ricardo introduced her to me like she was his little baby sister, what—I'm gonna try something with the sister of my *compay*?"

"Yeah, except, she's not Ricardo's sister, is she? She's

his *wife's*. Kay is *Dana Alexander's* sister. And she actually wanted you to try something with her, am I right?"

"Okay, maybe, but . . ." He shrugged. "It didn't happen."

"But you took her to meet your family?"

"Sure, why not? One time; *once*. In fact, it was my family who warned me about Kay. Like it says in the song, '*No te deje por mala, yo te deje por loca.*'"

"Translate, *por favor?*"

Yoandy reached for her hand and kissed it. "'*I didn't leave 'cause you're bad, I left 'cause you're crazy.*'"

"Kay is crazy?"

"I could tell you things, but it's . . . not very nice things to say about a friend. It's just my opinion, but I think Kay needs to be in a hospital."

"Really? Then why isn't she?"

Yoandy shrugged. "I think sometimes she *is*. Kay goes away sometimes, very suddenly. And there's no communication. Then she comes back and tells everyone that she went to Europe, or to Brazil to visit Ricardo's family. When we were spending time together, I wondered about that. And there were other things."

Candace could tell from the way Yoandy was talking that there'd really never been anything between him and Kay. So why did Dana Alexander send a hit man to the house? Oh wait, that was because of Lucy. Or was it something else?

No. Too confusing. She needed someone to explain it to

her again. None of it made any sense.

Yoandy lifted her chin with one finger. "Baby, are you okay? You look worried. Don't be. You're my girl. Kay never was."

She looked at him, feeling flustered. "Sorry, I was thinking about my sister. She . . . she's had some bad news. I think maybe that's why she was kind of a downer tonight."

"What bad news?"

Candace flushed. "Oh, you know." She pretended to frown. "Girl stuff."

"Your sister is a good person," Yoandy said. "I can see that. Grace has a really good heart. Maybe she was a little quiet tonight, but I think she wanted everyone to be happy."

"Whereas I only wanted you and me to be happy?" Candace said, biting her lower lip provocatively. "Gee, I guess that makes me the bad girl."

His hands dropped to the small of her back, palms encircling her waist. "Ha, so funny. That's what I like about you, *chula*. You wanted them to be happy—even more than Grace."

She was drawing him to her for another kiss when she felt her cell phone vibrate in her back pocket. Yoandy slipped his fingers inside the pocket and pulled it out. "Better tell your sister you're safe and that you aren't getting attacked by a very sexy Cuban boy," he said, handing her the phone with a mischievous grin.

Candace couldn't return the smile. Hearing the word "attacked" triggered a powerful shiver, a reminder of the totally heinous news she and Grace had just received. *A hit man had come after Lucy. John-Michael had killed two people.* These were facts. Impossible facts, that she was somehow expected to absorb. Ri-*diculous.*

From the edges of the olive grove, she heard voices, and then Lucy was calling out, "Hey, you guys, we're gonna watch a movie—wanna help choose?"

Candace flushed and rose quickly to her feet. The housemates had stopped at a discreet distance, she noticed, not quite close enough to have seen her kissing Yoandy. She peered at the phone in her hand. "Oh no. Not this, not now."

Yoandy stood up, too. "What's wrong?"

She didn't reply for a few seconds. She just reread the glowing message.

Do you really think this is over? My stars shine darkly over me; the malignancy of my fate might, perhaps, distemper yours.

"Dana Alexander . . ." Candace managed to say, through a clenched but trembling jaw. "She's doing it again."

LUCY
NAPA POLICE DEPARTMENT, MONDAY, JULY 6

Lucy and Grace hit the Napa police precinct nice and early. But it didn't help. "You're telling me that even though a man's life is in danger, you can't talk to me until Wednesday? That's bull*shit*. And I thought things were bad down at the precinct in Venice."

Lucy tried to temper her scorn, but the female police officer's eyes narrowed the instant Lucy swore. "Miss, I'm going to request that you watch your tone and your language with me," said Officer Alvarez. She was polite, but her voice had enough edge to make Lucy fume. Alvarez handed Lucy a form and a pen. "Leave your name, address, and contact details. I'm making an appointment for you to be interviewed at eight a.m. on Wednesday. If there's a cancellation today or tomorrow, we'll be sure to call you."

Lucy took the pen, resentfully. It had been pretty much the same story at Venice, but at least there'd been evidence of a busy office. The Napa department was quiet.

"We've got a lot of casework to catch up with after the holiday," offered Alvarez, her tone slightly kinder now. "I'm sorry about your friend in San Quentin. But really, one more day isn't going to make any difference. Why don't you call him and let him know that it's all in hand?"

"Two more days," muttered Lucy. She filled out the form and handed it back. She was afraid to look Grace in the eye.

To her surprise, Grace placed a hand on hers. "It's okay," she said.

It couldn't be easy for Grace to say those words, or to smile, but she did it anyway; she was full of gestures like that.

Lucy bit her lip. Paolo didn't deserve to get anywhere near a girl like Grace, and Lucy had been the one to encourage them. Last night, she'd interrupted what looked like a hookup in the making. *If it doesn't work out, that's another thing I'll owe Grace*, Lucy thought, grimly.

What a mess. It felt like Lucy would be turned away from cold, disinterested police departments forever. Always searching for justice, never quite getting close enough.

With a rush of heat, she realized that this must be how Grace felt. Times a thousand.

In the street outside, Lucy looked around for a distraction. It would be too horrible to return to the *casita* having accomplished precisely nothing.

"We should pick up some ice cream," she said, spotting a parlor. "Let's make up some containers with different

■83

flavors. How about chocolate Oreo, blueberry cheesecake, peanut butter cup?"

Lucy's fake enthusiasm didn't appear to move Grace. "Sure, whatever."

They bought the ice cream and headed back in Paolo's car. It was still early—Grace had insisted that they return to the house before midday. Lucy had no idea why.

When they got back to the *casita,* everyone was in the pool. The instant Lucy announced they had ice cream, the housemates and Yoandy joined the two girls in the kitchen. Soon they were sitting beside the pool, swooning over each spoonful.

Grace was making an effort to look happy. She smiled when anyone addressed her but Lucy wasn't fooled. After watching Grace awhile, she made up her mind. She needed to talk to Grace—to really *talk.* She was desperate to tell her friend why it'd taken her so many years before she'd remembered what happened at the Hollywood party.

Suddenly, Maya was at her side. "Can you help me with something? It's in the bedroom."

Mystified, Lucy followed her back into the *casita.* But Maya stopped short in the kitchen. "What are we gonna do now?" she asked, rounding on Lucy.

"About what?"

"Don't be idiotic, Lucy. About Yoandy. How long do you think Candace is going to keep quiet, now that she and Grace know?"

Lucy took a deep breath. It was bad enough that Maya

seemed to have moved in on Lucy's best friend in the house, John-Michael. Friday night had turned the two into coconspirators. Jealousy didn't sit well with her; it reminded her of middle-school rivalries, that time in band camp when a particularly annoying girl from the dorm tried to "steal" John-Michael.

"Who put you in charge?" she said, irritated.

"Who put me . . . ?" Maya looked exasperated. "Don't you care what happens to John-Michael? Or Paolo?"

"Course I care," Lucy spat back. "I've *always* had JM's back. And yeah, you're right, Yoandy is a definite complication. Although I gotta be honest, he seems like a good guy. I like him for Candace."

Grudgingly, Maya nodded. "Yeah, me too. Good, I'm glad we're on the same page. I'm sorry if I came across kinda bossy."

Lucy took a breath. Maya's anger seemed to turn on and off like a faucet. "Whatever."

Maya opened the fridge and took out a can of grape soda, which she shared between two glasses. "My brain's hardly stopped since Friday."

"Humph," conceded Lucy gruffly. "Same."

"Could you talk to Candace, try to find out if she's going to say anything to Yoandy? You're roomies; if she's close to anyone other than Grace, it's you."

"Actually, I was thinking of talking to *Grace*," Lucy admitted.

Maya agreed. "Grace *is* less scary."

"I'm not scared of Candace. It's just that she's more likely to hear it coming from Grace."

Maya gave Lucy a long, curious look, as though she were turning something over in her mind. "That could work," Maya said. "I'll go get Grace."

Then she was gone.

Lucy couldn't quite get a handle on what was going on with Maya. She seemed to have grown up in the space of two days. All those months living together, she'd seemed so sweet, so quiet, so nerdy. Sitting on her bed, working on her laptop, chunky headphones cutting her off from the rest of the world. But the way she'd been on Friday night . . . the way she'd kept her cool. Lucy would never have expected it from the youngest housemate.

"I guess we never really knew you," Lucy said aloud.

A minute later, Grace appeared, holding the empty ice cream bowls. "Maya said you were loading the dishwasher?"

Lucy took the bowls and opened the dishwasher. "Listen, Grace, there's something I've been meaning to say," she began. "I'm so sorry that we have to wait another two days before we can get your dad free."

Grace blinked. "It's not your fault."

"Yeah, but I promised you last night. And it didn't happen. That's on me."

Grace gave a minimal shrug. "It is what it is."

"I . . . I should have told you," Lucy stammered. "Sooner, I mean. About seeing a woman drowning Tyson Drew."

Grace didn't react, so Lucy went on, talking faster. "I know I already said some of this, but I want you to know that I feel bad about what you've been through, because of this. I mean, I feel just *horrible*."

Grace tried to smile, but this time a tear appeared in her eye. Hesitantly, Lucy touched Grace's shoulder. "I promise you, I swear to God, Grace, if I'd ever believed that those dreams were memories, if I hadn't spent so many years persuading myself that it was some kinda psychological damage . . . y'know . . . all those drugs I did? I would have found a way to say something."

Trembling, Grace managed a single nod.

Lucy withdrew her hand awkwardly. This wasn't coming out as sensitively as she'd intended. "Jeez, Gracie. I'm sorry. I shouldn't dump my issues on you."

Grace just nodded. "Lucy, okay. I understand . . . I think."

"I just want to know that we're cool," she said. Which was lame, and she knew it.

Grace nodded. "We're cool."

"Okay," Lucy said. Grace's reaction was less emphatic than she'd hoped. It didn't feel like she had bridged the divide between them, at least not enough to start trying to persuade Grace to get her sister's boyfriend to up and leave. So, very cautiously she added, "Hey, everything okay between you and Paolo?"

To Lucy's amazement, Grace's eyes flared. "Why do you want to know?"

"No reason," Lucy replied. "Just that the two of you seemed, ah, a little closer. Yesterday."

There was a pause. "Paolo's upset. Which I guess is understandable. I'm just trying to be there for him."

"Yeah, nice. Our boy Paolo could probably use some moral support."

"So you don't think he's a bad person?" Grace sounded hopeful.

The question struck a little too close to the bone. "Because of what happened Friday night?" Lucy flashed back to those terrible events. "Look, it all just sorta *happened*. I tried to stop it, but they didn't listen."

Grace looked her in the eye for a moment. "You tried to stop them?"

"Yeah," Lucy said wearily. "A couple of times. I said we should go to the cops." She regretted her words almost instantly. She couldn't seem to say anything that didn't hurt or disappoint Grace. And that was the very last thing she wanted.

"They didn't want to?"

"They just couldn't hear it," Lucy told her. "Scared for John-Michael, I guess. Y'know, what with the whole thing about his father dying the same way."

"But Paolo, he wasn't afraid of the cops, was he?"

"Yeah. He was, G. That dream of being a lawyer dies hard, I guess."

"You think that's why, because he's afraid of getting a record?"

"Yup. They don't give criminals a license to practice law."

Grace hung her head. "You think it'll come to that, to convictions, to jail?"

"God, I hope not," said Lucy. "Guess that's why we're lying low. Until it all blows over." She glanced at Grace, who appeared a little calmer. "Which, by the way," she said, carefully, "would be a lot easier without Yoandy."

"Oh, Yoandy," Grace said, sighing. "I wish Candace would send him away. But you know, after all the stress, I'm worried if I ask her to, she might totally freak on me."

CANDACE

The instant she heard her sister's voice on the patio, Candace sat up. Stretched out in the sun lounger next to hers, Yoandy had on his headphones, sunglasses over his eyes. He was moving his shoulders in a gentle rhythm.

"I'm going inside, Yoandy," Candace told him. "Can I get you anything?"

He lifted the sunglasses and grinned. "How about a little iced coffee?"

Candace stood up, looped an arm through Grace's, and led her sister to the kitchen, where Paolo and John-Michael were preparing a salad. "Could you guys make some iced coffee?" she asked. "And take one out to Yoandy?"

"Sure," Paolo said.

Candace steered Grace toward the bedroom. In the instant they turned away from Paolo, Candace caught the hopeful smile he reserved for Grace.

Seriously—Paolo? For a minute, she forgot about the news that she'd been dying to discuss with her sister—Dana

Alexander's text. It was yet more gloomy-doomy stuff, of which they already had plenty. Grace's love life, on the other hand—that was a real conversation starter.

Candace plopped down in the center of the double bed and faced her stepsister. It was time for a little honesty. She'd gotten to know Paolo. The more Candace thought about him, the more questions she had.

Paolo played the part of the cute, friendly jock. Was he, though? Or was he a player? As an actor, Candace was learning to tell when someone was using technique. Paolo too often took a fraction of a second to compose his sentences and even his features.

Her sister was too complex, too thoughtful, to be taken in by some idiotic player. If Grace found something in Paolo that was worthy of admiration, or even love, then it had to be there—somewhere.

Candace didn't admit it nearly often enough—actually, almost never—but she was fiercely devoted to the girl she'd come to think of as a blood sister. She knew she had to prod at this apparent attraction to Paolo, if only to protect her.

"You and Paolo, hey?" she said with a hint of accusation.

"I think we've got more important stuff to talk about."

"Oh, you mean, like me and Yoandy?"

Grace frowned. "Well . . ."

Candace groaned. "Or you mean the fact that our housemates have gotten involved in a little light *manslaughter*? You might wanna take a look at this text." She handed

Grace her phone. "Because if you're not in the mood to talk about you and the hunk, I can always heap a little more crap onto your cheery day."

"Jeez, Candace. It's not my fault," Grace muttered.

"Ah, yeah, 'fraid it is. You're the one who insisted they 'fess up. Me, I was blissful in my ignorance."

Grace rolled her eyes. "You were pretty blissful in your knowledge, too. I was awake half the night, but you were snoring."

"I never snore," Candace said loftily. She sat up, plucked her cell phone from the pocket of her shorts, and showed it to Grace. "Lookit. From Dana Alexander. She seems really mad–I'm guessing she's heard about what went down Friday night? Quoting Shakespeare at us again, like the malignant *fruitcake* she is. I looked it up–it's from *Twelfth Night*."

Grace read the text and handed back the phone. "She sent this last night? Why'd you wait until now to tell me?"

"You were pretty sleepy when I got back from my walk with Yoandy. I didn't like to bother you. By the time I woke up this morning, you'd already gone to Napa."

"Liar," Grace said affectionately. "I brought you breakfast in bed, lazybones."

"Grac-ie," she whined, "I almost never get to sleep in! No fair blaming me when I take the chance."

"You poor actors, it's practically abuse."

They both smiled, relieved to have a light moment.

Then Candace returned her attention to her phone. "This is such a mess."

"If Dana's involved in what happened on Friday, then she knows about it, I'd have to agree. Why did she text you?" Grace asked.

"Because she knows my number? Her husband has the numbers for the entire cast of our TV show. She knows Maya's number, too—the last text went to her, remember, 'O judgment,' blah, blah, whatever? I guess Maya was serious about keeping her cell switched off."

"Yes, Maya seems very serious about us being 'on the lam.'"

"You know what though, Gracie? Now I'm officially irritated," Candace said.

"Irritated?"

"I'm all for trying to make the best of this little super-secret vacay. But . . ." Candace shrugged and gazed at the ceiling. To her surprise, she felt herself welling up.

Grace put an arm around her shoulders. "It's okay, sis. I'm scared, too."

Candace threw herself back onto the bed, tugging at Grace's sleeve until she joined her. They both lay there, staring up at the ceiling, at the shadows cast by the chandelier.

We should never have agreed to come to Napa.

Candace began to think of a way out of it—whatever *it* was. Eventually, she spoke again, this time quietly. "So, come on. What's with you and Paolo, anyhow? Doesn't seem like your type."

"He's a good friend," Grace managed to say. "And no one chooses who they fall in love with . . . right?"

"Seriously—gross!" Candace mimed sticking two fingers down her throat. "You can't mean that."

In a small voice Grace replied, "But I do."

"You're stressed out. Not a reason to completely lose your mind."

"No. It's more than that. It's . . . it's been there from the very beginning. Almost since the first time I saw him. And before you ask, it's not because he's so good-looking."

This attitude didn't surprise Candace at all. Grace didn't want to be thought of as shallow, and the truth was, Candace knew perfectly well that she wasn't. That's what was so odd about it.

"Oh, please. Let's not kid ourselves here. 'Disney Channel'? He's a hot dude with muscles and a cute smile, but all the personality of vanilla pudding."

Grace bit her lip. "Paolo's more complicated than you think," she began, but stopped.

Okay—now we're getting to it.

"Still waters run deep, is that what you think? Gracie, if those waters are deep, then they're hiding something you maybe don't want to see."

Grace went very still. "What makes you say that?"

Candace thought for a moment. There were things that she could share, opinions about Paolo that might alienate her from Grace. Especially if anything serious ever did develop between him and her sister. But she loved Grace. Surely it was her duty to point these things out?

"I already told you back when we had the first party. All that talk about being a human rights lawyer? Pfft. Now he's gotten involved in an actual, serious crime? C'mon, Grace. Paolo's more interested in being liked and respected than in what he actually does to earn it."

Grace seemed to consider this. When she did reply, it was without bitterness or suspicion, but with a definite undercurrent of hurt. "Did it ever occur to you that the reason Paolo is too freaked out to go to the cops is because he needs a clean record if he's ever going to be a lawyer? Anyhow, what's so bad about wanting to be liked? Doesn't everyone?"

"Everyone? No. Lucy could care less, me either. Look, sis, I meet some heavy-duty snake-oil salesmen in the entertainment business."

By now Grace's cheeks were burning bright. Was it possible that her feelings for Paolo were clouding her judgment? From what she'd observed, her sister had been trying *not* to fall for the hot guy. Falling for a boy who was not just super-hot but also *bad* was more her own style than her sister's.

And she could guess what Grace thought of that: the worst cliché under the sun.

Candace knew she was right when Grace turned to her with an apologetic smile. "So, I might as well just shoot myself in the foot and get it over with? Is that what you're thinking?"

Candace sighed. She really didn't want to hurt Grace, but now that she'd started, there were things that had to be said.

"Honestly, nothing is turning out the way I expected, either," she said. "Like, what happened on Friday night at the house? If my mom gets even a hint of all *that*, she is going to *seriously* freak. And we can forget our cozy crib on Venice Beach."

"You think *your mom* is our biggest problem?" Grace asked.

Again Candace sighed. "Obviously, she's not. Not for Paolo and JM, anyhow. I'm just trying to think about you and me, the house and everything. If anything does happen, I guess I'd go live with Katelyn in Malibu. Ever since I got the TV shows, she's finally showing some interest. But, Gracie, I'd want you to come live with me, too. I couldn't face living in that house without a friendly face. And I'd miss you like crazy if you went back to San Antonio."

"But . . . with Dana Alexander mad at all of us," Grace said doubtfully, "don't you think you might have a problem with your new TV show? Isn't her husband one of the main guys?"

"Holy crap, you're right," Candace said, deflated. "But I'd still need to stay in LA. You're my girl, right? Gracie? You won't abandon me?"

Grace turned to face her sister. She raised a finger to

lift a strand of honey-blond hair out of Candace's eyes. "Of course I wouldn't," she said softly. "That's why I came to LA, Candace. You and me. You're my only sister in the whole wide world. I was all alone with those crazy lil' brothers, and then you came along like the answer to a prayer. We're going to be best friends our whole lives. Our kids are going to grow up together, like brothers and sisters. 'Cause you don't get rid of me that easily, okay?"

JOHN-MICHAEL
POOL, FLOR DE CANELA, MONDAY, JULY 6

Around three in the afternoon, Candace, Yoandy, and Lucy went hiking. There was a tacit agreement among the housemates to keep Yoandy distracted—and to stop Candace from being alone with him, in case the pressure of keeping the secret got to be too much and she cracked.

Now alone beside the pool, John-Michael peeled off his wet T-shirt. Gingerly, he prodded at the bruises on his ribs. They were yellow with a halo of purple red. He'd been taking Advil every day since Friday night, but now he'd run out. Luckily the pain had receded to a dull ache.

The smell of toasting cheese distracted him. He picked up a shirt that Paolo had discarded earlier and put it on, a little surprised at how loosely it fit He wandered into the kitchen, where Paolo and Grace were laying slices of cheese on wheat bread. Two grilled cheese sandwiches were already finished, cut into four triangles. He reached for one, but Paolo tapped his fingers with a spatula. "Hey! Those are mine."

John-Michael watched hungrily as Grace put two more sandwiches onto the griddle. Hot butter began to sizzle into the bread.

Paolo gave John-Michael a crooked grin. "Dude, I asked you a question."

"Yeah? Sorry. I need that sandwich."

Paolo smiled. "It'll be ready soon. So I was telling Grace my top five movies ever, and now we want to hear yours."

John-Michael cleared his throat. "Well, *Up* has gotta be in there. I mean, I cried—at least two times."

Grace sighed. "Oh, *Up*. I love *Up*."

"Then *Dance with Me*, because of Chayanne, a very cute singer from Puerto Rico."

"You do enjoy the Latino gentlemen," acknowledged Grace.

"Oh yeah," Paolo said, "what's the deal with you and that guy from Lucy's band—Ruben?"

John-Michael had barely thought about Ruben since Friday. Would he ever see Ruben again? Safer not to think about him at all.

"My cell phone has been switched off since Friday night," he said. "Like we *agreed*."

"Hey, if I took a call from my mom," said Paolo, "it was only to keep her from reporting me as a missing person."

"You took a call?" John-Michael asked.

"For like, two minutes. What, you want our folks searching for us on top of everything else?"

There was an uncomfortable silence. Grace gave each

boy a thoughtful look. "Who are you more afraid of—the cops? Or those hit men's buddies?"

Silently, John-Michael cursed Paolo's big mouth.

Paolo turned to Grace. "Gracie, I haven't ever denied that we came to Napa to hide from *someone*."

"I'm not an idiot; we guessed you guys had gotten into trouble. And yes, in our worst nightmares it was because you'd killed someone. But you understand, don't you: we didn't expect *actual nightmares* to come true!"

Expectantly, Paolo glanced at John-Michael.

"I really didn't intend to kill that guy," John-Michael said quietly. "But he was shooting off his gun. Any one of us might have gotten hit."

"Yes, I know," Grace said, somewhat resentfully. "You said. And if we'd known, Candace and me, I don't think we'd have agreed to come to Napa."

"I'm sorry," Paolo said. "We honestly thought it would be the safest thing, for all of us to stick together."

Grace appeared hurt by the misdirection, but not surprised. The dynamic between her and Paolo intrigued John-Michael. It had shifted in the past few days. Now Paolo was the one chasing Grace, whereas before, Grace had seemed like a girl with a crush, afraid to pursue the guy in question.

"Paolo's right. You're definitely safer here than in Venice," John-Michael said. It was time to leave these two alone. "Okay," he said. "I'm gonna head back to the pool."

John-Michael picked up one half of a grilled cheese. This time, Paolo didn't stop him. Standing outside on the deserted patio, he ate the whole thing in four bites. Then he took off the T-shirt and lowered himself onto the metallic steps at the end of the pool. Yoandy wouldn't be back from the hike for a while–John-Michael could swim without a shirt for at least half an hour without any difficult questions about bruises.

Soon he was drifting on his back in warm, lightly salted water, staring up at the darkening azure of the sky. He became aware of the faint, high-pitched buzz of crickets in nearby undergrowth. Above, swallows congregated in the air thermals, swirling as they began to flock. From inside the house he heard music.

John-Michael's neck relaxed enough that water began to trickle into his ears. He didn't resist, just let them fill up until the sounds of the birds and the crickets melted away. His limbs felt heavy and tired. There wasn't enough water in the pool to buoy him up; it would take an ocean.

He tried to think about other things, but when he closed his eyes, the memory of his father's death was empty. Not just faint and undefined, like shapes seen through condensation on a mirror, but gone: replaced. Now when he remembered holding a man down under a cushion, he only saw the hit man, felt only implacable resolve running through his own muscles: *keep holding him down until he stops moving.*

The deep blue sky seemed to bear down on him. The valley felt oppressive. He longed to be alone at the edge of the ocean, gazing out at the horizon. John-Michael had spent many nights that way when he'd been homeless. When dusk fell, people liked to come to the beach with empty hands, jogging or simply strolling, out to watch the setting of the sun. Who was rich and secure, who was poor and hungry? You couldn't tell; eventually everyone was reduced to a silhouette. On the beach, you could be anyone.

"Hey," Maya said. He opened his eyes to see her leaning over him. "You okay?" She winced through her teeth. "Yikes. Those are nasty bruises, JM. I'm sorry."

John-Michael stood upright, chest high in water. "I know."

Maya sat down, dipping her bare legs into the water. "So listen," she said. "I was thinking. Even though Grace and Candace know, we should probably still keep some stuff locked down. Because, y'know, Yoandy."

A faint smile. "Tell me about it; I'm still hiding under a shirt because of him," he said ruefully. "Are you working on the big escape plan? Want me to help? 'Cause I can help."

"Later, when I've thought of a better place to hide the money." Maya's legs swayed, creating ripples on the surface of the pool. "Just, y'know, I got to thinking about what might happen to us all—after this."

"If there is an 'after this,'" John-Michael muttered. He wondered if he should tell Maya about his desire to float away. She'd probably take it literally.

He raised his eyes to look at her. "Where would you go?" Maya asked.

The question caught John-Michael unawares. "Costa Rica," he replied.

"Have you ever been?"

"I dated a boy from there, once. Tito."

"Oh yeah, I remember. Your chem lab partner, right?"

"Right. Tito used to talk about how when he was a little kid, his dad worked in this gigantic banana plantation. They grew this kind of banana . . . you know anything about bananas?" When Maya shook her head, he went on. "These days, most of the world only wants to buy one kind of banana. It wasn't always that way. One day the supermarket fruit buyers said that they were only taking Cavendish bananas from now on, not the strain that grew where Tito lived. The banana plantation closed down. And pretty much the whole town went bust."

"That's why Tito's family moved?"

"Yep. The way Tito described Costa Rica, it sounded amazing," said John-Michael.

The pool lights turned on then—a blooming of blue around him that startled him for a second. "He told me about the beaches. Pale turquoise water, crystal clear. Shallow sands, palm trees, hammocks suspended between them. Mountains covered in green. The rain forest, sloping up from the coast toward the volcanoes. Food like Yoandy cooked, but even better. Warm nights all year round. And salsa music."

He stopped for a minute. This wasn't getting him anywhere close to what he wanted to say and meanwhile Maya was listening with a curious expression. John-Michael tried again. "There's got to be someplace, somewhere, don't you think? Where we can feel truly free. Like a nonstop dance party all bursting with energy. But you don't ever get tired, and you never feel lonely."

Her brow furrowed as she thought about it. "Heaven, maybe."

He shook his head as though that could erase the sheer impossibility of her comment.

"Costa Rica seems like a long way to go," Maya said.

"I like the idea of just getting lost out there. A place where nobody knows me."

Maya drew in her breath. "You aren't afraid of that?"

"I'd make friends."

"Could you take that risk, if you're on the run?" Maya looked closely at him. "Be careful, John-Michael. People are like sheep. Only a very strong person can live apart from the flock."

"You could."

"Maybe," Maya conceded, "I'd be fine. But *you* definitely need people."

John-Michael slid back under the surface of the water, eyes wide open. The night sky and the golden, flickering lights around the patio stretched above him, a wavering membrane. He'd have to get out soon.

Maya was right about it being hard to live that way.

But to live, you had to *survive*. Things were getting rough for the housemates; in such a storm, only the smartest and most cunning would stay afloat.

Maya might do it. John-Michael wasn't sure he would.

CANDACE

They returned from the hike just after six. Candace held back as they passed through the olive grove. She asked Lucy to go on ahead to the *casita*. It was obvious that Lucy was reluctant to leave her alone with Yoandy. But Candace stood her ground.

As they watched Lucy go, Yoandy turned to Candace. "*Nena*, I think it's better if I go."

Candace snagged the tight elastic of Yoandy's shirt and tugged until he'd joined her against the trunk of an olive tree. She'd been wondering how to bring it up, or if she even wanted to. Why should she make Yoandy unhappy by asking him to go just because her friends wanted to jabber on about something she'd rather not discuss?

Plus, they had to know they could trust her not to go blabbing their business to someone, even a boyfriend. She may not be down with what they'd done, but they were still her friends. And Candace was loyal.

Stalling, she asked, "What are you talking about?"

He shrugged. "Your friends. They'd prefer it if I left."

Now she felt protective. "Did someone say something?"

"No."

"John-Michael or Paolo, last night? Is it having to sleep in a hammock?"

He laughed and brushed a lock of her hair behind her ear. "No. They are nice. The hammock is beautiful."

"Then what?"

"It's a very strange atmosphere in this house," Yoandy said.

"How so? I don't understand."

He looked at her. "I think maybe you do."

"You don't believe me?"

Candace had lied to boys before to protect their male pride. What girl hadn't? But lying to Yoandy made her stomach itch, like it was crawling with ants.

He touched her face, caressing her cheekbone with the edge of his thumb. "Something is wrong here. You really don't feel it?"

This was her chance to come clean, but that was a step further than Candace was ready to go. To confess her fears to Yoandy would make them official, real.

"Everyone had a good time last night," she said, deflecting.

"Yes, last night they were happy. You worked very hard

to make that happen." Yoandy tipped her chin so that for a moment, he could look into her eyes. "That didn't seem like you."

"I can be sociable," she protested. The nearness of him, the tenderness of his every touch was beginning to undo her—again. But Candace knew that this time, she had to resist. She couldn't betray her housemates.

"Evidently."

He began to walk again, but this time Candace blocked his path through the olive grove. "Yoandy," she said seriously. "Do you mean it? You want to leave?"

"You didn't notice how your friends won't leave us alone? Why won't your friends let me sleep in the sofa bed with you?"

"That's just Grace being weird," Candace lied.

"*No lo creo.* Paolo and John-Michael *insisted* that I sleep in a hammock next to them. Like they wanted to keep an eye on me."

"Look," she said, "we're a bunch of American teenagers. What do we know about being hospitable?"

He smiled affectionately at her. "Nice try, but no way. American people can be very hospitable. Anyway, Maya is from Mexico, *sí o no?* And I think Maya is the one who would most like me to leave."

"Well, you gotta know that she's all kinds of jealous," Candace said, rolling her eyes.

That made Yoandy laugh. He wrapped her up in his arms and squeezed her. *"¡Ay, mi madre, que mujer!"* He kissed the top of her head and then bent lower to kiss her mouth.

Candace didn't resist. She drew him in for a deeper kiss than he'd intended, until he pulled away, breathless. "Beautiful *and* talented *and* funny."

"I'm not even a little bit funny," she said, pouting. "Your problem is that you don't understand me. I get what you're saying. But I don't want you to leave."

"Then leave with me."

Candace paused. To get away from this house of angst! To leave would be perfect. But Maya and Grace and the rest of them had gone into this whole lockdown mentality. She didn't dare to leave without asking them. She was pretty sure that they wouldn't agree, but it was worth a try.

Together she and Yoandy headed for the patio, where Grace, Paolo, and Maya were enjoying the last rays of the sunset. While Yoandy went into the house to get a glass of water, Candace used the moment to draw her stepsister to one side and tell her about his suggestion.

"I agree that Yoandy should leave," Grace said after a few seconds.

"Oh?"

Grace's answer was very frank. "Because we've got problems here, and I don't think he'd want to be involved if he knew."

Candace had to admit she had a point. "Okay, then I'll go, too."

"No, Candace, that's not safe."

"Don't worry; I know how to keep my yap shut."

"I know you do; that's not the problem."

Candace stood up as Yoandy came sauntering back from the *casita*. "You were right," she told him. "Maybe you should leave. We got some, ah, stuff going on here. I don't want it to affect you."

Yoandy gazed at her coolly, and then took both of her hands in his. *"Amor*, I'm not leaving without you."

"No," Candace said miserably. "I should probably stay."

He looked at her hard. "I knew it. Something happened, didn't it? Yesterday, when I made the mojitos. One minute was all dancing and laughing. Then–I don't know! You all got *so* sad."

"Yoandy!" Candace blurted. "There are things going on here that, well, I can't tell you about."

"What kind of things?"

No one would answer Yoandy's question. After a moment, Grace rose from her chair. "Candace is right. It's not fair to get you involved."

He looked imploringly at Candace. *"Mi amor*, what happened?"

"Look, man," Paolo said, "it's ancient history. And it really does not concern you. So why don't you do like your girlfriend says and bounce?"

Yoandy glanced at Candace for confirmation. When she nodded, he released her hands. "All right. I'll get my bag."

"You don't need to leave right away," Candace said. She was starting to feel a little desperate. Why hadn't she been more convincing? How hard would it have been for everyone to just chill out for one more night? "He can stay until tomorrow morning, can't he?"

Yoandy looked sad. "I don't think so. Anyhow, you don't really have space for me to be here overnight. I'll go."

"But it's late!"

"I'll find a motel."

"Really? Which one? I'll call you."

Candace dreaded the passing of each minute. She watched in silence as Yoandy fetched his suitcase. Then he took her hand in his, and they walked toward the driveway. By the time they reached the car, they were no longer in the housemates' line of sight.

Yoandy turned to face her. "Come with me," he murmured, raising her fingers to brush against his lips. "I asked the orishas to help me protect you. We should be together."

"If the orishas are so powerful, let them protect me themselves." She smiled, unconsciously touching the necklace he'd given her. It was in honor of Cuba's patron saint.

"The orishas act through people," Yoandy said doubtfully. He bent forward, touched his forehead to hers. "I should stay near you."

"I'll come as soon as I can," she whispered. She felt a tug of sorrow deep inside her chest, exquisitely painful and entirely new. Her heart began to pound. She'd made a mistake, a stupid mistake. She didn't want Yoandy to go like this, not at all. "I promise. It won't be long."

GRACE

Paolo peered toward the driveway, but Candace and Yoandy were just out of sight. "You think Candace is mad at us?"

Grace noticed how he glanced first at Maya, and then at John-Michael. It wasn't the first time the other three housemates seemed to defer to Maya's judgment.

"It's kind of irrelevant," Maya said eventually.

"Oh, really?" Grace asked. "Why's that?"

"It's nothing personal. I like Candace, I like Yoandy. I don't want her to feel bad. But right now, tonight, it doesn't change anything," Maya replied.

Grace waited for one of the others to object, or at least to say something conciliatory. But no one did.

"Are you guys actually saying it's okay to make Candace feel bad?" she sputtered.

"Don't get your panties in a bunch," Maya said. "Like we say, it's nothing personal."

"Like *we* say? Since when do you speak for everyone else?"

"Gracie," Paolo began soothingly. But when he stretched out a hand to touch her forearm, Grace snatched it away.

"No, Paolo! You've been dancing around this whole thing since we got here. But I've been thinking, ever since you told us what happened. We should call the bodyguard, my father's friend."

"A bodyguard?" Lucy looked around, alarmed. "No one told *me* about a bodyguard."

"Grace's father recommended someone," Paolo admitted.

Lucy stared at Grace. "He did? Why?"

"Like I told you, Lucy, from the minute he knew I was suspicious, my dad guessed you guys got into a fight, or worse. Well, now we know. And now that I know, I *don't* feel safe here," Grace said.

There was an extended silence. It grew more awkward with every passing second. Grace felt her ears sizzling as realization hit. Not one of the other housemates was denying it.

"So you agree?" she asked stiffly. "We're not safe?"

There was another painful pause. "We're safe, so long as no one knows where we are, but if . . ." Maya trailed off.

Everyone turned toward Candace, who was storming back toward the house. Grace tried to meet her eye, but Candace swerved away from her. There was fury in her glare. "Stay away from me!" she yelled, when Grace tried to follow her into the house.

In shock, Grace returned to the patio, where the others stood openmouthed.

Grace attempted to smile. "That didn't go very well."

"She'll be okay," Maya said.

"I've been where she is," Lucy added. "You get over it."

Grace shook her head, feeling a little hopeless. "I don't know. Until now, she's been in denial. Right from the time we were in the house on Friday night, waiting for you to come home. We knew—I knew—that something bad happened. But Candace, she *wouldn't* see it. Even after you actually told us!"

"She took some time to get there," Lucy commented. "But she sure as hell sees it now."

"Yeah, but it's going to hit her hard," Maya said. "This could be trouble."

"Oh yeah?" Grace said. "How? I mean, why?"

"Yeah," Paolo added. "What trouble?"

"Candace is no snitch," Lucy said.

Maya shrugged. "We all had our secrets, didn't we? Now, not so much."

"I think Candace is the *only* one of us who didn't have a secret," John-Michael said. "Unless you count that she was seeing Yoandy."

"That's exactly what I mean," Maya said. "Candace was dating someone connected to Dana Alexander, and she didn't tell us."

"But she didn't know that there was anything going on with Dana Alexander until Friday," Grace pointed out.

"I just hope she calms down, and soon," Maya said. "Because I got a bad feeling. We were supposed to be here in secret. Now Grace's dad knows we're here. And Yoandy knows, too. Yoandy's heading back to LA. What if Dana Alexander gets to him?"

Grace shot her a worried look. "You think we should have made him stay?"

"No," Maya said, with a little toss of her head. "It's not like he could stick around indefinitely. Better he's out of the way before he finds out anything."

"So you *are* glad he's gone?" Grace asked.

"I'm glad," Maya conceded. "But I still don't think we're safe."

"I say you're paranoid," Paolo told her. He put an arm around Grace's shoulders. "And anyway, if there's one person that Dana Alexander isn't likely to hurt, it's Yoandy."

"That's right," Lucy said. "Her lil' sister is sweet on the boy."

"Won't keep him safe from Dana," Maya said, scowling.

"But the fact that she and Yoandy are connected might," Paolo said. "It's pretty risky to hurt people who have any known connection to you. It leads to questions from the cops. So far Dana's been pretty careful—no one really knows about her connection with us."

"True," said Grace. "She *has* kind of stayed in the shadows."

"What about those texts?" Maya pointed out. "They're kind of a giveaway. I mean who'd send *us* Shakespearean quotes?"

"I wouldn't get your hopes up about those texts," Lucy said. "If she sent them from a burner, they'd be useless as evidence."

"You're all forgetting that Dana asked me to spy on you," Maya said. "Dana's connection to the house is clear enough. And it didn't stop her sending her goons."

"She only sent the first one," Lucy said. "Y'all decided to summon the second guy." She glared at Maya. "That was your particular piece of genius, if I recollect."

Grace put out a hand to silence them. "I think," she said, slowly, "that we need to call my dad's bodyguard friend, Pete Martens."

"Veto," Maya said quickly. "We need to know more about him first."

"There's no veto," Grace said, quietly. "Just a vote." She raised a hand. "I say we call him. Who agrees?"

One by one, Lucy, Paolo, and John-Michael raised their hands.

MAYA

CASITA, FLOR DE CANELA, TUESDAY, JULY 7

The next morning, Maya was the first out of bed. She moved barefoot and silent through the living room. Beneath the crumpled white quilt on the sofa bed where the Deering sisters slept, she spied tresses of blond hair.

Maya barely gave the girls a glance before turning into the kitchen. She poured herself a glass of water, and then walked back into the living room and opened the French doors that led to the patio.

John-Michael and Paolo appeared to be asleep in their hammocks. Maya walked by, watching to see if they woke, but they didn't. When she reached the edge of the pool, she peered into its still depths. A pool vacuum cleaner lurked there like a slumbering turtle. The sky was pale gray, completely overcast, a thin haze that the white sun was gradually burning away.

She sipped some water and flipped open her laptop, waiting for the screen to fire up, and quickly read her most recent email.

Hey there! You okay? I know you're probably busy with
your mates, but I wondered if we could have a quick hello
on Skype.

Jack Cato. She'd known him for a little over a month,
but she'd come to rely on his advice to steer her though
major decisions. Jack was so good at navigating complex
problems, whether they were chemistry or business. Now
she had problems of a whole different kind—but Maya felt
sure he'd have good advice for her.

Without Jack as a sounding board, her thought processes felt lackluster. Every time she hit a bump, her hand
went to her cell phone. Once she'd even selected his number before she'd remembered that they were supposed to be
keeping radio silence.

The only way she even dared to check in on Jack was
via the development server for her app, Promisr. Jack knew
that Maya uploaded new files there. She recognized the IP
addresses Jack used to access the server—at home or at the
library at Caltech. He was still checking, day and night.

Even that indirect method of communication gave
Maya a warm feeling. Now that she had an actual email
from him, she wondered if maybe they could risk a very
quick session via Skype. Even if she couldn't give him any
hint of what was going on with her housemates, she could
at least say hello.

Jack could have helped now in ways that no one else
could. He was brilliant. His sharp mind was ruthlessly

logical, quicker and was more insightful than anyone she'd ever met. No housemate could help Maya with this—not when possible scenarios included one of them being thrown to the cops.

There was the whole issue about the cash. What kind of insanity had gotten ahold of them, taking that bag of money? *Major* error of judgment. Not even remotely easy to undo, either.

To be caught with the money could mean jail or even death. They had to get rid of it—fast. The best plan she could come up with was to hide the cash somewhere and return for it someday. Maybe even years later, after the storm had settled.

There was still the matter of breaking the law. Self-defense or not, if those two deaths were ever linked to the housemates, there'd be a case to answer. Maya couldn't see any way to save everybody. John-Michael or Paolo might have to hand themselves over to the cops to save the others. It was that or risk calling in the bodyguard guy that Grace's dad had recommended—Pete Martens. But a new person in the mix meant a new risk.

All the solutions pretty much sucked. None of them left her safe beyond any guarantee. Most of them would cause enough scandal that Maya could imagine her investor, Alexa Nyborg, withdrawing her substantial support. It would most likely scare other investors away, too.

After another second or two of doubt, she called Jack on Skype. When he answered, she could see that he'd propped the laptop up in bed. Maya carefully turned her chair and laptop screen so Nyborg's pool wasn't in view.

"Well, hello! The wanderer returns!"

"Hey. I'm sorry I didn't reply. Not much phone reception, here. No Wi-Fi, either, just a LAN. I guess my friends *really* like to get away from it all."

Jack's open, curious face filled the screen as he peered at the image of Maya on his own computer. "Where's 'here'?"

"I've been staying at a friend's house," she lied. "A friend from, ah, school."

"Oh, one of your *rich* friends," he said. "Getting into practice for when you're the one hosting the parties?"

"Ha, yeah, I guess so," Maya said evasively.

"So, what's up? How was the Fourth?"

"I miss you," she said, and then stopped talking and just gazed at him.

He seemed surprised and pleased. "Well, I miss you, too. Wish you'd invited me."

"Yeah, next time."

"You're looking *amaze*, by the way."

"I am not," she laughed. "I'm in my pj's."

Jack winked. "I have an excellent imagination."

They chatted for a few more minutes. It wasn't difficult to steer Jack clear of specific questions about what they'd done for July fourth. Once he'd started flirting, Jack seemed perfectly happy to relax and enjoy the banter.

When she'd finished the call, Maya's eyes came to rest, wistfully, on the main house at Flor de Canela. Morning light streamed through adobe-painted archways and cast romantic shadows across the ceramic tiles of the floor.

This place was going to haunt Maya, she could already see that. It represented everything she thought she wanted out of life. Security for herself and her family, a dazzling career in the technology industry, a house more beautiful than anything she'd dreamed of.

But it all paled beside the thought of Paolo or John-Michael in prison. Or her mother prosecuted for document fraud and deported. Nothing could make Maya feel okay about that; not riches, not fame. To keep them safe, she'd give away all possibility of a future sponsored by Nyborg.

As the decision solidified, Maya felt relief wash over her. The law could go to hell. They'd started something. Now they had to finish it.

"We're all getting out of this," she muttered fiercely. "No one gets hurt, no one goes to jail."

"Who're you talking to?"

Maya spun around to see John-Michael ambling toward her. He was still wrapped in a fleece blanket. "I was just, ah . . . Nothing."

"Thought maybe it was Candace. Where is she?"

"Candace? In bed, I guess. Or the bathroom."

John-Michael yawned. "Uh-uh. I just went to use the bathroom. She's not in the bed. She's not in the bathroom. Or the kitchen. I thought maybe in the pool, 'cause you're standing here . . ." He shrugged. "Guess not."

Maya stiffened. There was another possibility. But

surely Candace wouldn't be so crazy impetuous?

Maya broke into a jog. "No . . . no." As she rounded the *casita*, the full length of the driveway came into view. "Candace! Candace!" she shouted.

John-Michael joined her a second later. There was just one car in the driveway—Paolo's Chevy Malibu. Yoandy's car had gone. So had Candace's Prius.

"But—but I saw Candace," Maya said uselessly. "She was in the sofa bed."

"There was only one person there a few minutes ago," John-Michael said. "And that was Grace. You must have walked right past and not noticed that she'd gone."

Maya didn't want him to be right, but as the wave of shock passed through her, so did another sensation—a rush of ice-cold lucidity.

Candace had gone. Despite their warnings and pleas, she'd left the group.

Once again, this changed everything.

One by one, their options were closing down. And there was no endgame in sight.

PAOLO
PACIFIC COAST HIGHWAY, TUESDAY, JULY 7

"Stupid, stupid, stupid!"

Paolo's hands gripped the steering wheel, his muscles bunched with tension. He'd never seen Grace this distressed. She'd been running the entire incident over and over for the past two hours.

"You think Yoandy made her go?"

Paolo suppressed a groan; they'd been through this about twenty minutes ago. "I don't think so."

"But before, you said that you couldn't believe how easily he agreed to leave! You said: 'I'd never walk away from my girlfriend without making a huge deal about it.'"

"And you," he replied, "told me that a *nice* guy would respect his girlfriend's wishes and just leave."

"I said that?" Grace sounded dazed.

"Yes, you did."

"Well, then I don't know. Surely if he really cared about Candace he'd try a little harder to stay, right?"

"Exactly," Paolo said, relieved.

"Which means that he was only *pretending* to leave without making a big deal. All along, he had a plan to get my sister to leave."

"That's a shade paranoid, don't you think?" Paolo asked cautiously.

Grace groaned in frustration, bringing a clenched fist down on the car's dashboard.

"Why don't you try calling Candace again?" Paolo suggested.

"Because—argh! It's too depressing when she doesn't pick up. Makes me think that Yoandy's strangled her and chopped up her body into little pieces."

"Gracie!"

"I know, I know, I'm certifiable. It's just, Paolo, you can't imagine how scared I am."

"Baby, I can see that." Paolo took one of her hands in his and knitted their fingers together. "Look," he said, "they're probably, y'know, *doing it*. They looked pretty hot for each other yesterday. And we didn't leave them alone the whole time. All that unresolved tension. Maybe they arranged it all ahead of time? And now . . . ? I'm guessing that the last thing your sis is thinking about is taking calls from you."

Despite herself, Grace seemed a little calmer. "Maybe. I'll feel better if we find her at the house in Venice. Just in case you're wrong, and she's there already . . ."

A ringtone sounded—Grace's burner phone. He looked hopeful. "You think it could be Pete Martens calling you back?"

Grace examined the number. "It's my cousin Alice—the one in San Francisco. I had to give her a number where she could reach me and we promised not to use our own cell phones."

Paolo groaned. Still the burner rang.

Grace eyed him pleadingly. "It could be important."

"Any reason why she'd reach out? You just saw her two days ago."

Grace seemed anxious. "Maybe it's about my dad?" When Paolo agreed, she touched the answer button and listened. He heard a catch in her breath, and then a horrified gasp.

"What is it?" he whispered. But Grace didn't respond, only grew more rigid. Then she began to talk, a flurry of soothing words. Alice had to be incredibly upset, judging by Grace's reaction.

After what seemed like far too long, Grace said goodbye.

"Someone came to visit Alice," Grace told him. "A man, a stranger. Asking questions, Paolo! Questions about *us*!"

Paolo's mind raced. "They must have been watching the prison or something."

"No, no, it can't be that, because, think about it: if they did, then why would they need to talk to Alice? They could have just followed us when we left."

"Yeah," he agreed, instantly relieved. "Gracie . . . did he threaten her?"

"Not exactly, not from what she said . . . but he was

obviously scary. Alice is totally spooked. She's left home, she's staying with friends. A man came to her apartment, Paolo, knocked right on her door! Can you imagine that?"

"Can I imagine it?" he echoed.

But Grace stopped him. "Omigod, you *can* imagine it, can't you?" Now she simply stared at him, aghast. "That's what happened to you on Friday. Isn't it?"

"It did kind of end up being a lot worse," Paolo admitted. "Although, obviously, that really sucks for your cousin."

"She couldn't tell him anything, but she said the guy was real insistent. Made her show him her cell phone contacts, checked the house for messages written on paper. Alice told him over and over—she thought we were in staying in some motel near the prison."

"You told Alice that? Smart."

"No, Paolo, I didn't tell her anything, but I guess she assumed. I mean, that's what we did last time."

Paolo blinked. "So whoever called your cousin, they've gone to check the motels?"

"I guess. By now they must've realized we're not at home in Venice."

"What makes you think that Candace would go home? Wouldn't she go straight to Yoandy's?"

"I don't know where he lives," Grace said. She sounded dangerously close to anger. "I do know where our house is. We've got to hurry, check to see if she's gone there and get her out, as fast as possible."

Paolo wasn't about to argue. They drove the rest of the way in silence.

He glanced over at her every now and again, wondering if she wanted him to be more physical with her. Sometimes people liked more physical contact when they were anxious. With anyone but Grace, he wouldn't have thought about it twice. Now that they'd almost kissed, he was on shakier ground. If she thought he was being comforting, fine. But what if she thought he was making a move?

Okay, he *would* be making a move. But did she want him to? In this mood, Grace was particularly difficult to read. He'd never had to work so hard to figure out a girl.

They arrived at Venice Beach shortly after noon. Paolo parked the car and walked around to the trunk. He wanted to have something, anything, to protect them in case anyone besides Candace and Yoandy was waiting inside. His dad's Weedwacker was pretty much the only thing that fit the bill. He grabbed it, and then hurried to catch up with Grace at the front door.

"Let me go first, just to check," he warned.

He watched Grace turn the key and softly slide it back out of the lock. Then he pushed the door open gently and advanced, fingers wrapped tightly around the Weedwacker. He took two steps, enough to capture the whole living room at a glance. It was empty.

A third step, and a turn to his left. Paolo peered around the corner into the kitchen-dining room. It was empty and bright with the afternoon sun streaming through the windows, the chopping board and knife just as they'd been after John-Michael had finished slicing vegetables on Friday evening. Nothing in either room had changed since they'd left.

He and Grace quickly checked all the rooms upstairs. No one.

They returned to the living room, where Paolo checked the French doors. They slid apart smoothly at his touch. He winced. "Look. We left them unlocked."

Grace joined him. "They'll have to stay that way; Candace has the full set of keys. We'll have to close the drapes and hope it's okay."

Paolo held one edge of the drape aside and slid the door open again. "In that case, we should leave by the backyard. Better if no one on the boardwalk sees us go." He followed Grace into the backyard, and then slid the door until it clicked.

They made their way to where he'd parked the Chevy in the street behind the house. They'd almost reached the car when he remembered the shovel. He'd cleaned the hit man's blood off it on Friday night. But it was probably safer to remove it completely.

He blipped the car doors open and handed the key to Grace. "I'll be back in a minute. I left the shovel in the yard. Just going to pick it up."

He hurried back and grabbed the shovel. He was about to leave when he heard a woman's voice from inside the house. It was someone he didn't recognize.

Paolo froze for an instant, and then moved. He pushed up against the outside of the French door and carefully slid it open about four inches. The gap was safely hidden by the drapes.

The voice had stopped. The person was standing still, silent, taking a moment to get the measure of the house. Paolo held his breath tight, muscles rigid, his bloodstream soaking with adrenaline. He couldn't see anything, but he could hear footsteps.

Through the frantic beating of his heart, Paolo reasoned that it *could* be Candace. After all, he'd done the same thing just minutes ago; he'd entered the house warily, like a burglar. But it wasn't Candace's voice that he'd heard.

A stranger had entered their house.

He sank to his knees, crouching as low as he could, and folded his legs beneath him, straining to listen to the movements of the intruder inside.

Whoever this person was, they were not familiar with the house. They were taking time to look around. The fridge was opened for more than a minute, then the pantry.

An idea struck Paolo—could it be Ariana? Lucy's former rehab roommate could have made a copy of her key. Had she returned? It certainly fit the facts so far.

He took out his burner phone and sent a text to Grace's burner: Someone in the house. Not Candace. Come back? I'm around back. QUIETLY!

He waited anxiously until her reply came through: On my way.

Briefly, Paolo relaxed. Then he heard the footsteps approaching—the intruder was in the living room. A second later, the intruder sat down on the red sofa. There was a scraping sound, metal against the wooden floor. For a moment Paolo struggled to identify that sound, and then remembered with annoyance that he'd left the Weedwacker somewhere in the living room. Their unexpected visitor seemed to be examining it now.

Could it be Dana Alexander herself?

Paolo hardly dared to breathe. A cough, a sneeze, and he'd be discovered. His eyes were drawn to the shovel beside his right knee.

It was all starting to feel like a replay of Friday night. This time he had to be smarter, calmer. Or else he could end up with blood on his hands again. He felt his cheeks flush with sudden heat.

What if the person inside is armed?

CANDACE

Yoandy gazed up at the yellow spiral of the staircase. "The stairs are *in front of* the door?"

Candace turned the key in the front door of the beach house. "Yep. Pretty weird, I know. I think the guy who built the house lived on the first floor and rented out the upstairs rooms to pay his mortgage."

Affectionately, Yoandy placed one hand on the small of her back. "Then your bedroom's upstairs? So we should be going up the stairs, no?"

With a wry smile, she held him away. "What happened to waiting until I'm eighteen? We need to check the living room. I'm kinda worried I left the French doors unlocked."

Candace pushed the door open and stepped inside, turning to him. "So—welcome to the infamous Venice Beach house—" She broke off abruptly and peered into the living room.

There was a woman sitting on the red sofa, brunette with shoulder-length wavy hair, pale skin, and bright red lipstick. She eyed Candace with mild interest and sipped from a glass of what looked like Coke. She was smartly dressed in a two-piece, tailored pants suit, black trousers and a white jacket with black lapels, and black kitten heels.

At first glance, she looked just like Dana Alexander. But Candace realized almost immediately that she wasn't.

The young woman sitting on the sofa didn't move at all.

Then Candace laughed, awkward and incredulous. "What the holy heck?"

Yoandy moved quietly to Candace's side. "Kay, what are you doing here?"

Kay Alexander was in their house.

"How'd you get in?" Candace demanded. She was getting over her surprise pretty fast, but a note of anxiety entered her voice as she approached the red sofa—and then stopped.

Kay ignored the question. She bent down to put the glass of soda onto the floor beside the sofa, and then leaned over, picking something up in her left hand. It was a Weed-wacker.

Candace sensed that Yoandy had stopped moving, too. He didn't say anything. Candace, for a brief moment, couldn't think of anything to say that she'd want Yoandy to hear. She had just opened her mouth to test out a polite reprimand when she froze.

Kay still had the Weedwacker in one hand. With the other, she was picking up a large kitchen knife from between the sofa cushions. She seemed to admire her own reflection in the blade for a moment before glancing up at Yoandy. She eyed him sternly, like a warrior princess.

"Kay," urged Yoandy. "Please. Be reasonable."

Candace said nothing at all. Her nervous system was overloading with adrenaline. It amazed her that she could control the urge to turn and run. Yet Yoandy sounded almost calm. He knew Kay a lot better. Maybe this was just the kind of melodramatic thing that Kay did?

Yoandy would know how to handle Kay. Better let him take over.

For the first time, Kay spoke. "Reasonable," she said, as if tasting the word. Her accent was American, totally Californian, not British like her older sister's. "Reasonable . . . ?" There was a long pause as she dragged the Weedwacker across the floor.

"What do *you* call 'reasonable,' Candace? Do you call it 'reasonable' to steal a man from right under his girlfriend's nose? Do you have no discretion, no shame? Or maybe you're just too stupid to realize how wrong that is? Please, do tell, I'd honestly love to know."

"Don't talk like that," Yoandy warned her. "Kay, you're doing it again. Come on, let's sit down. We'll call Dana, yes? Or Ricardo."

The Weedwacker clattered to the ground. The noise of it was like an electric shock.

"Shut your goddamn lying mouth!" snarled Kay.

The sheer animal sound of Kay's sudden rage had a wrenching effect on Candace. Terror soaked into her muscles and bones.

They were in the presence of someone very, very dangerous.

"You're a lousy sonofabitch bastard betrayer," Kay howled at Yoandy. She sounded unhinged. "I warned you, I told you a thousand times, if you ever left me, I would kill myself, I'd cut myself, I'd tie the laces of my sneakers around my neck until I choked . . ."

"He told me you weren't his girlfriend!" Candace sounded utterly horrified.

"Candace, come over here . . ." Yoandy said.

"Don't move!" Kay screamed.

Silence. Then Kay spoke again. Her voice was lower, dripping with menace. There was a pathetic tone of underlying misery—pitiful, but also desperate. "You told me you liked me. I told you you'd made me happy. That's all I ever wanted. You know how hard it is for me to be happy." She began to sob. "You know how hard things have been for me. You *know*."

"Kay," Yoandy said, his voice filled with sorrow. "Kay. Please. Put down the knife and we'll call your sister."

Candace followed Kay's eyes to the knife. Kay turned back to Yoandy with a muffled sob. "My sister. My *sister*? Sure. I should be the sister. Then people wouldn't realize how *old* she is. That she slept with who-knows-which married bastard to get ahead. That she lied to the whole world, said I was her little sister, yeah, that was fine." Another sob. "She should have had an abortion!"

There was a bare, crackling pause as this settled in. Yoandy spoke first, still reasoning with her. "Kay, listen, Dana loves you no matter what. Look at how she's taken care of you."

"How she's taken care of me? *She owes me!* Do you have any clue what I *did* for my precious *mother*?"

"She worries about you," he said.

"But I want to die!" moaned Kay. Her left hand relaxed and the Weedwacker fell, clattering against the floor. "I want to be dead, *dead*! You have no idea how many times I've tried . . . and she will *not* let me go."

Then with a movement that was as quick as it was shocking, the blade flashed as Kay sliced her left wrist.

Candace took two faltering steps toward Kay before Yoandy held her back.

"No, Kay," Candace blurted, "don't cut yourself, please don't do that, just don't!"

Kay's attention switched to Candace—a terrible moment. Her expression was devoid of any emotion; it was blank, like a corpse. Meanwhile, blood poured freely from the gash in her wrist, a horizontal wound, splashing onto the butterscotch-colored wood of the floor.

Yoandy and Candace gasped, appalled.

"Take a good look, blondie," Kay said, narrowing her eyes. Her tone had shifted. Now it was full of malicious intent. She moved toward Candace. "Look, you ridiculous bimbo. See? This is what it looks like to be hurt by the one you love."

"Candace, go. Go outside," Yoandy warned.

"Noooo!" Kay said. The knife went to her own throat, its point wedged just below her mouth. "You take another step and I'll do it. I will slit my *goddamn throat*, right here."

Kay wasn't a danger to her, Candace realized, with a flash of insight. She was suicidal. And maybe not even that. Horizontal cuts wouldn't bleed enough to kill her; surely everyone knew that?

Okay. This was most likely a desperate cry for help. You could see from Kay's eyes that she was having some sort of episode. It was pretty freaky. Electrifying, in fact—she noticed that all the hairs on her arms were standing up. Her whole body prickled with tension. But maybe, just maybe, with some gentle persuasion, they could talk Kay off the ledge.

"Kay," Candace said very calmly, holding out both hands to Kay. "Come with us. Why don't you come with us? We'll take you to Dana. She'll help you. Okay? Let's go to your sister."

But it was as though Candace had flipped a switch. Inside of Kay, something had broken. Without a sound and with no change to her expression, she moved. In seconds, she'd cleared the distance between them.

Candace was eye to eye with Kay. She felt a hard blow to her chest. Breath stuck in her throat as she tried to scream.

Kay's eye was like a shark's—open and wide and gray.

As she stepped back, Candace caught a glimpse of the knife in the young woman's hands. It was covered halfway to the hilt in blood.

The pain in Candace's chest bloomed like a burst of colors, shades of agony for which she had no language. She tried to gasp, but it hurt too much. Breathing shallowly, she looked down, only faintly surprised to see that her top was stained. An expanding circle of bright, bright red.

"Oh God," Candace managed to say. Her words were barely audible. She heard a roaring sound, like a distant river rushing toward her. Her knees went next; it was as though they'd turned to water. She saw the floor rushing toward her. A fraction of a second before she hit the ground, Candace blacked out.

PAOLO
BACKYARD, VENICE BEACH HOUSE, TUESDAY, JULY 7

Paolo pressed a button on his burner phone impatiently. A text. It wasn't from Grace—he could see her in the street, approaching the backyard.

It was from Lucy.

Ariana called my parents' house. Said I lent her some nail polish, she needs to pick it up. Ariana is going to Claremont to get THE NAIL POLISH DANA GAVE ME AFTER SHE KILLED TYSON DREW. PAOLO, DO SOMETHING.

The bottle of nail polish. So far as Paolo understood, the nail polish was a crucial piece of material evidence. Without it, Lucy's testimony might fall apart. The last chance to save Grace's father from execution would be gone.

Lucy was right—Paolo had to do something.

He watched Grace climb the steps that connected the backyard to the street below. He signaled her to stay quiet as she joined him, crouching behind the gap in the French doors at the back of the beach house. Placing his mouth next to her ear, he whispered, "I think Kay Alexander's in there. Candace and Yoandy just showed up. I'm pretty sure that something happened to Kay. Candace was begging her not to cut herself. Then I heard something fall. I think maybe Kay collapsed."

Grace looked at him, alarmed. From inside the house, they heard the choking, almost strangled voice of Yoandy. "No! No, *por Dios*, Kay, what did you do?"

Wide-eyed and confused, Paolo and Grace stared at each other.

Then Grace couldn't contain herself any longer. She tried to push him aside. Paolo stopped her, pulled her close to him. "Wait. Lucy sent a text. We can't stay."

In silence, he showed her the text from Lucy.

Then once again, Yoandy's shattered cries filled the living room. "Call nine-one-one, Kay, *please*."

"No." The reply–presumably Kay's voice–was toneless. "No. She stays like that. It's better like this. I didn't want to die alone. Now, we'll go together. Like sisters. The little sister I never had."

Yoandy must have lunged or something, because there was a scream, and then sounds of a heavy scuffle. Grace began to move toward the doors, but Paolo held her back.

Kay screeched and bawled throughout the very brief struggle. When it was over, there was only the sound of Yoandy's sobs, his groans of "Candace, *mi amor, no, no, no.*"

Yoandy was audibly crying. Grace had stopped moving. She was listening intently, gasping for air. Paolo drew her to him. "Breathe, baby, c'mon. In. Out."

As he spoke into his phone, Yoandy's tearful voice carried clearly to where they crouched outside the French doors.

"This is an emergency. I need an ambulance. Two friends of mine, knife wounds. It's very serious. They're both girls. I don't *know* if they're dead. There's a lot of blood, please hurry." Another pause. Then impatience: "I don't know the address! It's right on the front of Venice, the beach, man. Ocean Front Walk? I *don't know* the number! Okay, wait."

Paolo heard Yoandy go to the front door, open it, and disappear–probably going outside to check the house number.

Now, when Grace tried to push him aside, he didn't stop her. Paolo merely closed his eyes, took a deep breath, and followed her into the house.

Grace was standing just inside the living room. Two young women lay on the floor, only a foot apart. Paolo barely managed to handle a glimpse before he had to look away. He caught a flash of pale blue tank top awash with blood. Honey-gold hair was strewn about her head, face turned to the floor. Candace.

When he looked back at Grace, her hand was clasped to her mouth. She seemed to be fighting for air. He squeezed her hand and led her as fast as he dared toward the doors to the backyard. He practically had to drag her away from the bleeding bodies on the living room floor; Candace in her shorts and sneakers, Kay Alexander in a two-tone jacket in black and brilliant white; a canvas for blood, so much of it, on her sleeves, the front of her jacket, flowing from a gash at the base of her neck.

The blood was everywhere. The ceiling, both sofas. The knife was the last thing he saw, gleaming and slick with red, lying in the palm of Kay's hand.

By the time he and Grace had reached the backyard again, she was incoherent. Paolo felt pretty faint himself, but managed to lead her down the steps and to the street where he'd parked the car.

Once out of sight of the house, however, Grace stopped, reversed direction, quivering as she tried to return to the house. He had to block her with both arms to stop her. After a moment she relented, practically collapsing in his arms.

He held her tight. "Grace. We can't go back. We can't help them now. Yoandy needs to handle it."

"I need to," stuttered Grace, gulping. "She's my sister."

"No, baby, we can't. Yoandy will take care of her, he already called nine-one-one; you heard him. We gotta go. Lucy needs us to do something. For your dad, Grace. To save him."

Grace stared at him. "For my dad?"

Paolo nodded, patiently. In her distress, Grace seemed not to have understood the text from Lucy. But there was so little time. The police would arrive any minute.

"They'll say that Yoandy did it," she pronounced slowly.

"No, no, how could they? Kay is *insane*. I mean she was sounding pretty nutso before you got here, but you heard her say she wanted to die, right?"

"She said she wanted to die with her sister," Grace said. "Why would she say that?"

Paolo looked at her helplessly. "Because she doesn't have a sister. Dana is her *mom*."

Grace was stunned. "How . . . did she . . . ?"

"That's what I heard. Yoandy heard it, too. I don't think he knew."

He watched Grace try to swallow. "But if we leave him?" she managed to say. "No one knows what happened but us."

Now Paolo understood why Grace was so worried. The danger to Yoandy hadn't even occurred to him, and now that it had, it horrified him. To leave Yoandy to face a possible accusation of two murders? Unthinkable.

"But, baby, we gotta get that nail polish. It's the only evidence that can connect Dana to the murder. We have to get to it before Ariana."

"I'll stay," Grace said.

"No, no, we stay together. There's nothing you can do for your sister. She needs a doctor. And I will not abandon you."

"I can't leave Yoandy to deal with this."

"Grace, please, we have to."

Stubbornly, she shook her head. "No. Then we're the same as Lucy. Walking away from what we saw. I would never do that to anyone, Paolo. No one should go to prison for something they didn't do."

He touched the backs of his fingers to her cheek. "Gracie," he said tenderly. "What if you call the cops, right now? On your burner. Say you're a neighbor, that you were passing by. Tell them what we saw. We'll tell them everything else later. But now, we have to go."

"They'll say we're making it up," she said, but he could tell she was starting to yield.

"Not if you call them. We know what we heard. Kay said she was going to kill herself. Yoandy tried to stop her."

Reluctantly, Grace took the burner phone from the pocket of her jean shorts. She began to dial 911. "Why wouldn't I stick around, if I were a neighbor?"

"It'll be okay. It happens a lot. People don't want to get involved," Paolo said. "Later, we'll describe it all. How we saw them on the floor. How they lay, what they were wearing. Yoandy, what he did. Grace, they'll question us separately. When they hear that our story is the same as Yoandy's, they'll know. He's not going to jail for this, Gracie, I promise."

"I couldn't bear it if he did. I couldn't live with myself."

"Do you remember what you heard, what you saw?"

She nodded, silent as tears rolled down her cheeks.

"Okay," he said, relieved to see that she was finally breathing normally. "You'll call the cops from the car. From your burner. Then we'll toss it. Okay, Gracie?"

Her skin was so pale it was practically translucent,

the light in her eyes dimmer than he'd ever seen. It was as though something had switched off inside Grace. Paolo's instinct to protect her surged like a wave crashing over his head.

"All right. We're gonna drive to Claremont now. And we'll talk about what happened here; we'll write it down or record an audio. Better to do that while it's fresh in our minds."

Grace's chest began to heave. "I . . . I can't leave my sister that way."

Paolo put an arm around her shaking shoulders. Gently he began to lead her past a palm tree and a Dumpster, toward the car.

His heart broke for Grace, for Candace, for Yoandy. He was desperate to leave that place of horror, of violence that exploded from nowhere twice now. A place where he'd once felt so safe and so happy, where friendship had embraced him like the warm sea. Now it was all gone, forever lost, those sweet memories replaced with blood and terror and despair.

LUCY

Lucy glared at Maya and John-Michael. "If anything happens to Candace, that's on us, you understand?" She felt belligerent, provocative.

John-Michael's only reaction was a quick, sideways look at Maya, as if to gauge her reaction. But Maya didn't seem to have heard Lucy. She put down the plate of peanut butter toast she'd been holding and pursed her lips, apparently deep in thought. Then she opened her mouth as if to speak and then shut it again, with a cautionary glance at John-Michael.

Lucy couldn't handle it. "JM, what *is* it with you? It's like you can't say a damn thing without getting Maya's okay."

"I'm not getting anyone's okay on anything," replied John-Michael, remarkably calm. Lucy knew him well enough to know that beneath the surface he was angry.

Maya spoke up. "It's not on us, Lucy. We *warned*

Candace not to leave the group. We made that abundantly clear."

"We should have told them what was what right from the beginning!"

"I really don't recall you advocating that on Friday night," Maya said. It was impossible not to hear a touch of superiority in her tone.

"Oh yeah?" Lucy began to pace up and down the patio. "You wanna know what's *abundantly* clear to me, today? You wanna know what I'm *advocating* as of right now?"

Maya closed her eyes. Lucy could see her lips moving in a slow count, probably in Spanish. "Okay, Lucy. What?"

"I may have agreed to what happened up in Malibu Canyon. But I did not agree to keep our friends out of the loop. I didn't want–"

"Yeah, you did," interrupted Maya.

". . . to delay going to the cops," Lucy finished, glaring at her.

"Could have gone to them a lot earlier."

Rage boiled up inside Lucy. She made herself sit down, gripping the armrests of the white enamel–painted metal. Maya was maddeningly unperturbed.

"Lucy, I don't get why you're so mad at us, why you're trying to blame Maya for anything," John-Michael said. "She didn't deserve to be dragged into all our messes. Look at what Maya's got going for her. Even if we walk away from this with our lives and our freedom, Maya could lose everything she worked for. And we all know how hard she worked."

"Maya? Uh-uh. That would be *Candace*! Candace is the one who's done nothing wrong. None of this has anything to do with her! She might lose her job, too. And what are you saying, that Maya didn't choose to get herself involved? Because from where I'm sitting, Maya was playing on Dana Alexander's team until about fifteen minutes ago."

This, finally, seemed to make Maya lose her cool. She crossed the space between the two girls and stuck a finger so close to Lucy's face that she almost poked Lucy in the eye. "Lucy, the *minute* I saw what Alexander was all about, I stopped reporting anything useful or *even* truthful. I promise you *on my mother's life*, I've been trying to think of ways to help all of us. To get us out of this nightmare!"

Lucy didn't move. She was too transfixed by Maya's sudden change in mood.

"Keeping the group together was a big part of that plan!" Maya snapped, but the passion was already draining away. "I didn't want Candace to leave," she said. "I didn't want Paolo and Grace to leave. I *literally* can't think of anything worse, right now, than us splitting into two groups. Our strength comes when we're together, the six of us, like a family. *Then* we protect each other. *Then* we support each other."

"Well, Grace was always gonna go after her sister," Lucy admitted.

"Yeah, sure, totally understandable."

"So . . ." Lucy hesitated. "This plan of yours. I take it there is one?"

"There was one," Maya said, sighing. "Now, with us in two groups, I gotta say, I'm going to need a rethink."

"Okay, Maya; how about you clue us in?"

"First of all, we need protection. In case Alexander's people catch up to us."

Lucy frowned. "Catch up, how? No one knows where we are."

"First rule of planning—have a backup for your worst-case scenario. We're toast if those people show up. Therefore, we need a plan." Maya hesitated for a moment. "I guess we need to bring in Grace's father's bodyguard friend after all."

Lucy couldn't resist. "It's good to hear you admit you were wrong about *something*." But Maya didn't react.

"Grace already called Pete Martens last night," John-Michael said. "Paolo took her to a payphone. I guess she's waiting to hear from him on her burner phone."

"He only has the number of Grace's burner?" Maya said, blinking slowly. "This is no good."

"Good luck getting Grace or Paolo to pick up," Lucy said. "I just sent a text about Ariana calling my parents' house in Claremont. And still no reply."

"We should call," John-Michael said. "Lucy's right. It's been a long time. They should check in." He took out his own phone and waited for a moment, attempting a grin as the call connected. "Hey, bro. What's going on, we've been trying to call . . . ?"

His sentence faded. Before Lucy's eyes, John-Michael's expression turned from mild relief to pale, stricken panic. "Oh God . . . no. No! Are you serious?"

Anxiously, Maya and Lucy watched him. Finally, Lucy demanded, "What's happened to Candace?"

John-Michael answered in a halting voice. "She's been stabbed. Kay Alexander attacked Candace with a knife! In the house! In *our* house!"

His words were like a punch to the guts. The air in Lucy's lungs seemed dense and heavy, moving through her like liquid. "Is she dead?"

"I don't know." John-Michael looked from Lucy to Maya, absolutely helpless. "Paolo says Grace is halfway out of her mind. But they're going for the nail polish like you asked, Lucy."

"Yeah, but when I sent that text I didn't know that Candace had been stabbed!" cried Lucy.

"Obviously Grace is going to want to get the nail polish," Maya said quietly. "I mean, that totally makes sense. It may be the key to her dad's freedom."

"Omigod, Candace! Why didn't she just stay here?" Lucy gasped.

"Paolo just kept saying, 'She's crazy, she's insane,' like that. You think he was talking about Kay Alexander?" John-Michael said.

"Dana's sister?" Maya said pensively. "You mean, like,

crazy jealous over Candace and Yoandy? That doesn't make a lot of sense; she wasn't his girlfriend."

"According to Yoandy," pointed out Lucy. "But who knows for sure?"

"There's obviously stuff going on here that we don't understand," Maya said slowly.

"Like what?" John-Michael asked.

Maya shook her head. "I have no clue. But I think we have to assume the worst. Which is that Dana sent Kay to the Venice house to look for us. God knows what happened and why." She paused, thinking. "Okay. What I think is this: our top priority is to protect Lucy. Which means we really gotta get ahold of that bodyguard guy. We need to let Grace know that." She took a deep breath. "And I need to hide the money. The cash and Lucy," she said. "Those are our two danger factors as of right now. We have to hide you both." With that, Maya stood and headed into the house.

"Hey!" called out Lucy. "Where d'you think you're going?"

"Need to make some calls," answered Maya, retreating. "I'm gonna contact some hacker friends of mine. And I'm gonna call Jack. I need to warn him. Ariana knew he and I were friends—it's possible that Dana may track him down. In fact, you should probably warn Ruben, too," she told Lucy. "If Dana's prepared to use her sister to attack us, then she must really be desperate. Our friends may be in danger, too."

GRACE
INTERSTATE 10, DOWNTOWN LOS ANGELES,
TUESDAY, JULY 7

Paolo had promised that they'd talk about it, but they didn't.
Grace simply could not.

The phone call to the police had taken everything she
had. It had felt like a betrayal to cut that off so early, too.
The officer she'd spoken to wanted her to get to the police
station immediately and had become quite angry when
she'd refused.

The burner phone she'd used to make the call was in
bits now, in a trash can outside a gas station near the house.
Luckily she'd sent a text to Pete Martens with the number
of both her and Paolo's burners. It wasn't strictly in line with
how her dad had insisted they make contact with Martens,
but things were moving fast now. They had to take some
risks or they'd never connect with the bodyguard.

Now all Grace seemed to be able to do was to stare
silently and unseeingly at the growing swell of traffic. Her
mind seemed to have gone into a suspended state where

thought moved at the speed not of sound, but sluggishly, like glacial flow. She could sense the approach of certain ideas before they hit smack in the middle of her consciousness. Like a goalkeeper protecting the net, she could ward some thoughts away.

Candace was dying, was maybe already dead. That had happened—Grace had seen the aftermath. And she'd run away; she'd run away from her dying sister. This was the most corrosive of all her thoughts, the most insistent. No matter how she tried to swat it away, it ate into her.

Then there was the nail polish. If Dana Alexander had realized the significance of that element of Lucy's story, it meant Grace had severely underestimated how much Lucy had told Ariana.

Which, she realized with a sinking sensation, was probably *everything.*

Lucy had pretty much admitted it. She'd looked physically sick when she'd put two and two together, realized that Ariana had been spying on her for years, reporting back to Dana Alexander. Even so, Grace hadn't seen the need for urgency. They shouldn't have gone north to Napa; they should have gone straight to Claremont to get that nail polish.

"Breathe, baby, breathe." She felt Paolo's hand on her shoulder.

Incredible to think that yesterday she'd been preoccupied with her feelings for him. Now she felt hollowed out, numb. Behind it all, one idea niggled away, uncertain and small, yet growing as she turned it over in her mind.

It took her a few seconds to realize that Paolo was speaking to her again. She looked out the window, vaguely surprised to see that they'd already reached Downtown Los Angeles.

"Did you know?" he asked. "About Kay? Did you know she was *actually* insane; did Candace talk about it?"

Dully, Grace shook her head. That kernel of uncertainty—could it be the key to everything? Or was it just Grace's imagination? "Did you see how she was dressed?" she began. "Kay . . . did you notice?"

"Gracie." Paolo hesitated. "You sure you wanna talk about Kay right now?"

Grace ignored him. "She was dressed so oddly. Did you notice? Like for a business meeting."

The traffic was starting to move again. Paolo pulled into the outside lane and rushed ahead, aggressive as he shifted gears. "What's your point?"

Grace shook her head, as though that might clear her thoughts, but it didn't. She turned to look at Paolo, willed herself to feel what she'd felt when she'd looked at him like that even a day ago: yearning, sadness, anxiety, warmth, love. Where were those feelings now? What had happened to all that desire? How was it possible that a whole segment of her emotions could be shut down, as if the entire circuit had been switched off?

Paolo seemed to notice her scrutiny, because the skin of his forearms turned to gooseflesh under her gaze. "Gracie?"

She spoke slowly, considering. "Candace told me that Kay was one of those wannabe urban hipster types. The way she was dressed just does not feel right. It's like in Lucy's TV show—jelly with pie; two things that seem like they'd go together, but they really don't."

"But Kay was dressed just like Dana Alexander," Paolo said. "And if it's really true that Dana is her mom, then, y'know, it's just imitation."

"Oh, Paolo." Grace looked up slowly as understanding dawned on her. ' "That's *it*."

"What'd I say?"

"The way she was dressed today. You're exactly right. She looked like Dana Alexander." Grace clamped her lips together for an instant to stop them from trembling. When she spoke again, the words were almost inaudible. "What if . . . it was Kay . . . dressed like Dana Alexander . . . who drowned Tyson Drew? And that's who Lucy saw?"

He mulled it over. "Not Dana, then?"

"Not Dana—Kay. Her daughter!"

"That would be messed up. This was nine years ago, right? Kay might still have been a minor. What we saw today . . ." He twirled a finger in the air. "You think she was crazy back then, too?"

"Do we know that she is crazy *now*?"

Paolo raised an eyebrow. "You didn't hear what I heard. She was totally suicidal."

"Yet she attacked Candace," said Grace.

"I don't know why she did that. It was so fast. One minute Candace was talking and then, nothing."

"*Crazy* is too easy," Grace said. "More like she believed that Candace was dangerous to her."

"Because of dating Yoandy?"

"Because of what Candace might know. What if Lucy got it wrong; what if Kay killed Tyson Drew?"

"Kay?" Paolo shook his head, firmly. "You're forgetting. This was nine years ago. Kay would have been a teenager. And why would she kill Drew?"

"That's the easy part," Grace said. "Kay was Dana's big secret. What if Tyson Drew somehow knew?"

Paolo sucked in a slow breath. "You think he was blackmailing her?"

"Dana's awful eager to use blackmail as a weapon. Maybe she's experienced it herself?"

Now that the theory was out there, Grace felt the will to pursue it evaporate. Creeping numbness began to overtake her once again. The memory she'd been resisting burst through her carefully constructed lattice of thoughts.

Candace, stabbed in the chest.

Paolo was oblivious to her changing mood. "If Kay killed Tyson Drew," he speculated, "then I guess it explains how come Dana Alexander had an alibi, right?"

Candace, bleeding to death.

Grace tried to close the thought down again, but it was too late; it was inside now. A shiver went through her. Paolo put a hand gently on top of hers. She felt the warmth of him seeping into the clammy surface of her palm. She tried to smile, but she couldn't.

"You may have something here, Gracie," he said. "A parent would do anything to protect their kid. Especially if Kay was a minor at the time. Although I guess 'insane' is better than 'guilty,' right? Then you don't even do any jail time."

"They lock psychopaths away—in hospitals," Grace said slowly.

"If Dana thought her teenage daughter was in danger of being locked away, don't you think she'd want someone else to take the blame?" Paolo said. "The cops will never link Dana to those hit men. But we're gonna get that nail polish from Lucy's old house. Then we'll see."

Grace was drifting away again. She'd left her sister lying seriously injured, perhaps dead. When you added it to the list of things she'd done over the years, mistakes and compromises and lies to keep her father a secret; when you added it all up, it was enough, she thought. Enough to be the actions of a bad person; not the person Grace wanted to be.

She gazed at Paolo. Who was she to judge what he and the other three had done the other night in Malibu Canyon? Were they any worse than she was, or was it all a matter of degrees?

Maya had said it and she'd been right, reflected Grace. *If it's blame you're looking for, there's a lot to go around.*

MAYA

CASITA, FLOR DE CANELA, TUESDAY, JULY 7

"Jack's not answering," Maya said. She frowned at her phone. "John-Michael, did you call Paolo from your burner?"

He nodded.

"Okay, I did the same thing just now," she continued. "Hopefully, that's why Jack won't pick up—he doesn't recognize the burner's number. I'm gonna Skype him from my laptop."

"Your hacker friends," Lucy said. "Are you calling them, too?"

"Those guys don't just hand out their contact details. I sent out a message over the dark web."

"The 'dark web'?" Lucy said, looking worried.

Maya took a breath. Many who'd heard of the dark web tended to assume it was the exclusive haunt of criminals and perverts. But if you wanted to deal with some of the world's best coders, there was no other way—they were paranoid as hell. Those hackers wanted every transaction conducted via peer-to-peer encryption, so that the

■157

government couldn't snoop.

Who'd have thought Maya herself would need that level of privacy, too?

I'm really a criminal now, she thought grimly. "Dark Web is a secure place, like a private internet that the government can't track. Hackers prefer to exchange information that way. They like their civil liberties, those guys. I'm gonna look for a Bitcoin miner—one who'll sell us the coin for cash."

"A 'Bitcoin miner'?" John-Michael was as clueless as Lucy.

"Some dude whose computer is part of the Bitcoin network, doing the blockchain verifications." When both Lucy and John-Michael continued to stare at her blankly, Maya continued. "Some miners collect a lot of Bitcoin. They earn it as part of the process of making the whole thing work. A few of them are prepared to do the occasional cash transaction as long as someone they know can vouch for you. There's no other way any of us is going to make this cash disappear, fast, to someplace where we can still get to it—not without a lot of questions. Lucky for us, in the San Francisco area we're likely to find a high density of miners."

The answer seemed to satisfy them—for now. Maya returned her attention to her laptop. She started up Skype. Jack wasn't online, so she sent a message.

Hearing about Candace had made Maya more nervous than she was letting on. They hadn't told any of their friends that they were at Alexa Nyborg's place in Napa.

There was a chance, however, that Jack would figure it out. He'd known about Nyborg's offer to Maya. He didn't know where the house was, but someone as resourceful as Jack could probably find out—eventually.

Just to be safe, Maya positioned the computer on the coffee table facing the sofa. Only a plain section of white wall was visible in the background. There'd be no way to know where Maya was Skyping from.

"Maya, your Skype," John-Michael said. He nudged her laptop across the coffee table. "It says Jack Cato is calling you."

Maya used the trackpad to click "Answer with video."

A face swam into view. It wasn't Jack's.

The shock of this made Maya recoil. Lucy and John-Michael made to approach, but she held them off with both arms outstretched. She stared at the screen in horror.

The face staring back at her wore a navy blue ski mask. She guessed that he was male and white from the glimpses of pale skin around his mouth and eyes. When he spoke, she didn't recognize the voice. "Well, hey, Maya, we've been looking for you. But I think you already knew that. Question: Where's Lucy Long?"

Maya's gaze went, involuntarily, to where Lucy stood, directly behind and to the left of the laptop's screen.

The man in the ski mask caught the shift in her eyes. "Oh, I see she's with you. Good. Then this shouldn't take long, not long at all."

"Where's Jack?" Maya said, finally managing to speak.

"Jack? Good question." Then he cocked his head to one side and called out, "Oh, Jack! Hey, Jack! Make some noise, wouldja?"

A blood-curdling scream tore out of the laptop's speakers; a sound that reached deep into Maya's belly and clutched at her insides. She watched, frozen with dread, struggling to understand what she was seeing.

The video feed on-screen switched swiftly to a second camera. Crumpled up on his knees, in the corner of a dimly lit room, was Jack Cato. He arms were somewhere behind his back, presumably bound. There was no indication of what had caused him to scream, but now his eyes looked wild, terrified.

The video feed switched back to the man in the ski mask.

"They tell me that you're a smart girl, Maya. Now listen. This is what's going to happen. You're going to tell us where Lucy is. When we have her, we're going to let Jack go. We'll even dump him at a hospital—how d'you like that? We barely touched the kid—he'll be good as new in a week. And that's it. You down with that?"

"What . . ." Maya cleared her throat and then tried again. Behind the screen she could see Lucy shaking her head desperately. "What happens to Lucy?" she said.

"What happens to Lucy?" The man in the mask seemed surprised at the question. "If I were you, Maya, I'd be more worried about Jack. Should be worried about

Jack, shouldn't she, fellas?" he called out to some unseen accomplices.

A second later another burst of screaming ripped through the laptop's speakers. This time, the video feed didn't switch to show what they were doing to Jack. But the scream conjured dark, vivid scenes in Maya's mind—unbearable images of Jack suffering.

The man in the ski mask faced down the webcam of his own computer, peering at Maya with grim determination.

"Now listen to me, Maya Soto. You're gonna tell me where we can find Lucy. You're gonna put her in front of your webcam and make damn sure she stays there until we arrive. Get it?"

Maya couldn't even make herself lift her eyes to look over the laptop at Lucy.

"Jack goes to a world of pain," said the man in the mask, taunting her. "Unless we get Lucy."

JOHN-MICHAEL
CASITA, FLOR DE CANELA, TUESDAY, JULY 7

After way too long, John-Michael snapped out of it. Maya was practically catatonic, hunched over her laptop, her eyes as empty as the desert. With empathic gestures, he signaled to her: a great big "no."

Lucy sank to her knees. Her head was bent, shoulders crunched together. Total despondency.

Finally, Maya spoke. "Please." Her voice broke, and she began to sob. "Please. You can't hurt Lucy."

"Why would we hurt Lucy?" the voice said. It was difficult to tell much about the person behind that voice—other than he sounded youngish.

John-Michael wondered if Maya knew the man. From what he'd heard of the conversation, the man knew about Jack Cato, which must have come from Ariana, which in turn led straight to Dana Alexander.

"Lucy's gonna be taking a little vacation with us, is all. She'll have a bed, her own room; she'll get food and water.

And when we've decided that all's well in the world, we'll release her."

"You mean when Grace's dad has been executed," Maya said flatly.

"Hey," continued the voice. "I don't know what you're talking about. Look, you have my word that no harm's gonna come to Lucy."

"I don't know you," Maya sobbed. "How can I trust a word you say?"

"You girls, you and Lucy, you're being very brave," the voice said. "As to *trust*, well look, honey, didn't I keep my word about Jack so far? Trust me on *this*: I will hurt your pal. I'll hurt him bad. Maybe even kill him. So, Maya, you're gonna need to decide."

"*Promise* me you won't hurt Lucy," Maya begged, tears streaming down her face. John-Michael longed to speak, but so far the kidnappers only knew that Lucy and Maya were together. They probably assumed the others were with her, too, but they didn't know for sure. Any uncertainty could turn into an advantage—one that John-Michael couldn't risk losing.

"And you gotta let me talk to Jack," Maya said. She wiped her tears with the back of her hand. "I mean it. I'll give Jack our address."

"Kid has no idea where he is, miss, if that's what you're thinking. We brought him here with a bag over his head."

She sniffed. "I just want to talk to Jack, to see he's okay.

Please. Let him out of that room."

John-Michael watched, fascinated. Like Jack's kidnapper, he suspected she was planning something. But what?

There was a pause. Finally, the voice said, "Okay. Bring the kid up."

A moment later, Maya burst into tears once again, obviously shaken at the sight of Jack on her computer screen. An angry red bruise on his cheekbone was already swelling up. "Jack," she said, brokenly. "Oh, Jack, Jack. I'm so sorry, so sorry, please, please—"

"All right, enough," interrupted the voice. "As you can see, he's still reasonably pretty. See—I'm holding up my end of the deal. If you cooperate, then he ain't goin' back in the basement. You got my word. Maya, I'm gonna need that address now."

"Can I look at my phone?" she asked. "I don't actually know the address of where we are. We used GPS coordinates to get here."

"But it's Napa, right?"

Maya nodded. "Yes, Napa."

"Now, you wouldn't lie to me, would you, Maya? Because if we show up at some address where you ain't, or find Lucy gone, then it's so long, Jack."

"No," she insisted. "I can prove I'm telling the truth. My phone has an app that will let Jack locate it. I can show you my phone, right now, and you can watch Jack locate it. You'll see my phone respond."

John-Michael shook his head. Lying about their location

was the single play they had left! If Maya blew their location, then Lucy was as good as dead.

On the other side of the screen, John-Michael heard the kidnapper chuckle. "Now, that *is* smart. Okay, kid, lemme see you locate her phone."

Jack mumbled something inaudible, and Maya nodded. She held up her smartphone to the webcam. After a few seconds, it vibrated, and the screen lit up. The kidnapper read out a zip code. "Okay, Maya, I see where you are. But that's a pretty wide area. Where's the house?"

"There's a side road, see it on the map? It goes right past the entrance to the driveway. The house is at the end."

"Maya, you did good. You bought your pal some time out of the basement. If you and Lucy are there when we show up, he gets painkillers. If not, we go to town on the kid."

There was a despairing grunt from Jack, and the sound of a struggle.

"Get something for his bruises now, please, please," urged Maya.

"All right. Now listen: put Lucy in front of the camera," ordered the voice.

John-Michael and Maya turned to Lucy, who was crouched low to the floor. She tried to rise to her feet, shaking as she went.

John-Michael grasped both of Lucy's shoulders, helped to steady her. Then Maya was leading her to the sofa, where she took Maya's place before the webcam.

A lamb to the slaughter. And they'd led Lucy there. John-Michael felt sick. But part of him wasn't ready to let go of hope. Maya had to have a plan. She couldn't have simply walked them into surrender—could she?

"Lucy! It's good to meetcha," came the kidnapper's voice, eerily cheerful. "I was a fan, back in the day. Okay, girls, now you just hold tight. We'll be with you in a little while."

"How long?" Maya blurted anxiously.

"Oh, you let me worry about how long. Now, Maya, you wouldn't call the cops on me or anything, tell them how far away we are, get 'em to triangulate our location or anything?"

"No, no," Maya mumbled. "It's just that Lucy and me, we might need to go to the bathroom."

"Bathroom breaks are fine, so long as one of you stays in front of the camera at all times."

"Can I go right now?" Maya asked. "I'm sorry, but this has made me really nervous. I really, really need to ping the john."

The kidnapper gave a nasty snigger. "'Ping the john'? Is that what you kids are calling it these days? Okay, you go right ahead. But be quick. And leave your phone with Lucy, where I can see it."

Maya was out of there like a fury. Once she was out of range of the webcam she clutched at John-Michael, dragging him away and into the bathroom with her.

"What the hell?" he hissed. "Are you crazy?"

Maya's eyes flashed. "What choice did I have?"

"You could have lied!"

"No, I couldn't; I don't know how to hack the Fone-Trackr app. And I needed to find an excuse to let Jack touch the keyboard."

John-Michael pulled away. Was it possible that Maya had outwitted their enemies?

"You did something . . . ?"

"Give me your phone," she said, snatching it out of his hand.

Hope flickered within John-Michael as he watched her fingers trace patterns on his phone's touchscreen. "Maya . . . ? There's a plan?"

"The server." Maya brought up a browser window running what looked like code. "The one where I've been developing the app. Jack just pinged it from the computer he's using. It only takes a second."

"Pinged the john?" He gasped. "You were giving him a hint?"

She raised her head, her eyes met his: piercing, sharp, lucid. "Jack *pinged* the server," Maya repeated. "And now *I* know exactly how to find *him*."

MAYA

Maya's thoughts were chaotic, charged with negativity. Jack's agony had been a wake-up call. It had lit a fire inside of her; a bushfire. If she didn't get it under control, everything would burn.

Candace stabbed, Jack captured, the housemates scattering across the state—and it had all happened in the past few hours. More than ever, Maya needed to find that inner resource of cold determination, the will to tackle one problem after another. Jack's screams had derailed her, but now she had to get back on track.

Her hands shook a little as she sent off a hastily written communication on John-Michael's phone. He was trying to catch her eye in the bathroom mirror, but she didn't have time to respond. This was literally life or death.

If Maya didn't receive an answer from the hackers within an hour or so, Lucy's life was in the balance. She handed the phone back to John-Michael. "Stay out of sight. Get ahold of Grace," she told him. "We need her to send that bodyguard guy here, to Napa. *Right away*, John-Michael."

He nodded, standing aside as Maya pushed past him. She had to get back in front of the laptop's webcam so the kidnapper could see her. She took her seat again, next to Lucy on the sofa. Neither girl looked at each other.

Maya longed to tell Lucy that she hadn't simply handed her housemate over to the kidnappers. That she'd merely lit the touch paper of a rescue plan. But they couldn't communicate: it would look suspicious. Even appearing too calm was suspicious. The only viable position was to act scared, really scared; so scared she was likely to wet herself every twenty minutes if they didn't let her go to the bathroom.

Then again, Maya didn't need to be the one to go to the bathroom. Lucy could go. John-Michael would tell her what was happening. Yes. That's how they'd do it. There was no need to talk.

Maya had done everything she could. Now she was in the hands of her hacker "friends."

She'd never met a single one of them, knew them only from the code-debugging boards of the dark web, where anonymous hackers helped each other out for no other reward than the cooperative spirit of open-source. She usually asked for tips on programming; now she was asking someone to do something illegal—to hack the database of an internet service provider.

Jack had picked up on her cue. He'd pinged Maya's server. But an IP address wasn't something you put into a car's GPS and expected to lead you to a building. It would still need to be translated into a geographic address.

It wasn't easy to get access to the databases where IP addresses translated to actual physical locations. Internet access providers held such data; police and courts could demand access. Hackers were proud of their ability to crack such data. Highly illegal, naturally. There wasn't much chance that someone would provide that information for nothing, so she'd offered a reward: twelve hundred dollars. Then another four thousand if the address was accurate.

The total sum of what Maya had in her Bitcoin account was $1,248 —earnings from various programming jobs she'd picked up, plus the trickle of advertising revenue from her Cheetr app. Even if someone was willing to risk breaking the law for that much Bitcoin, Maya would have no way of knowing if the information was reliable. It amounted to trusting her life to a hacker—to someone she'd never met in real life.

Some of the hackers might be pretty douchey people—Maya knew that. But there was a code of honor, too. She trusted at least two hackers she'd worked with before to honor her offer. If anyone other than those two hackers took up the offer, Maya would have to say no thanks. It would be too much risk.

"Can I go to the bathroom now?" Lucy asked. Her voice sounded plaintive and small, not like herself.

On the computer screen, the masked man bared his teeth. "Nah. I changed my mind. Better I keep my eye on you two girls. Matter of fact, get your hands up where I can see them. We don't want you passing notes in class."

So that was it–there was no way to give Lucy even an ounce of hope.

Maya maintained her facade of meek anxiety. But inside, she itched with nervousness.

There were only two hackers that she trusted in the whole wide world. They might be on the other side of the globe, asleep in their cozy beds. They might be playing a video game, noise-canceling headphones blasting a soundtrack in their ears. They might be just about anywhere except where she needed them right now; in front of their computers, distracted by a distress call.

Urgent help needed. Five thousand dollar reward.

On a sudden impulse, she grabbed Lucy's hand. *There,* she thought. They were together in this; she needed Lucy to know it. Maya said a silent prayer for both of them; she prayed for the hackers to save them.

JOHN-MICHAEL
FLOR DE CANELA, TUESDAY, JULY 7

A Buick Century pulled into the driveway of the main house. John-Michael watched as the car was parked with fastidious care. His father, Chuck, had been the same way—had treated his car like it was a baby.

The man who got out of the car walked over with careful purpose. He was not a tall man—no more than five nine. He wasn't particularly powerfully built. He looked disheveled in a dark gray suit jacket over blue jeans with a navy checked shirt. His top button was unfastened, no tie. His short hair was very light brown with a lot of gray, and it fell in greasy strands straight down to his ears. He swept it aside as he peered over at John-Michael. His face had a worn, weary quality, sallow and heavily lined. He looked tired of life.

John-Michael stood up and shook the guy's outstretched hand. "Peter Martens," the man said, releasing him from a firm grip. "You can call me Pete."

"Hello, Pete. I'm John-Michael."

"I talked to your buddy, Grace. Heard you're having some trouble. So." Martens took a moment to take in the main house, the *casita*, the patio and pool in between. "Girls are inside?"

John-Michael nodded.

"Grace?"

"In Claremont."

"Claremont? Now, how am I supposed to protect Grace, all the way up here in Napa?"

"Grace isn't the one in danger."

Martens glanced off to the side. "John-Michael," he said. "Listen carefully; I'm gonna explain how this works. Grace is the one who called me. *Grace* is whose daddy I'm working for. And when I spoke—*to Grace*—she somehow neglected to mention that she was all the way down in Claremont."

"Look," John-Michael said. "Grace's friends are inside the *casita*. The people who tried to kill us on Friday have kidnapped someone important to one of us. They beat him up—to get us to reveal where we are. And now they're on their way over."

"And now they're on their way over," Martens repeated. "I see."

"They're holding on to our friend, just in case Lucy or Maya turn into a flight risk."

Martens nodded a couple of times. He looked pensive. Then he turned. "All right. Well, so long."

"What?" John-Michael darted ahead, catching up.

"You're going? I already told you—Grace isn't the one in danger, we are."

"And good luck to you. But I'm paid to look after Grace." Martens continued on his way.

John-Michael called after him. "Grace is fine! She's with Paolo. They're running an errand. The *danger* is *here*."

"Who's Paolo?" Martens asked over his shoulder.

"Another friend. You can trust him, dude." John-Michael was beginning to sound desperate, and he knew it. "If money's an issue, we can pay! How's ten thousand sound?"

Pete Martens stopped. "Pay me with what?"

John-Michael stalled. He didn't know this guy, except that he'd been in prison with Grace's dad. There was no way he could risk telling him about the bag of cash. "One of the girls in the *casita* is an internet entrepreneur. She's got this covered."

"I see. In that case, fifteen is more realistic, John-Michael. Fifteen, in cash."

"Deal."

Martens turned and smoothed down the lapels of his jacket. "Let's get to it. I'm gonna need a tour of the grounds, get an idea of the defensible areas."

"First we have to go rescue our friend. Before their guys get here. And then we're leaving."

Martens eyed him with a narrow gaze. "Leaving? On a rescue mission? Fifteen was my offer to defend you and your girlfriends, right here. A rescue mission—now that's a horse of a different color."

John-Michael waited nervously. It didn't look as though Martens was opposed, and yet, when it came to a deal like this, who knew what to offer? "We have to rescue our friend," he pleaded. "What other option is there?"

"The other option is to stay here and defend your girls," Martens reasoned. "Or else they wind up with three hostages, not one."

John-Michael could feel desperation clutching at him. Martens was right. If they tried to rescue Jack Cato, they'd leave the two girls defenseless. All he could think to say, rather desolately, was, "But if we don't give them Lucy, they're going to kill Jack."

"You or the two girls, any of you know how to use a gun?"

He brightened up. "Maya does. And I'll give it a try."

Martens considered this. "That'll have to be enough. Now, about this rescue, you got an address? Know how many people to expect when we get there?"

"Not yet, and I don't think we know."

Martens rolled his eyes. "That's a no to both things, is it?"

"Yes. It's a no. To both. But we're working on the address."

"No address, no intel. But you can pay fifteen large in cash?"

"We can pay anything." John-Michael regretted the words the instant he saw the effect they had on Martens, who scowled.

"Son, don't ever tell a criminal that you can pay anything," Martens said.

"Grace's dad trusts you."

The bodyguard chuckled. "You don't meet a lot of guys like Alex Vesper in prison. A genuinely innocent man. Some folks don't respect that, but I did."

"We have the cash," John-Michael said, standing his ground.

Martens screwed his eyes up, mouth twisting in contemplation. "Normally, I require more notice. Planning and preparation time, if you will. There'll need to be some accommodation of that."

John-Michael nodded. "Of course. Name it."

"One wingman isn't enough for this job. The girl can cover me with a weapon, but we're going to need you, too. So—any experience?" He waited. "Anything . . . at all?"

"I've killed three people," John-Michael said.

This got the bodyguard's attention. "You've shot three people?"

"I didn't say that. Suffocated two of them. The third guy, well, I pushed him off a cliff."

There was no doubt about it; Pete Martens' manner changed instantly. He took a minute to scrutinize John-Michael's eyes, as though he might find the history of his crimes inscribed on the back of the boy's retinas. "Takes a lot to kill someone with your own hands."

John-Michael's honesty got the better of him. "They weren't in a position to fight back."

"You killed people who were no direct threat?"

"I didn't say that."

"You made a judgment call, though, correct?" Under his breath, Martens chuckled. "Decided it was too dangerous to let them live, so you killed them?"

If any friend had said this, John-Michael would have dismissed it. But there was something about the bodyguard's interest. A curiosity more professional than it was morbid. "I guess," he admitted. "Dangerous for them, or dangerous for me."

Martens smiled, skeptically. John-Michael stuck out an empty hand. "I'll take a gun to Maya."

Martens pressed the pistol into John-Michael's right hand. The edge of a clip was visible in the handle. John-Michael let his hand fall to his side, fingers loose and relaxed around the weapon, conscious of the weight of death he held there. Then he turned away, ready to reenter the *casita*.

"John-Michael?" Martens took a deep breath and released it slowly. "The address of the place where they're holding your girl's buddy? We're gonna need it real soon."

PAOLO

CHIPOTLE MEXICAN GRILL, WEST COVINA, TUESDAY, JULY 7

They sat at an outdoor table, unwrapping burritos. Paolo watched as Grace tried to take a bite. She couldn't.

After a moment she put the burrito on the table, screwing her eyes shut. Tears began to spill, but she made no sound. Paolo's fingers stretched toward hers.

"Gracie, you've done everything you can. You finally got ahold of that Pete Martens guy; by now he should be in Napa."

She spoke then, brokenly, through sobs. "But . . . *Candace*! I should call my mom, I *need* to."

"Hold on a little longer, babe. We'll be at Lucy's parents' house soon, we'll get the nail polish. And then you can call your mom, the cops, everyone. But if you say anything now, we'll have to talk to the cops right away."

Grace plucked a napkin from the small pile on their tray. "You're right; Ariana might find a way to get the nail

178 ■

polish before us," she said, wiping her nose. "Maybe we shouldn't even stop to eat."

"We stopped to use the bathroom and to plan how to get into the house," he said kindly. "And it doesn't look like we're gonna eat."

Tentatively, Paolo raised his right hand, trailed fingers through her hair. Grace closed her eyes and leaned in to his touch. Her eyes opened slowly, gazing into his. She filled his field of vision, the dazzle of her eyes never bluer, the soft pink of her lips never more tempting.

Paolo held his breath. His whole body was rigid as he willed himself not to kiss her. "Grace . . ."

"Tell me everything's going to be okay," she whispered.

"Everything's going to be okay."

Any other day, any other hour, he'd be kissing her by now. Did Grace have any idea what she was doing to him? In that moment she looked utterly vulnerable, full of hope and trust. He would do anything in his power to keep her safe. He'd go to prison for her if he needed to. The only thing he wouldn't do, couldn't do, right then was kiss her. Not while she was still mourning her sister, not unless she asked.

The moment probably lasted only a few seconds, but it left him reeling. Then Grace drew her knees toward her chest and wrapped both arms tight around them.

Did people get used to this? Did people survive unexpressed desire?

"We should go," he told her. "We can eat in the car."

"Lucy isn't answering her phone," said Grace as they made their way through the parked cars. "Maya isn't picking up, either."

"You spoke to John-Michael on his burner, though, right? You told him that Martens was on his way?"

"Not yet. I'll try John-Michael again."

"We need Lucy to call her folks' house," Paolo admitted. "Or else we're gonna get stalled by the housekeeper, just like Ariana."

"What d'you think Ariana's plan is?"

Paolo was pretty sure that by this time Dana Alexander would have heard about Kay's violent suicide. If Kay was her daughter, that news would be hitting her pretty hard. "Ariana takes orders from Dana." He opened the passenger door for Grace. "And Dana's sister-I-mean-daughter just slit her own throat. I'd say that's a major distraction." He got into the car and started the engine.

Grace waited for him to maneuver out of the parking lot and back onto the San Bernardino Freeway. Then she handed him his burrito. He ate it in six bites, listening to her talk about how strange John-Michael had sounded during their last phone call. "Almost like he was afraid to talk to me," she said. "Like there was something else on his mind."

"What you have to understand is, JM is having a tough time dealing with what happened on Friday," Paolo replied.

"Because the two of you killed that guy who broke into the house?" She didn't look at him, but Paolo couldn't help hearing the accusation in her voice.

"I hit the guy with a shovel," Paolo said, far more gently than he'd expected. "I was trying to defend Lucy, not kill him."

"But when John-Michael finished him off," Grace said, "he intended to kill. That's what you said the other night, right?" She paused. "It would make sense. He's done that before."

Paolo's mind flew. Did she know? Or was she guessing? John-Michael had as good as admitted to Paolo that he'd helped his father to die by smothering him with a cushion. It didn't feel right to discuss that with anyone else, even Grace.

He felt her eyes on him. "Is that what you mean, Paolo?"

"*I* was supposed to shoot the second guy. Did you know that? Did Maya or Lucy tell you?" He stared straight ahead so that he wouldn't have to see her reaction.

"No," Grace said quietly.

"I was supposed to do it," Paolo continued. "Maya offered, said she knows how to shoot a handgun; we said no. It was supposed to be me. John-Michael had already taken the first guy out; the second guy was my responsibility."

Grace was close to tears again. "Why didn't you just call the cops? Lucy told me, she said she tried to make you, but you wouldn't."

"Because we'd committed a crime! Because if they investigated . . . John-Michael . . . if they started asking about how he smothered that guy . . ."

"Then they'd ask about his father," Grace concluded sadly.

"Not only that. We'd committed conspiracy, too; we made it look like the guy died in a hit-and-run in Malibu Canyon."

"Like that woman from your tennis club?"

Paolo's heart practically stopped. Her words echoed in his brain, thoughts with the power to stun. Luckily, a traffic light turned red. He took his hands off the steering wheel for a moment so Grace wouldn't notice his hands shaking.

"Woman?" he said, finally. "Which . . . which . . . one?"

"Didn't you hear? It was in the news. One of the members of that tennis club where you coach was in a car accident. This would be a few weeks ago. I read that her head was bashed in, and some hit-and-run driver left her for dead on a road in Malibu Canyon."

Grace said all this with a detached curiosity. Paolo didn't think she had any idea of his connection to Meredith Eriksson. He sensed, but did not see Grace turn to face him. "Is that how you got the idea, Paolo?"

Close to panic, Paolo focused on the flickering of the traffic lights. Red. Yellow. Green. He stepped on the gas. He put his right hand back on the wheel—two o'clock.

He'd told John-Michael about Meredith; he'd confessed all to the guy that was now his closest friend. Paolo had hoped to lighten the burden. But it hadn't. Instead, sharing his secret had bound the two of them in a pact of guilt.

And now, Grace was waiting, giving him the chance to tell the truth.

Paolo ached to tell her, but he was afraid. More than he feared the police, more than the disapproval of his parents, he was afraid of disappointing Grace, of doing something that might lock him out, forever.

JOHN-MICHAEL
FLOR DE CANELA, TUESDAY, JULY 7

The plan was simple. They'd wait to see who showed up to drag Lucy away. They'd let them believe they'd gotten away with it, then follow them back to where they were holding Jack Cato.

John-Michael and Pete Martens would stay out of sight. If things looked like they were getting sketchy, well then, Martens would take care of anyone who tried to hurt either Lucy or Maya.

"Better hope that doesn't happen," he warned John-Michael. There would be no rescue for Jack unless his abductors believed they'd successfully taken Lucy.

"Then we'll head for the house where they're keeping Jack. I'll deal with the men inside. I'll release Jack—assuming he's still alive. Then we secure Lucy's release."

John-Michael listened with ever-wider eyes. "Any chance we can avoid shooting people?"

The bodyguard's expression didn't alter. "Feel free to explain how."

"Negotiate?"

"Sure," he said, flatly. "If Henry Kissinger shows up, we'll get around a table; will that do?"

John-Michael had heard vaguely of Kissinger, but he didn't really get the reference. From the tone Martens was taking, he guessed his idea had been dismissed.

John-Michael checked his watch. It was twenty minutes since Pete Martens had arrived and three hours since the kidnappers had first made contact. If they were sending someone from Los Angeles, it would be another hour or two before they arrived. If they'd sent someone from San Francisco, it could be any minute now.

Martens had settled into one of the lounge chairs on the patio and was reading from a slender gray e-reader. He seemed relaxed. John-Michael wasn't sure whether to be reassured or not. The plan was simple, but it had one huge flaw: What if the gang didn't take Lucy to the place where they were holding Jack Cato? What if they killed her in the car, or took her to some isolated place where her body wouldn't be discovered and shot her?

John-Michael raised this with Martens. The man listened with an air of feigned politeness, and then said, "Springing someone from captivity is a three-man job. One to take out the opposition, one to cover the main guy, and a driver. John-Michael, you're the driver."

So Martens wanted Maya to get involved—presumably to shoot at anyone who tried to interfere with their escape. Another friend would have blood on her hands. The very thing that John-Michael had worked so hard to avoid last Friday night.

At the edge of the pool, an empty Coke can suddenly toppled over and scraped along the ground. John-Michael and Martens leapt to their feet. Martens had attached the Coke can to a cotton thread that ran all the way to the threshold of the driveway, about 150 yards. If the can shifted that fast, it could only be because a car was heading down the driveway.

Both girls hurried to the hiding places that Martens had identified—Lucy in the bedroom with the door bolted, Maya in the living room with a handgun, covering the patio through a window that had been cracked open. They'd locked all the doors to the house except the kitchen. Martens had a clear line of sight to the living room. "Now we wait," he'd said. "If these guys are cool, they'll take Lucy without firing a single bullet."

"And if they're not cool?" John-Michael had asked.

"Then we'll be prepared."

John-Michael was tucked out of sight behind the pool equipment shed, near the patio. The moment that he'd found out that John-Michael had never shot a gun, Martens had forbidden him from getting involved in this maneuver. "People who don't know how to shoot tend to get themselves killed when they point a gun at someone who has. So stay out of the way. The gun is an absolute last resort—don't forget that."

John-Michael waited and watched. From his vantage point, he could only see Martens, who lurked at the edge of the French doors. He couldn't even see the kitchen door, the main entrance to the *casita*.

The minutes ticked by. John-Michael crouched behind the pool shed—the only structure large enough to hide him while he kept an eye on the *casita*. He caught sight of a distant hot-air balloon, a rainbow checkerboard puffing across the landscape.

The early evening stillness was sudden ripped apart by the sound of a single gunshot. There was a scream. The sound of running. Another shot, then a flurry of gunfire. Then, unmistakably, "Kid, get over here!"

John-Michael flicked off the gun's safety as Martens had shown him. He gripped it with both hands, shifted in one smooth movement from the back of the shed to the rear of the pool, where he threw himself to the ground. Now he could see the driveway. A second later, he saw one man bursting out of the house and scrabbling across the gravel toward an old Volvo parked on an angle about ten yards around the corner from the kitchen door. From their vantage points, neither Maya nor Martens had sight of the driveway.

"Shoot him, John-Michael," Martens yelled. "Shoot, goddamn it!"

This time he didn't think about it. His finger was squeezing the trigger as soon as Martens shouted. The first two shots missed, but the third caught the intruder in the right flank. The man went down, clutching his gun hand to the wound.

"Shoot again, he's armed!" Martens insisted, louder.

Four, thought John-Michael, as he shot yet again, and again, and again, until he'd seen the man's body jerking.

Four people he'd killed now. *Four.*

He clambered to his feet. Both hands gripped the automatic pistol, which was trained on the crumpled figure of the man he'd shot.

John-Michael approached, slowly, weapon outstretched. One of the guy's legs still twitched.

This must be how hunters feel, he thought. *Walking up to take a first look at the kill.* When he saw the man's face, his stomach heaved. He gagged, swallowing bile and acid. The man was young, and his face was twisted in pain and exhaustion. Now—judging from the blood that had soaked the shirt around his heart—he was dead.

John-Michael heard the sound of gravel crunching behind him. He spun around, still brandishing the gun. Pete Martens was there, dragging a second man along. The fingers of one hand bunched into a fistful of the younger guy's camel-colored leather jacket. Martens' other hand held a gun, its muzzle inches from his captive's temple.

John-Michael relaxed enough to lower his pistol. Martens glanced briefly at the body on the ground. His eyes flicked upward to John-Michael's. "Dead?"

John-Michael nodded, swallowing hard.

Martens prodded the second guy, pushing him toward the parked Volvo. He got the man to open the car door and hand over the keys.

The man Martens had captured was about thirty years old, white, with a shaven head and light stubble. He looked wary and quietly furious. "What happens now?" he asked.

Martens ignored the question. "Go inside," he instructed John-Michael. "Get your friends, bring them out here. We're leaving."

"In the Volvo?"

"I think it'd be less of a surprise if they used the same car to take Lucy back, no?"

"But . . . but . . . the dead guy," John-Michael stuttered. "We can't leave him here."

"Put him in the trunk."

Lucy and Maya emerged. They looked shaken, cautious. Martens scraped his gun against the shaven-headed man's cheek. "Call your compadres. Tell them you're bringing in Lucy. Just that: 'We're bringing Lucy in.' Say a single other word, and I'll shoot you in the eye. Now, are we clear on that?"

Pale eyes glared in silence at Martens. After a second, the man gave a single, reluctant nod. Martens stepped back, let him slide across into the rear passenger side–seat.

Martens took some plastic handcuffs from inside his jacket. He told John-Michael to cuff the stranger and to get into the back next to him. Then he turned to Maya. "Now, miss, I didn't get a chance to see your shooting; you didn't exactly have a favorable angle. Would you mind giving me a demonstration?" Martens gestured toward a tree about thirty yards away. "Show me. Hit that olive tree halfway up the trunk and in the middle of that big branch."

Maya nodded once, raising the pistol John-Michael had passed on earlier. She fired off two shots. Martens walked to the tree and inspected the trunk. "You'll do," he said. "We're gonna need you in the car. Any trouble from our friend back there and I want you to shoot him in the knee, you got that?"

John-Michael watched Maya climb into the opposite side of the backseat. She barely gave John-Michael a glance. All her attention was on the man they were guarding. In her right hand was a gun, which she trained on the guy's kneecap. Ruthless focus, deadly intent.

It was a side of Maya he'd not yet seen. Ever since Friday night, he'd suspected that this side existed. And yet, John-Michael was the one who'd racked up four kills.

In theory, Maya might feel okay with the idea of hurting someone to protect her own.

In practice, it was soul scarring. A bloodstain that had seeped into John-Michael's skin. It marked him just as surely as any tattoo. If Maya couldn't see that, she was blind.

GRACE

The text from Lucy arrived just after six in the evening. With the help of Martens, the three housemates in Napa had managed to hold Lucy's would-be kidnappers at bay. Now they were on their way to rescue Jack.

Lucy had also sent the code for her parents' burglar alarm. Now they knew when the housekeeper would leave the house. They knew more or less what time Lucy's mother would return from her office on campus. They knew that Lucy's father had returned to Washington DC earlier that afternoon. Everything was set for what Paolo referred to as "a little light breaking and entering."

Grace was glad of his attempt at humor, even if she didn't have the heart to laugh. But she could tell Paolo was trying to cheer her up. He kept checking up on her.

It had been many months since a boy had made a play for Grace. She'd almost forgotten what it was like. The way a boy might tip-toe around her, all attentive, looking at her like she existed within a circle of eggshells he was scared to break. It was strange to see Paolo behaving like that. Not what she'd expected—or dared to hope for.

Paolo parked the car some way from Lucy's parents' house. He switched off the ignition and lifted his eyes to hers, silently asking for permission to take her hand. She nodded and they shared a hopeful smile.

"Ready?"

"Two-four-seven-eight," Grace said, reciting the code for the burglar alarm.

They locked the car and made their way down the tree-lined avenue. The homes were grand, with much of the architecture obscured from view by huge, mature trees—California oaks, cottonwoods, spruces. Lucy's family home was a three-story Craftsman-style house; a gabled roof, deep overhanging eaves, exposed rafters painted a rich olive green. A front porch extended below the main roof.

Paolo climbed the porch stairs and peered through the windows. "Looks empty enough." He trotted back down to where Grace waited on the front lawn. This time she took his hand, leading him to the side passage and toward the rear door. It had a half window divided into four panes. Paolo picked up a blue-and-white ceramic plant pot from the path and used it to smash the glass of one pane. With his elbow, he knocked out the remaining glass.

The warning alarm went off, a high-pitched squeal.

Then they were barging through the door. "We've got fifteen seconds," Grace said.

Paolo bolted ahead, making for the utility room next to the main staircase, where Lucy had told them to find the keypad. A few seconds later, the whining noise stopped. "So far, so good."

Nervously, she nodded and took his hand again. Like Gretel with Hansel.

They started up the stairs. Grace was fascinated by just how wrong it felt to be in someone's home without their invitation. The hairs on the backs of her arms were raised. Undeniably exciting, once she forgot to be scared and remembered to breathe.

Lucy's bedroom looked ready to receive its occupant at the end of a school day. There was a neatly made bed. From beneath a shiny purple satin coverlet, the black cotton of the quilt cover showed. Posters of Billie Joe Armstrong, Rancid, the Sex Pistols, and the Dead Kennedys hung from the walls. Hand-drawn artwork adorned the wall behind Lucy's bed: finely drawn pen-and-ink illustrations. Grace had seen so little of this side of her friend, she couldn't even be sure if it was Lucy's art.

Paolo turned to her, holding a framed picture. "Look. It's the cast of *Jelly and Pie.*"

Grace studied the photo for a second or two. "Lucy was so cute," she said. "It's hard to imagine what it would do to a little kid like that, to see someone you know kill someone else."

Grace could see why Lucy hadn't been able to talk about what she saw. In the meticulous order of Lucy's childhood bedroom, Grace saw the opposite of her own childhood. Quiet. Lonely. Introspective. The room of a child who understood the danger of secrets.

"It's like Lucy's folks think she's coming back one day," Paolo said.

"Wonder if my parents think that about me?"

He turned to her, still holding her right hand in his. "I'm not going to live with my parents again, you know that, right? You and me and the others, we stick together."

Grace felt her lower lip tremble. She couldn't reply.

Beneath the whitewashed pine bed, a thick layer of dust had collected on the antique-stained pine wood floor. Kneeling, Grace bent low to get a good look. It wasn't as tidy as the rest of the room. Abandoned sneakers, purple Vans worn thin in the soles. An old PlayStation box.

The box of Lucy's treasures stood out—it was covered in burgundy fabric shot with gilt thread. Grace grabbed one corner of the lid and pulled it out. She sat on the bed, wiped the dust with the edge of her hand, and blew it away. Paolo sat beside her as she lifted the lid.

"Lucy has a box like this in Venice," she said. "Snapshots and letters, mostly."

They stared at the contents of the box. Playbills and flyers for stage shows. Lyrics from songs that Lucy must have learned for performances. Ticket stubs, show programs. Newspaper cuttings with photos of the cast for one or other dramatic performances featuring a tiny, cherubic Lucasta Jordan-Long.

"My mom has a collection, too," Grace said, barely audible. "For Candace."

Paolo began to rifle through the objects. It didn't take him long to find what they were looking for—a bottle of peach-colored Chanel nail polish.

"Don't touch it," Grace warned. "It's evidence." She put the box aside and stood up, looking around. "We should have brought a Ziploc bag."

"Grace," Paolo said, "why don't we just take the whole box?"

"Of course." She was quivering now. He stood and placed both hands on her upper arms. They watched each other for a second nervously. His gaze moved from her eyes to her lips, and she licked them self-consciously, acutely aware of the tension between them, of grief that was welling up inside her at the thought of Candace's box of stage memories and her mom and her brothers and her stepfather, who would soon be feeling so much anguish far away in San Antonio. How was it possible that she was avoiding it, here, with Paolo? She longed for the world to reduce itself to the touch of his lips on hers.

"Kiss me," she whispered, wrapping both arms around his neck.

Paolo didn't need any more encouragement; he teased her lips with his own for a second, then grabbed her hips, drawing her to him as they kissed.

After a moment, he tried to break away, but Grace resisted, raking her fingers in his hair, breathless as she held him against her.

"Is this okay?" he murmured, his lips buzzing against her neck. "I feel like . . . like we're not supposed to do this."

Grace's mind was clouding, her thoughts fuzzy and unformed. She kissed his throat, felt his pulse there, and then leaned back in his arms as he did the same to her. Her legs buckled and gave way. They stumbled backward toward Lucy's bed.

The irony wasn't lost on Grace. But from the way Paolo was kissing her, she doubted that Lucy was anywhere in his thoughts.

PAOLO

LUCY'S FAMILY HOME, CLAREMONT, TUESDAY, JULY 7

Paolo drew back and looked at Grace. Her cheeks were flushed, her pupils dilated. Girls had looked at him like that before, and he'd felt nothing but amusement and the hunger of raw lust. Yet the sight of Grace just wrecked him. He wanted to fall to his knees and make eternal promises of love. To say things that sounded ridiculous even in his own head. He wanted to tear off Grace's clothes and his own, to slide into the bed with her and completely lose his mind.

Every other coherent thought had been banished by the simple act of kissing Grace. He didn't care, not even a tiny bit.

His thoughts must have showed on his face because Grace broke away from him for a moment. "Paolo, not here," she said breathlessly. "We should go."

She was right. It felt like he'd been waiting his whole life to feel what he'd experienced in the last three minutes. And now it had to stop.

■197

Grace sat up. With light pressure to his shoulders, she pushed him away. It was quietly devastating. "That was . . ." She took a deep breath, blushed as their eyes met. "Wow. Bad timing, right?"

Paolo was still recovering from the disappointment, but he managed a halfhearted chuckle. "Really, really bad."

She stood up, waiting for him to pick up the box. They left the room and quickly headed back downstairs and into the kitchen. There didn't seem to be any point to resetting the alarm and anyway, Lucy hadn't told them how.

They hurried back to the car. Paolo placed Lucy's box of memories in the trunk, and then got into the driver's seat and pushed the key into the ignition. "It's getting late," he said. "Too late to drive back to Napa. The house in Venice is gonna be crawling with cops. But I could take you to the airport?"

"Why?" Grace turned to him, her face open. She wasn't hiding her desire from him any longer.

Utterly distracted, Paolo stumbled over his response. "Don't you want to go to San Antonio? I figured maybe you'd want to be with your family."

Grace shook her head. "We need to go to the cops with Lucy. She's being interviewed tomorrow morning. I want them to have the nail polish right away."

Paolo nodded. Of course, saving Grace's dad from execution was their main task. He needed to get a grip. Her kisses might have been brimming with desire, she might be gazing at him with frank devotion, but right now, her priorities were elsewhere.

"We could go to a motel, rest awhile, and then drive up tomorrow morning early," he suggested, wishing he had the courage to ask her outright, here and now, so that he wouldn't have to face the crushing disappointment later. *Go to bed with me. Please. Let me make you forget everything that's happened today and yesterday and since Friday. Let me make you feel incredible just for a little while.*

"Yes."

Paolo started the car, pretending that she'd answered the real question, not simply the practical one. There'd likely be disappointment later, but at least for a little while longer, he could dream.

"I'd do anything for you, Grace," he said, turning to look into her eyes. It frustrated him that he didn't have the kind of skill with words she deserved. A girl like Grace should have poems; she should have songs. "You know that, right?"

She inhaled, shakily, and tried to smile. Was she regretting what had happened? Just the idea that she might made him feel sick. He was painfully aware that Grace was thinking, her mind whirring.

Paolo glanced in the rearview mirror. About fifty yards behind them, a white car had just pulled away from the curb. Now it was motionless, partway into the road, as though waiting for someone to come out of the nearest house.

"Use my burner," he said suddenly. "Call your mom. She needs to know you're safe. Then we'll break the phone up, and I'll get another." He rummaged in his shirt pocket and handed her the tiny cell phone.

Grace's hands quivered as she made the call. When she got through to voicemail, she sobbed in frustration. Paolo could barely stand to hear Grace's quiet tears as she stumbled through her message, telling her mother that she was okay, that she shouldn't worry on her account. That she'd be in touch very soon, that she was doing something that would help her father.

Paolo placed a hand on her shoulder, caressing the edge of her face with his thumb. When she ended the call, he plucked a Kleenex from the box in his car door pocket and handed it to her.

Grace accepted it and dabbed at her nose. When she finally spoke, her voice was broken with sorrow. "I guess they're on their way to Los Angeles. Someone has to identify Candace's body." She paused. "I wonder if they'll run into Dana?"

He leaned across to kiss her cheek. It was hot, damp, salty. "Why would they?"

"Kay died. Dana will have to identify her daughter. Poor Dana."

Paolo was astonished. "It's not 'poor Dana.' That woman tried to have Lucy killed! It's because of her that your dad was about to be executed."

"I know." Grace closed her eyes and leaned into his

touch once again. "I know. It's just that to lose a daughter that way . . . must be so awful. Look at what Dana did to keep Kay out of an institution. She must have been out of her mind with worry about her kid—for years. Now she's lost everything."

Their fingers intertwined. "You have way too much sympathy for the devil," Paolo murmured.

"Paolo," she said quietly. "I'm so tired. Let's go to a motel."

He nodded and reluctantly released Grace from his touch. He pulled the car away from the curb. Behind them, the stalled white car began to move. Paolo hardly registered its presence.

At the end of the road the car behind them made the same left turn. Paolo didn't notice that, either.

MAYA

Maybe she shouldn't have agreed to take a gun. A Glock Gen4 semiautomatic handgun—she'd used one before, at the range where her mom had taught her to shoot. Now that it was in her hand, Maya itched to fire one again.

The last ten minutes at the *casita* kept replaying in her mind. Martens had given his instructions from behind the laptop, after he'd signaled to Maya to mute the sound on the laptop so Jack's kidnappers couldn't overhear the conversation. The instant they'd detected the intruders' car in the driveway, they'd launched into action. Maya knew that Lucy had felt the full force of her own powerlessness when Martens had ordered her to lock herself in the bedroom. But it had been the best way to ensure her safety.

Martens had been definite about one thing: he had enough firepower to stop anyone taking Lucy, but not necessarily without casualties.

"There's a chance someone will die today," he'd told them. "Let's make sure it's not one of us."

Minutes later, she heard an explosion of gunfire outside the *casita*.

From her position in the living room, Maya had shot steady rounds of covering fire. She'd made it impossible to cross the patio. Martens had shot from inside the kitchen. Those guys had rolled up expecting to find a bunch of defenseless teenagers. They were not prepared to find Martens, Maya, and John-Michael armed and waiting.

Sitting in the car, Maya's fingers curled around the handle of the automatic pistol. Across from her, she could sense John-Michael's fear. He was sweating profusely. The guy between them—presumably sent by Dana Alexander—was strangely detached. He seemed eager not to upset her or John-Michael.

Would they reach Jack only to find him already dead? Or would something happen on the way, something that might alert the cops? No one in the car wanted the police involved—Maya was sure of that. At this point, it would mean jail for everyone.

Pete Martens had guessed that the men sent by Alexander were coming from LA, so he'd headed down the 5. Moments ago, one of Maya's hacker friends had finally texted the information they needed. Her burner cell phone now had a physical address to match the IP address where Jack Cato had last accessed the internet: a place in the San Fernando Valley.

Maya couldn't risk touching her phone, not while she was supposed to concentrate on guarding Alexander's goon. Lucy was sitting up front with Martens and handling any calls.

All that mattered now was guarding the man who sat between her and John-Michael. And getting to Jack as fast as they could.

During the journey, Maya had plenty of time to study their captive. Her eyes roved over the two-day stubble on his cheeks and scalp and the ruddy skin beneath. She watched his brown eyes, lazily hooded as they stole covert glances at her. *You can tell how badly I want to use this gun,* she thought. *You can feel my anger through the metal. You hurt my Jack; now I'm begging you, make a mistake, just one. Let me use this gun to smash up your bones.*

It took several hours to drive down Interstate 5 to San Fernando. A lot of time to speculate, to reflect.

The language of mirrors, Maya thought. If she were to stare into a mirror right now, what would she see? The eager, fifteen-year-old high school app developer that she'd been until Friday? Would she see Maya, who was born in the USA? Or would she see sixteen-year-old, Mexican-born Julia, who carried the burden of all that new knowledge?

It was dark by the time their car rolled up across the street, about twenty yards across from the address that Maya had been sent. Martens rolled down his window.

For a minute or two, they all studied the house opposite. She saw a large bungalow with a gray-tiled roof. A tidy lawn led to the tree-lined sidewalk. In the corner of the front yard stood a large jacaranda, empty of all but the last of its purple-blue-colored blossoms. A house like millions of others, with no hint of the horror within.

"Gun, please," Martens told John-Michael. When John-Michael handed him the weapon, Martens removed the clip, emptied the bullets into his palm, and replaced the empty clip in the gun. He got out of the car, opened the rear passenger door, and let them out, handing the now harmless gun to their captive.

He indicated the driver's seat. "Okay, kid, you're up," he told John-Michael. Then he beckoned Maya over and whispered, "When their man has his back turned, I want you to take cover behind the nearest tree on the sidewalk. It's easily within your range. I'm gonna come out of the house with your friend Jack. Anyone comes after us with a weapon, you take 'em out, got that? Once I'm in the car, I'll cover you while you head for the vehicle, okay?"

Maya managed to nod. She glanced at Lucy, whose fingers were twisting around and around, anxiously. It made Maya conscious of her own right hand, slick with perspiration on the warm handle of the gun.

Martens turned their prisoner to face the front door of the bungalow, pushing him slightly ahead. He used a concealed box cutter to slice through the plastic cuffs that had knotted the man's hands for the past few hours. Martens raised his own gun and pointed it close to their prisoner's kidneys.

"There are twenty-two places where you can shoot a person and he won't die. Five of those will floor a person, instantly, rendering him helpless. Three of *those* will leave him a cripple for life, unable to take a leak, or walk. And of course, there are three different places where a bullet will *kill*. Now, if you want me to avoid the three places that kill *and* the three places that cripple, I'm happy to oblige. But I'm going to need you to stay out of my way. Tell me you understand, and we can begin."

The man took a long look at Martens. "Dude, you're not the one I'm afraid of. And you shouldn't be afraid of me. Forget maiming the guys inside there—either shoot to *kill* or die. Tell *me* that you understand *that* . . . and we can begin."

Martens almost smiled. He pushed the man ahead again and withdrew to the side, just out of sight. When he nodded in Maya's direction, she backed along the sidewalk toward the nearest tree. Then Martens pushed Lucy and their captive in front of him. It looked as though the captive had a gun on Lucy, but it was empty. And Martens had a box cutter to their captive's back.

Maya peeked around the trunk just enough to see the front door open a crack. Lucy stepped aside as Martens rushed forward, barging past the shaven-headed guy. There was a muffled shot. Lucy jerked backward, visibly stunned. Their captive suddenly abandoned her, turning and pelting across the lawn and down the street into the shadows. Left stranded, Lucy hurried back toward the car.

Once Maya saw Lucy was safely in the car, she turned her attention to the front door. From inside the house, she heard muted gunfire. That sound on this friendly-looking street was chilling. Maya glanced around, both relieved and horrified that no one else was around to hear it.

Inside the bungalow, someone was using a silencer or shooting up close. After about three minutes, she heard Martens's voice. "Maya. Could you get in here, please?"

She hesitated. It had definitely been the bodyguard's voice. And yet they'd agreed that she would stay outside. What if someone inside had taken Martens prisoner and was forcing him to say those words?

But when Martens appeared in the doorway with an unreadable expression, Maya lowered her gun. She paced across the lawn swiftly and followed him into the hallway.

When Martens put both his hands on the walls to stop her, Maya knew something was wrong. She tried to look past his slim frame, but he swayed, blocking her view. "Maya, it's not good news."

That was enough. She pushed hard on the bodyguard's chest, shoving him out of her way.

She stumbled into the kitchen, where she found the kidnapper. Blood was pouring from an injury to his right eye. He was immobilized, handcuffed to the faucets by the sink. Maya felt his fierce glare follow her as she stepped into an adjacent corridor. She forced herself to keep walking, to round the corner into the first bedroom.

When she caught sight of Jack, she stopped moving. He lay motionless on the floor, faceup. A cry lodged in Maya's throat. She moved closer, kneeling beside his head.

Then she saw the blood. It had seeped out of a hole under his jaw and from the top of his head, from where the bullet must have exited. His fair hair had turned to rust around the wound, matted with blood.

"I take it this is Jack? I'm sorry. He's been dead awhile," Martens said. "They never intended to keep their word."

A single word escaped her. "Why?"

"Kill all the witnesses," Martens said. He tilted his head, regarding her with a hint of sympathy. "Look at how they were in Napa—they came in, shooting. These men, they're pros. Your friend was marked from the minute they took him. Same would have happened to Lucy."

Maya felt like she'd run into a wall. Air stuck in her chest.

Jack was dead.

Everything he'd done for her. Everything she'd felt for him. He was the only one who understood her. Now he was gone. And it was her fault.

Martens helped her to her feet. Taking her left hand, he led her back to the kitchen. Jack's murderer was still there, cuffed to the faucets and glowering.

Martens raised his gun and placed it against the man's heart. "What about this one? You want him dead?"

Maya felt her whole body shaking. Tears obscured her vision. She choked down a sob, and then nodded.

"Kill all the witnesses. Isn't that what the pros do?"

LUCY

Lucy scanned Paolo's text several times before she read it aloud.

Sending this from a new burner—I destroyed the old one cuz we had to call Grace's parents. No word yet about Candace. Good news, we got the nail polish. We'll come back tomorrow morning, it's too late now.

No news about Candace. That was a tough blow, especially on top of losing Jack Cato. It overshadowed the news that Grace and Paolo had retrieved the bottle of nail polish that could incriminate Dana Alexander.

Maya and John-Michael listened without comment. Both seemed too emotionally drained to react. Only Martens was impassive as the car moved smoothly along Interstate 5.

What now?

Shell-shocked. That's how Maya was reacting. Lucy had sensed the truth the moment she saw her housemate stumbling blindly into the parked Volvo.

Jack Cato was dead. The kidnappers had lied. They

had never intended to trade hostages—only to kill them.

For a long time, Lucy had simply hugged Maya as they sat together in the backseat. At first the younger girl had sobbed, quietly shaking with grief and rage. Lucy had stroked Maya's long hair and murmured words of comfort—anything she could think of, really.

"At least they didn't hurt him any more," Maya kept saying, in shaky whispers. "They gave him a quick death."

Then she made an awful sound—a low, agonized wail—and the crying started up again. Lucy buried Maya's head against her shoulder. "It's okay now, sugar. You're safe with us—no one's gonna hurt you."

Lucy longed to ask, but didn't dare. It was pretty evident that the kidnappers had all been killed—aside from the one who'd made a break for it. The question was, had Martens done the killing? Or Maya? She'd gone into the house with a gun. Even though she'd come out without one, Lucy couldn't help but wonder.

You couldn't know ahead of time how a thing like murder would take you. To see the dead body of a close friend and to have their killer right in front of you, armed and dangerous . . . that would be a lot of temptation. Only a very forgiving person could resist. Revenge didn't seem like Maya's style; it was driven by passion. Lucy had gotten the impression that Maya had all that under control. But Jack's death seemed to have broken her.

After about thirty minutes, Maya calmed down enough to sit up. She pulled away from Lucy and gazed into the desert night around Interstate 5. Her eyes seemed dead, her expression blank.

Then Maya spoke. Her voice sounded faded. "This happened because we killed the second hit man. Because I made us send that stupid text. Because I made the boys kill him."

There was a long moment. "No, Maya. You didn't *make* us do anything," John-Michael said at last. "If we hadn't acted on Friday night, that guy would have gone for Grace and Candace."

"We don't know that. It was Lucy that they wanted."

"Exactly," John-Michael said. "And they would have done anything to find her. Grace and Candace would have been the ones in their basement, not Jack."

Maya's voice cracked. "You think that makes me feel better?"

"I know it doesn't. I'm just trying to point out—we acted to protect Grace and Candace. There was nothing else we could do."

"That's a crock, and you know it," she said. "We could have called the cops. Like Lucy said."

"If we'd called the cops from Malibu Canyon, I'd be in jail by now," John-Michael said, and he glanced over his shoulder at Lucy. "Maya," he said, "you and Paolo *and* Lucy would be in jail for conspiracy. Look, we made a difficult decision, and we made it together."

"You're lying to yourself again," Maya said, shaking her head. "Lucy never agreed."

"I don't think we should be going over and over it," Lucy said slowly. "I said what I said because I thought it was the best thing at the time. But I wasn't thinking through all the angles."

"I never thought Jack would get hurt," Maya sobbed. "I did not risk my *friend* . . . Jack helped me!" Her cries became inconsolable, heartbreaking. "I let him worry about me . . . How did they even . . . ?"

"Ariana," Lucy pronounced bitterly. "Ariana knew about Jack. She knew about Jack because . . . because I let her into our lives. It's on me, Maya, as much as anyone else."

"No." Maya wiped fresh tears, and turned to her. "You didn't know that Ariana was dangerous. Lucy, you did nothing wrong."

At last, Martens spoke up. "The truth is, you kids were in way over your heads from the start. In my experience, once someone fires a gun at you or someone you care about, your life changes forever, right then and there."

The bodyguard's words resonated with Lucy. Her life had changed forever the night she'd watched Tyson Drew being drowned. It was like she'd switched to a different track—her first destination as a star of the screen had gone forever. Now she was stuck in a life of compromises—half-begun plans and searching, always searching, for something to fill the gaping hole inside her.

Sometimes it was as though she could see and even touch that other Lucy, the whole one. She could dream of her, but she couldn't become her, not ever again.

"A total of five hired guns came after seven of you," Martens went on. "The six of you and your pal Jack. Now four, count them, *four* of them are dead. For just one of you. And you guys had nothing in your arsenal when all this got started. I've been doing this a long time, kids. In my book, you've won this war."

"Not 'just one' of us," John-Michael murmured. "Candace might be dead, too."

Into the quiet that followed, Maya said, in a strangled kind of gasp, "Oh God. He's really dead. Jack is dead. He's dead. And it's because of me."

"Not because of you, Maya!" John-Michael said, turning around to face her. He touched her knee. "You did the best you could. They'd *already* decided to kill him. It's not like they did it because you and Pete walked into that house."

Jack's death isn't even half of it, Lucy thought, but she kept her thoughts to herself. Now John-Michael was a killer, several times over. Candace might be dead. None of it would have happened if she'd only remembered what she'd seen the night of Tyson Drew's murder.

"In a little while," said Martens, "we're going to ditch the dead guy in the trunk, find someplace to bury him. Once we get back to your place in Napa, you can pay me what we agreed. Then we need to dump this Volvo. My guess is that we'll be busy until around three in the morning. After that, you can get some rest. From tomorrow, my advice would be this: buy yourselves some camping gear. Get yourselves off the grid.

"I'm going to find my buddy's daughter; I'm going to find Grace," Martens continued. "You kids have gotten yourselves mixed up with some extremely unpleasant people. It may be that this isn't over."

GRACE

Paolo was asleep when Grace woke. She didn't move for several minutes, just watched him as he lay there next to her. He looked so relaxed. This was a rare chance to gaze at him in the kind of open admiration she'd never risked before. She held her breath, tracing a fingertip along the line of his cheekbone and toward the edge of his mouth.

The housemates joked about it, called him "Disney Channel." They teased him for the care he took over his diet while he was training, about his lifting weights on the balcony, practically preening over his muscles. About the tattoo that now adorned his right arm. Yet you couldn't deny it—Paolo was gorgeous. Hot. Sexy. He was all those horrible, terrible things. Everything that Grace had promised herself she'd avoid. The kind of "player" girls simply offered themselves up to.

If I had any sense, I'd have resisted, she thought. *Indefinitely.* It had to be possible to cure yourself of that kind of crush. Those feelings couldn't last forever, could they? Paolo was the hurricane you forced yourself to ride out.

At least, that had been the plan. Now her plan lay in shreds.

Grace reached out again, this time sweeping her fingertips lightly across his tattooed upper arm. The inflammation had disappeared, black ink all tight lines and curls on lightly tanned skin.

Last night, she'd managed to resist the urge to do anything more than let him hold her and kiss her. They'd agreed to sleep in their clothes. Paolo had suggested it, but Grace knew that if they'd been skin to skin, she'd have been the first one to cave. As they kissed, Grace had felt herself letting go more than once. She knew he sensed her weakness; she understood it with a knowledge that felt primitive, instinctual.

You wouldn't think a guy with Paolo's reputation would let a girl off the hook so easily. But he had.

His eyes fluttered open, green and clear, connecting with hers in a way that made Grace's heart race.

"Hey," she said, softly. Paolo caught her hand and brought it to his lips, kissing her fingers and then the inside of her palm, closing his eyes. *So romantic*, she thought. And then, *Stop it.*

If they'd actually done it last night, Grace knew she would be blushing by now. She might have slept a lot better, though, instead of waking throughout the night to a combination of frustration and fear; flying between thoughts of Paolo to the stark reality of what had happened to Candace.

He sat up, rubbed a palm over his jaw, as if checking to see if he needed to shave. "You okay?" he asked cautiously, as though he'd somehow sneaked into her bed and was about to get kicked out.

Grace smiled. In the middle of all that anxiety, this moment of happiness felt like bliss. "Mm-hmm. I was about to take a shower."

A flicker of interest appeared in his eyes. "Don't suppose you want . . . ?"

"For you to join me?" she said wryly. "I don't think so."

Paolo shrugged. He hid his disappointment well. "Okay, baby."

Grace hesitated. "Don't stop asking, though."

"Oh, don't worry," he said, flashing her a cocky grin. "I don't give up that easy."

She headed for the shower quickly, afraid to look him in the eye. Anything else would be too much temptation.

When she returned, he was watching tennis on TV. "It's Wimbledon," he said as she sat on the opposite side of the bed, reaching for the hair dryer.

"You'll play there one day," she told him affectionately.

He gave an ambivalent sigh. "Maybe. ATP Challenger in a year or two, I hope. Then we'll see. If that goes okay, I'll be playing a bunch of those Grand Slam tournaments." He paused. "Either that, or jail," he added ruefully.

She pretended she hadn't heard that last part. "What about law and human rights?"

"Law?" A sad smile. "I guess I'm not the law-abiding

type. Conspiracy to conceal manslaughter, remember?"

Grace chose her words with care. "You're not the one who . . . who killed that man."

"I did most of it. Just before John-Michael finished the guy off, he looked me in the eye, y'know, like to say, are we cool? And I nodded, Gracie. I told him—yeah."

There were no words she could offer. But in her heart, she knew Paolo was no killer.

"Grace, there's more," he started to say. "There's something else I want to tell you. That you need to know."

He stopped, as though something had stolen his words. Whatever he was planning to say next seemed to make him anxious.

There was a knock at the door. "Housekeeping."

Paolo rose to his feet. "Actually, I'm ready to get outta here. You?"

"You don't want to shower? It's only nine fifteen."

"I'd like to get back to the others ASAP, to be honest."

"We should call first."

Paolo nodded. "Okay. May as well take a super-quick shower, then." He strolled over to the door, opened it a sliver, and told the maid, "Hey there. We're gonna be about ten minutes, that all right?"

Grace watched him return to the bed, pulling off his T-shirt as he walked, and then blushed when he caught her looking at him. Instead of veering toward the bathroom, he halted directly in her path. Gently, he used a single finger to turn her face toward him. "Hey. Don't, Gracie, please. I like it when you look."

She tried to suppress the shiver that went through her, but couldn't stop her eyes roving over his toned torso, lean with taut muscles.

"You're so perfect," she murmured as his arms encircled her waist. Her fingertips tingled with the impulse to touch him.

"You won't say that when I tell you what I've done." He placed a kiss on the outside of her neck, and Grace closed her eyes, clenching her hands into fists. She wasn't going to be able to resist much longer. Why was she even trying?

But then she thought of Candace. All she could see was Candace, covered in blood, Yoandy on his knees as he wept.

Gently, she placed her hands on Paolo's. "Take your shower. I'm gonna use your new phone to make some calls."

Paolo kissed her forehead, sweetly. He walked backward toward the bathroom, letting go of her hands at the last possible second.

Grace found Paolo's new burner and dialed Lucy's number. It rang twice, and then Lucy answered. "Grace? Jeez, it's good to hear your voice. You okay? Is our boy Paolo looking after you?"

"He is; we're taking care of each other." Grace smiled, felt herself turning red when she realized what she'd said.

Lucy's awkward pause suggested that she'd heard it, too. "You hooked up?"

Grace couldn't stop herself from blushing. "Not quite."

"And that's all right with you?"

"Yes. I think it's better if we take things slow. I'm too tense, can't think about much except my sister."

There was another uncomfortable pause. "Gracie, there's something I have to tell you. There's been bad trouble up here, too."

Grace's knuckles cracked around the phone. "What? Didn't Peter Martens get to you?"

"Yeah, he was here. But they somehow got ahold of Jack Cato. Used him to find us. Martens and John-Michael got rid of them, but we had to leave the house. And, Grace—Jack is dead."

"What?" For a few seconds Grace was too stunned to make another sound. She heard the shower running, heard it stop. In the corridor outside, she heard a polite knock on the door and the soft female voice repeating, "Housekeeping."

Grace struggled to concentrate on Lucy. "Where are you now?"

"Waiting to talk to the cops, remember? I had that appointment in Napa."

Relief surged through Grace. "Oh yes. Thank God! *Finally.* And Pete Martens is with you?"

"Martens? No—he's on his way south, to you."

"What? No!" Grace clutched the phone. "Lucy, call Martens, make him turn around. It's *you* that we need to protect—you're the witness. Without your testimony, my dad will be executed."

"But, Gracie, what about you and Paolo?"

"We're okay, Lucy. We got the nail polish from your old house. We'll have some breakfast and check out of here, and then we'll head back north. Why don't you stay in Napa, and we'll meet back at the police department?"

"Okay, sugar, you got it," Lucy replied.

"Lucy . . . is this it? Have we done it, have we saved my father?"

Lucy took a deep breath. "Maybe. Yeah. I hope so, Grace."

Paolo emerged from the bathroom in a cloud of steam, T-shirt sticking to places on his back that were still damp.

"There's one other thing, Lucy," began Grace. This was probably a good time to tell her housemate her theory about Tyson Drew's murderer. She hoped Lucy wouldn't be too disturbed to learn that it might have been Kay, not Dana, whom she'd seen drowning Drew in the pool at that party nine years ago.

There was another light knock at the door.

"I said ten minutes, not five," Paolo muttered, striding across the room. But when he opened the door, there was a heavy shove from the other side. Off balance, Paolo stumbled back into the room.

Grace glanced up, too shocked to cry out as the chambermaid burst into the room. It took her a full three seconds to register that the uniformed figure was someone she recognized.

The phone dropped from Grace's fingers and onto the

bed. The door to their motel room slammed shut. Paolo backed closer to the bed.

A compact yet sturdy-looking pistol was aimed at Grace's face, in the grip of a hand with perfectly manicured, cherry-red fingernails. Peering at Grace with an air of imperious detachment was Dana Alexander. Dressed in the uniform of the motel's housekeeping staff, hair tied in a neat bun, her face stripped of all but the lightest makeup, the movie star's magnetism was barely diminished.

"Sit on the bed," Alexander said.

Grace felt Paolo draw closer to her, felt his fingers searching for hers on the mattress until he'd wrapped two fingers around her thumb. Her mouth felt dry, her eyes stung.

"Forgive the intrusion, my dears," said Alexander silkily. "And I do hope you won't think me jejune . . . if I expect you to hand over the item that I think we *all* know I'm rather keen to retrieve."

LUCY

"The line is still connected," Lucy whispered to John-Michael. "I can hear everything. *She's* there—Dana Alexander. Sounds like she's got a gun."

She covered the phone's microphone with one hand. John-Michael was sitting beside her on a bench in the waiting area of the police precinct. "Tell the cops!" he hissed.

Clutching the phone to her ear, Lucy made her way over to the reception desk, ready to raise hell if that's what it took to be seen instantly. But then, Dana Alexander's voice came on to the line: "Who's there?"

Lucy froze.

"Lucasta?" said Dana, obviously speaking into the phone. "Is that you?"

The shock of hearing the woman's voice again after so many years paralyzed Lucy. "I'm at the police department," she managed to say. "I'm gonna tell them what you did."

"What I *did*?" Dana mused. "How would you even

know? You didn't know who I was that night, Lucasta—you thought I was Kay. And as for talking to the police, my dear girl, I should very strongly counsel that you *do not.*"

"What . . . what do you mean, I thought you were Kay?"

"My sister, Kay. She had a penchant for dressing up as me. Kay befriended you, I believe. When you were a little girl. I got her a job as a runner on *Jelly and Pie.* You and Kay were friends—that's what she told me."

It was as though a manhole cover had suddenly been pulled away right above Lucy's head, and she was suddenly drenched in light. She staggered backward and caught herself on the bench next to John-Michael. She could feel his hand on her arm, heard his voice asking if she was okay, but mostly all she heard was a roaring sound, a white noise that blocked out everything that wasn't Dana Alexander.

"I've got your friends here, Lucasta. Paolo and Grace. If you ever want to see them again, I suggest you remember what we agreed the night of that party. It's a long time ago, I know, but I'd be happy to refresh your memory. You didn't see my sister down by the pool having a rather heated interaction with that wretched blackmailer, Tyson Drew. You didn't go to the bathroom and you didn't see me upstairs. You slept like a baby the whole night long."

"Kay . . . Kay killed Tyson Drew?"

"My dear girl, I don't see how you could possibly know. How could anyone? Tyson died years ago and Kay died today. As for you, we've already established that you *slept like a baby."* There was a dangerous pause. "Now," Alexander asked briskly, "do you have an Instagram account?"

"Y-yes. Why?" Lucy stammered.

"What's your account name?" demanded Dana.

"It's, ah, Lucy-JL."

"Splendid. Lucasta, I want you to take a photograph of yourself outside the police station and pop it onto your Instagram account. And then in twenty minutes, I'd like another photo, something to prove that you're on the interstate, forty miles from your current position, on your way to Claremont. I'll need a photo every twenty minutes, each one twenty miles farther south. Be a dear and repeat that back to me, just so I know everything is crystal clear."

Lucy did her best to comply. Before she could add anything else, Dana said, "It shouldn't be necessary to break the speed limit, but if you do happen to stop to chat to any police, you certainly won't make it back in time. If that happens, I'm afraid it's curtains for at least one of your friends. So be a good girl and run along. 'We are time's subjects, and time bids be gone.'"

The line went dead. Trembling, Lucy stabbed at the buttons of her burner phone, trying to end the call, and then remembered that Dana had already hung up.

John-Michael just stared at her. Something told Lucy that he was more scared by what he saw in her face than in anything he'd overheard from their call. "Luce . . . what is it?"

"Omigod. *Kay Alexander* killed Tyson Drew. Not Dana!"

"What?"

"I knew Kay," Lucy said, in a tone of wonder. Gradually, the facts of the mystery were settling. "Dana's younger sister. I was *friends* with her, John-Michael! I'd forgotten! How could I have forgotten?"

He didn't seem able to reply.

Lucy pressed herself backward on the wooden bench, desperate to feel the cool of the wall, something that might ground her. "Kay worked on the show. We were friends!"

"But wouldn't she have been, like twenty years old?"

"No, she was seventeen or eighteen. In fact, now that I think about it, I'm pretty sure she had her eighteenth birthday on the set, a big party with a piñata. I just, I don't understand how I forgot this."

"Lucy," he reminded her, "the psychotherapist warned you that you'd blocked those memories, that not even the hypnotherapy would release everything your subconscious mind tried to bury. What is Dana Alexander doing calling your burner phone?"

"She's not the one who called it." The full horror of it entered Lucy's voice. "*Grace* called me. Dana is in Claremont with Grace and Paolo. She took Grace's phone. Dana says she'll kill them if we talk."

"And when you said that we had to drive down south, Instagramming on the way . . . ?"

"Dana said I have to do it or else Grace and Paolo die."

John-Michael exhaled, trying to steady himself. "Holy shit."

Lucy stood up. "We gotta go. I have to post the first selfie right away. John-Michael, you need to talk to the cops for me."

"What? No, Luce, it's got to be your testimony."

"You can tell them what I was going to say!"

John-Michael shook his head. "That's not how it works." He stood up, too. "And anyhow, I'm not gonna let you head off alone. How are you even gonna do it? Did you tell Dana we don't have a ride?"

"We were about to buy a car."

"Dude! You really think we have time for that?"

Lucy started to walk out. "Not really. But we can use the cash to pay for a taxi."

"All the way to Claremont?" John-Michael was following her reluctantly.

Maya had taken the bulk of the hit man's money with her, leaving them with enough cash to buy a used car—the next errand on Lucy and John-Michael's schedule. Her plan was to meet with a Bitcoin miner near San Jose and change the money into the cryptocurrency. The thought that Maya might be able to take the whole fortune had crossed Lucy's mind, but she'd dismissed it instantly. No way. They were in this together, to the end.

"How much could it possibly cost for a taxi to Claremont?" Lucy asked.

John-Michael just shook his head in disbelief. "You're actually gonna do this? You're walking away from telling the cops what happened to Tyson Drew?"

Fiercely, Lucy grabbed the front of his shirt and dragged him out the front door onto the sidewalk. Then she turned on him. "Were you not listening to what I said? Dana has a gun on Grace and Paolo. Thanks to all this secrecy business, we don't even know where they're at. So how can we send the cops to them? Now, if we don't get our asses over to Claremont and frikkin' Insta the whole goddamn journey, our friends are dead. So stop talking, and help me pick up a taxi."

She headed for the road behind the station, peering into the road. John-Michael hurried after her. "We can give the cops the number of the burner phone. They can trace it."

Lucy's attention was fixed on the cars. "Assuming Dana leaves the phone switched on and doesn't smash it into little pieces."

John-Michael looked deflated. "Oh. Yeah. I suppose she could do that. But we should still try."

"Sure, but first I'm gonna do whatever I can to keep my friends alive." Lucy took out her own smartphone and snapped a selfie with the sign for the Napa Police Department behind her. She took a minute to post it to her Instagram account, and then switched the phone off just in time to see John-Michael flag down a red cab.

By the time she'd jogged over to join him on the sidewalk, he'd already begun to haggle over a price with the taxi driver, a woman of around thirty who wore a Sacramento Kings hat. They eventually agreed on $750 each way.

"We only wanna go one way," John-Michael said.

To which the driver replied caustically, "I hear you, Einstein, but *I* have to do both."

Lucy followed John-Michael into the cab. "All right. But can you drive kind of fast? We're on a clock."

Once inside, she asked John-Michael for his phone. "I'm calling Pete Martens. We need to make sure he's on his way to Grace."

"Does he know where to go?"

"No, for God's sake!" Lucy said, her voice rising in despair as she realized their predicament. "Paolo and Grace were obviously too busy getting it on to tell us what hotel they checked into!"

"How many could there be, in their price range?" asked John-Michael.

Lucy groaned. "A few! But I guess Martens can make a start when he gets to Claremont."

But when she dialed, Martens's phone just rang and rang; a death rattle in an empty room, until its rhythm matched the pulse of her heart, until she felt ready to burst into tears.

"Where the hell is he?"

PAOLO
MOTEL 6, CLAREMONT, WEDNESDAY, JULY 8

"Who's helping you?"

Paolo strained over his shoulder, trying to catch sight of Grace. It was pointless. Dana Alexander had arranged their chairs so that they were back-to-back. She'd ordered him to sit down and forced Grace to duct-tape his hands to the backs of his chair. Then Alexander had repeated the action, this time taping Grace into her chair.

Alone, Paolo would have risked tackling the woman. But with Grace's life in the balance, he didn't dare. Try as he might, he couldn't think fast enough to outsmart Alexander. She had to be absolutely determined to take things this far, to engage them in person. Paolo could practically smell the desperation in the air.

Someone was going to die in this room. The certainty was physically painful.

And it could have been avoided. That's what made it hurt so badly. He and Grace had driven south, chasing

Candace. No plan, no clue what they were walking into. Now it was too late—for everything. No one else knew where they were. They were alone and defenseless. At the mercy of a woman who'd lied and had people killed to protect her secrets.

Dana Alexander didn't just want information—she needed to guarantee their silence.

But last night, all Paolo had been able to think about was Grace and her grief. All she'd been able to think about was Candace. Both were lost in their emotions.

Where was Maya's icy clarity when they'd needed it?

Paolo's heart raced as the truth wrapped around him like a boa constrictor, crushing him. *We're going to die here.*

"I asked you a question," Alexander reminded them calmly. "The men I sent after you are missing. The Malibu police are asking witnesses to come forward about two dead males they've found up in the canyon. I've made some discreet inquiries, and from the descriptions, it does seem as though one may be a match. Now, let's not deceive ourselves; you and your hedonistic housemates lack the wherewithal to dispatch two armed professionals. Which means that you had help. It's not an unreasonable stretch to suggest that your father, Grace, has made certain contacts during his stay at San Quentin; the kind of individuals who could present a genuine threat to my associates."

She paused, lips pursed as she took a moment to study their faces. "I can see from your reactions that I'm on the right track. So, further hypothesizing that you did indeed recruit such a person to protect you, I'm left wondering where he is."

"He's on his way," spat Paolo with effort. Behind him, he sensed Grace tensing up.

Dana Alexander bent down to look him in the eye. "What you undoubtedly mean to say, then, is that he is *not* on his way." Bowing her head respectfully she told him, "Thank you, Paolo, your gallantry is noted. In your haste to defend fair lady, however, you've revealed the lie." She stood up. "I've been thinking about that incident in Malibu Canyon. And while the outcome undeniably points to the hand of a professional on your side, the manner of those deaths, I have to say, sparked a faint memory."

She peered into his face. "Do you know to what I refer, Paolo?"

This time, he forced himself to restrict himself to the most insignificant shrug. "No, what?"

"Ariana told me all about your proclivities, you know. The women that you so enjoyed at the country club. Your bratty little housemates did like to gossip about that, were you aware?"

"Paolo, I promise you," Grace blurted. "I never talked about you to that miserable snitch." She was on the edge of tears.

Paolo blinked back tears of his own. "I know, baby."

"Your loyalty is touching," said Alexander. "Notwithstanding, I thought it might be handy to do a bit of poking around of my own. So I dropped in on your tennis club. Sat in the bar, caught up with a couple of old chums, asked innocently about you, Paolo. And dearie me if I didn't have *quite* the chat with a certain coach from the Czech Republic. Tania, Talia, something like that? The dearest slip of a girl, but by golly, what a serve! And I heard that you'd recently been the naughty object of desire for a woman old enough to be your mother. For shame, Paolo, for shame!"

Paolo's cheeks began to burn. His most dreaded nightmare was coming true—Grace was about to discover his worst secret.

Alexander tutted, tapped his shoulder lightly with the muzzle of the pistol. "Although—poor you. Meredith Eriksson didn't strike me as the type of woman you'd wish to cross."

Paolo could almost hear the calculation in her timing. She was waiting for the best moment to follow up with the deathblow.

"And then, what do you know? Dear, formidable Meredith, glorious in her liberated ways, is found dead on her way to her cabin in the woods. Alone, apparently. Now, where do you suppose they found her, Paolo?"

He couldn't bear it. "Stop," he said in a low voice.

"Do *you* know, Grace?" Alexander continued. "You'll be fascinated, I promise."

"Please," begged Paolo. "Stop. *Please.* Don't do this."

There was a clucking sound. "Isn't it just dreadful? You really do have my sympathy, young man. It cannot be easy to turn down a woman like Meredith. After all, it's not as though you were getting a modicum of satisfaction from any of your housemates, were you? Poor, frustrated Paolo. And yet, my feminine intuition tells me that you and Mrs. Eriksson were not, after all, quite so ideally matched."

She turned away, pacing. "Meredith died in Malibu Canyon. Now, was it on Piuma Road or somewhere else close by? I really cannot remember—Paolo, care to help me out?"

He returned her inquiring gaze with a stony glare.

"Probably not in the exact same place, now I think about it. That might trigger unwanted attention, no? But it's more the manner of her death that fascinates me. A massive wallop to the head, poor thing. Side of her head bashed in, as though she'd run straight into an anvil. I didn't see her myself, you understand, but I did manage to get hold of a story from an eyewitness." Alexander curled her lip. "Absolutely horrid. Well, imagine my surprise when weeks later, there's another hit-and-run in Malibu Canyon, leaving someone with precisely the same injury."

Paolo held his breath. This time Alexander's scrutiny was unforced, without irony, searching his expression for the smallest sign that might betray him.

"Did you hit her, Paolo?" she said, tilting her head. "Was she becoming tiresome, needy? Was Meredith threatening to thwart your futile attempts to woo Lucasta? Or should I say *Grace*?"

Before he could stop himself, the denial was out. "I didn't touch her!"

"Well, someone did, Paolo," Alexander said. "All it really needs is for the police to connect you, Meredith Eriksson, Malibu Canyon, and a certain professional thug, and you'd have quite the battle to stay out of prison for what I fear will be *rather* a long time."

It was useless. Paolo couldn't stop himself from trembling with pure, indignant rage.

Alexander grinned, delighted, and took a position on the bed, legs daintily crossed at the ankles. Both her palms were flat on the mattress as she leaned back, watching him with great amusement.

"Shall I tell the police my theory, Paolo? Oh, I don't imagine it'll be easy to prove, but it's simply not possible that you'll have alibis for everything."

Paolo felt his voice quavering. "Grace, I didn't hurt that woman." Alexander didn't matter right then. Only Grace. Grace and the tears of betrayal that were sure to be streaming down her cheeks. "I swear to you, Gracie. I didn't cause Meredith's death."

"I want to know who's helping you," said Alexander. "I want to know where they are now. I want to know why my phone calls to certain other associates aren't being answered. We're in no hurry—Lucasta's on her way down from Napa as we speak. But I promise you, Grace, if you think you can use your daddy's prison chum to get you out of this, you're very wide of the mark. And in this case, I'm afraid that when I say 'wide of the mark,' what I mean, of course, is 'dead.'"

Alexander fell silent then, finally. Paolo's rage subsided, fear replaced by a wave of pity and shame. For Grace and what he'd put her through. For being denounced in this way, without being able to face Grace properly. For the fact it was now too late to confess to her as he'd planned. All he wanted was to throw himself on his knees and to beg for her understanding.

Behind him, he could hear Grace gulping as she struggled to form words. "No one is coming to help us," she finally managed. "We've done nothing to you, Dana. Nothing. Why do you hate us so much?"

Alexander's features twisted into an icy scowl. Paolo saw white in her knuckles as her grip tightened around the gun. When she spoke, her words were taut, clipped, precise.

"Nothing? Then why is *my daughter* dead? You and your friends tried to destroy my life. Now you have ended Kay's. And 'the croaking raven doth bellow for revenge.'"

JOHN-MICHAEL
PEA SOUP ANDERSEN'S, SANTA NELLA, WEDNESDAY, JULY 8

"What is this place—Swedish?"

John-Michael looked across the other parked cars toward the half-timbered, windmill-like structure of what looked like an old European barn.

"I'm going with Danish," he told Lucy. "Like Hans Christian Andersen."

He checked his watch. Dana Alexander's last message to Lucy had demanded a selfie in front of the restaurant. She'd allowed a total of ten minutes for a restroom break. Lucy took the selfie and posted it on Instagram.

A few minutes later, they were back in the car. "Luce, you think we should maybe discuss what's gonna happen when we reach Claremont?"

For a moment, Lucy pretended not to have heard. When John-Michael repeated the question, she shot him a look. "Why bother?" she said. "It's not like I have any choice."

"But what do you *think* is gonna happen?" he asked, as patiently as he could. Lucy *must* have thought about this. The hours they'd already spent in the car had been spent mostly in silence. Not much else to do but to speculate.

It didn't take a hardened criminal to figure out that as the key witness against Dana Alexander, Lucy had to be silenced. It was just possible that Alexander planned to negotiate. Maybe blackmail, maybe a bribe. But the sacrifice Alexander demanded was Grace's father—someone to take the blame for Tyson Drew's murder. He'd be executed in just over a week—unless Lucy gave her testimony.

"I don't see how they could convict Dana on what I'm gonna tell the cops," Lucy said. She spoke so quietly that he had to lean in close. "Even with the nail polish. All it proves is that she gave me the bottle. Enough doubt to get Grace's dad off the hook, maybe. But to convict Dana? How?"

"Well, having Dana's nail polish proves you're telling the truth."

"Am I, though?" Lucy sounded doleful. "On the phone, Dana said I thought she was Kay that night when she ran into me on the balcony. Which now that I think about it, makes perfect sense. I didn't know Dana Alexander. Why would she be sweet to a little kid? She's not that nice a person."

"Why would you think she was Kay?"

"I only ever saw Dana in her fancy outfits. And Kay usually dressed like a teenager. If Dana was in sweats or pajamas, it might have confused me."

"Wait, you're saying that you don't remember how Dana was dressed when she saw you, but you remember the color of her nail polish?"

Lucy sighed, exasperated. "Exactly. My testimony means *nothing* if I'm mixing up Dana and Kay."

John-Michael looked away. She was right. "Maybe they *both* wore the peach nail polish?" he said helpfully.

Lucy managed to chuckle. "Yeah, that works. Kay was copying her, after all."

"So it was the woman on the balcony who gave you the polish?"

"Yes."

"But if the woman on the balcony was Dana, and she was dressed in something casual, not like the woman who killed Tyson Drew . . ."

"I know. It means that Kay was the person I saw down by the pool. Not Dana. It means that Kay is the killer."

"And Dana gave you the polish," John-Michael suggested. "Because she wore the polish and you saw it on her hands and liked it so much?"

"I guess."

"Then you're right, Lucy. I don't think that the woman you saw in the house did the murder. Why would she give you any evidence against her?"

Lucy pondered. "I guess. Maybe Dana didn't know, when she gave me the polish, that Kay was wearing it, too. She was just looking for a quick way to get a lil' kid to be quiet. If she'd given me candy instead, we wouldn't be talking about this because I'd have eaten the evidence." She looked at him, beginning to feel more composed. "Kay killed Tyson Drew. Not Dana. Tyson Drew was blackmailing Kay. I wonder why?"

The more Lucy said it, the more sense it made.

"If anyone knows the answer to that, it's Dana. Makes you wonder," John-Michael mused. "What if Dana's doing all this to protect Kay?"

Lucy nodded. "And now Kay is dead."

"But without *Kay* alive to give her version of events, the suspicion falls on Dana. And it's going to be Dana's word against yours."

"Not if she gets rid of me first," Lucy said.

John-Michael blinked. In a way, it was a relief that he didn't have to be the one to say it.

"John-Michael," she said in a tiny voice. "I don't want to die."

Her hand found his. For a moment he rubbed the back of her hand, trying to send vibes of positivity through his fingers.

If Dana was hell-bent on staying out of prison, there'd be only one play left in her book—silencing Lucy. The full horror of the scenario seeped gradually into John-Michael's mind. *Grace's father would be executed. And Lucy would be killed.*

If he or Paolo or Grace tried to go to the police about it, Dana Alexander would blackmail them. She was the only person who knew of the link between the two dead hit men and the housemates. Everything would lead back to John-Michael—right back to his father's assisted suicide.

Death and prison. Both were in his future. Someone was going to die, someone he cared about. And someone was going to jail—most likely him.

"What if we went to the cops?" he said urgently, his eyes large with fear. With those possible outcomes, it had to be worth taking some risks to change their fates. "What if we went *right now*?"

Lucy simply shook her head. "Then she kills Grace and Paolo."

"That's what she wants us to think! But Alexander would never risk it. We'd have all the evidence they'd need to convict her. The phone calls," John-Michael insisted. "We can record them, with another phone. And the selfies."

"Nice idea. Wish we'd thought of it a few hours ago," Lucy replied sadly. "Even if I had, Dana knows I'm not gonna risk it. She knows how much I care about Grace and Paolo. Man, she's counting on it."

John-Michael held her hand, unsure if he was comforting her or trying to take comfort. Either way this played out, someone he cared about was going to suffer, maybe even die.

"Any word from Maya?" Lucy asked.

"Just the last text she sent," he told her. "Saying she'd found one of those Bitcoin miner guys. In San Jose. I guess she's with him now."

"Try Martens again." Lucy sounded faint with desperation.

"I keep trying. Dude isn't answering."

"Maybe he's on his way to Claremont. He's gotta be!"

"The minute you get a heads-up from Alexander about their location," John-Michael said, fighting the tremor in his voice, "I'm gonna send that information to Martens. If he's anywhere nearby, he'll come by."

Lucy smiled sadly. "What'd I do without you, JM? You give me hope."

John-Michael let go of Lucy's hand and wrapped both arms around her. For several minutes they just held each other, tightly, both giving and taking solace. He was dimly aware of the taxi driver glancing at them in her rearview mirror.

"I'm sorry I stole Ruben," he murmured against Lucy's ear.

That won him another smile. "Omigod, *Ruben*. I haven't thought about him in days."

"Me either," John-Michael admitted. "Guess I'd be a bad boyfriend."

Lucy pulled away a bit, brushed long strands of jet-black hair from John-Michael's brow. She looked at him, her brown eyes gentle, her gaze steady and warm. "Don't say that, sugar. You'd be the *best* boyfriend. You got things on your mind, is all." She paused; he heard the regret. "A lot has changed since Friday. Like, everything."

John-Michael could feel his chest bursting with sorrow. There had to be a way to save Lucy. After everything that had happened, after all the terrible things that he'd done, he might lose his best friend anyway.

It was more than he could handle. He clung to her, until he could feel her heartbeat against his chest, until his tears spilled onto her cheeks, too.

"Lucy," he said, holding down a sob. "Oh, Luce. There has to be *something*. We *have* to find a way."

MAYA

The limo dropped Maya in front of a house with a speed-boat parked in its front yard. Behind the houses, through the pines and spruces in the garden, she caught glimpses of fern-green water. Under a buttermilk sky, Anderson Lake looked matte and featureless. Rolling, sandy hills dotted with trees were visible on the opposite shore.

Maya took out her burner phone. She was scared to look at the power level. Jack's death had profoundly shaken her ability to think straight. She'd barely been able to concentrate enough to keep track of the duffel bag that contained the better part of a half-million dollars in cash. So she'd forgotten to charge her burner. By now, it was running on fumes. She might be able to risk a few texts, but nothing else.

Her smartphone was in better shape, but it was switched off to prevent anyone tracking them. She didn't dare to risk using it to access her Bitcoin account—any clue that she'd visited the Bitcoin miner would be dangerous. She'd have to use her laptop. If this meeting went well, all the cash they'd found would be safely nestled inside one of her two Bitcoin accounts.

Maya used the cryptocurrency Bitcoin for the earnings she made from her apps. She'd recently created a separate account for her business, but that account had to report to the other shareholders in her company—her parents. The money in the duffel bag would have to go into her personal account. Technically, her parents could make her show them those transactions. But they never had yet, and without good reason probably never would.

She watched the limo leave, and then walked down the road a little. She'd made sure that the driver hadn't known the exact address in case he had to answer questions later. The Bitcoin miner had insisted on it. It was a basic precaution, and Maya shuddered at the fact that she hadn't thought of it herself. But after Jack's death, her mental processes were anything but sharp.

She walked the last few blocks to the miner's house, a bungalow that backed directly on to the beach. Compared to the other properties, it was in shabby condition; no lawn, a VW Golf parked in the front. The rear driver's side had obviously been dinged at some point, and the owner hadn't repaired it.

Maya knocked on the front door and waited. A guy in his late twenties opened the door. He looked about as frazzled as Maya felt—his shoulder-length blond curly hair was greasy and in disarray; his eyes were slightly bloodshot.

When he saw Maya, he frowned. "Hey, I'm Seneca. You're Cheetah?"

Maya nodded. He'd insisted they use their handles from the forum on the dark web.

"What are you, like, twelve?"

"Ha," Maya said, without smiling. "Yeah, that's real funny."

Seneca opened the door a little wider. "No, seriously, though, you're really Cheetah, who wrote the Cheetr app?"

"Yup. I'm really Cheetah, who wrote the app. Dude, how about you sell me some Bitcoin?"

The guy stood aside, and Maya walked past him into the house. The entryway was lined with rack-mounted computer servers on sturdy metal frames. A tangle of ribbon cables poked out from behind the boxes, which winked their electric blue lights. "I put my servers against the wall," he explained proudly. "On the other side, I dry my laundry. You shouldn't waste energy."

Seneca led her into his living room. French doors at one end opened onto an open patio, which led directly to the lake. A neglected home in a wonderful location.

"Your message said you had four hundred and thirty large," Seneca said. He seemed skeptical.

Maya tapped the duffel bag, which she'd placed at her feet. "Minus another five thousand, yeah."

"Four twenty-five, then?"

Maya made a rapid calculation. She was taking five thousand—one thousand already spent on getting to

Seneca's home. Twenty of the original half million had gone to Pete Martens: his price had gone up when he'd agreed to attempt a rescue mission. Lucy and John-Michael had taken another five. Paolo and Grace had taken forty-five thousand, in case of emergencies. That should be enough cash to tide them all over.

"So—I'm assuming this isn't legit?"

Maya didn't answer, just fixed him with a flat stare.

"Hey," Seneca said. "I don't judge. But my commish goes up to twenty-five percent if it's not legit. There's a whole other accounting trail I gotta set up. A lot of work. Now, you don't pay that extra commish, and I don't set up the trail. That's both of us exposed, but you worse than me, 'cause if someone comes looking, I don't just hand over the transfer deets; I *blacklist* you, Cheetah, you got that? I send every known hacker your way, to take down you and all the work you've ever done. My bank, my rules."

Maya didn't doubt him for a second. Twenty-five percent seemed like a lot, but then again, it was "found" money. There was no point in getting greedy.

She nodded. "Okay, got it. Take your twenty-five percent." She opened the duffel bag and began taking out rolls of cash. After a minute, she'd laid them all out on the rug and handed one to Seneca. "Each one is twenty thousand."

Seneca flicked through a few of the tightly rolled bills. He didn't seem to doubt her word. He put out his empty palm. "Gimme your phone. I'll make the transfer."

Maya ignored him and reached for her MacBook inside

the messenger bag. She logged into the Bitcoin wallet and passed the laptop to Seneca. She watched him use an app to transfer Bitcoin worth $318,750 to her personal account.

Seneca handed back her laptop. She checked the screen. It showed a new total balance of almost $318,798 in her account.

Seneca stood up. "You want some breakfast or something? Coffee? I was just about to fix some eggs. Protein—good for what ails ya."

Their eyes met, and she realized he was hoping to hit on her. Maya just about managed to suppress a wave of revulsion, replacing it with a friendly grin. She made a show of looking at her second phone, sending a quick text to John-Michael to tell him that she was in Morgan Hill and would make her own way back to LA.

"Ah, sure," she agreed. "Something to drink would be nice. I need to call a limo. You know a good service for long distance?"

Seneca attempted a winning smile, which only made things worse. "Where are you headed?" he asked.

She closed the laptop and slid it back into her messenger bag. "Back to LA. In kind of a hurry."

"Speed might be an issue," he admitted. "The cars come from the airport. Why dontcha sit a spell?" he added, with another shot at geek charm. "I give great egg."

Before she had time to react, Maya's burner phone buzzed: a text from John-Michael.

We're headed to Claremont. Exact location not yet known. DA has P

& G. Trying to reach Martens. Please call him, too. It's urgent.

She replied instantly: Can I help? Still have the weapon.

The power on her phone was down to its last bar. It was getting too risky to leave it uncharged. But she couldn't spare the time. What she needed was a car-powered charger. And, ideally, a car.

As the adrenaline coursed through her veins, an idea came to Maya. "Dude, I really do have to leave right now. Is that vdub outside an automatic?"

"Sure is."

"You wanna sell?"

"You wanna buy?" he said, still trying to flirt.

"How's two thousand?"

"A little light, but ehh." He grinned. "I just made out like a bandit on a Bitcoin deal. Guess I can afford to lose out on a car to a hot girl like you."

"Could you throw in a phone charger for the car?"

"For your crappy little Nokia? Sure, why not? I prob'ly got one in a box somewhere."

Maya nodded, a watery smile pasted to her features. If she could just get this bozo to hand over the phone charger and the keys to his VW Golf, maybe she could reach Claremont in time to help Paolo and Grace.

Of course, it would mean driving a car on the freeway and on the interstate. She'd had driving lessons with her mom, but she didn't yet have a license.

The back of her neck felt suddenly cold, and her stomach muscles clenched. After everything Maya had been through in the past few days, she hadn't expected to seize up from fear of the simple act of driving on the freeway. But there it was. Apparently terror could exist in the ordinary, too. She clenched both fists until she could feel the bite of her fingernails.

Jack is dead, she told herself. *He's dead, he's gone. Jack can't help me. And I can't help him. So quit thinking about him and get back to thinking of a way out. Things can still get worse.*

GRACE

"I'm going to remove the tape from your face, Grace. Hold still now; I'll do this slowly."

Grace pressed her lips together, as she had when Dana Alexander first gagged her. With a deft movement, the woman peeled back the plastic enough for Grace to speak.

The last two hours had been morbidly fascinating. Witnessing how a movie star behaved while holed up in a cheap hotel room certainly stripped away any aura of glamor. While Grace and Paolo were taped up back-to-back on two chairs, Dana Alexander had stretched out on the double bed, watching the Wimbledon tennis championship on TV. She'd bark out the occasional disparaging observation about a player, while her attention flitted between the TV and her smartphone. The pistol had remained inches from her hand throughout.

Dana had gagged them shortly after her first attempt to question Grace and Paolo. Unable to talk to or even to see Paolo, Grace had relied on the comfort of his fingers touching hers. It was better than nothing, but she was still simmering with rage.

After talking to Dana Alexander, there was no way Lucy would have changed Martens's plan to find Grace. Not that he could help them now.

Why didn't we think to tell someone where we were staying last night?

There was no way to let anyone know where she and Paolo were. A simple text, that's all it would have taken. *We're in Motel 6 in Claremont, room 125.* A basic precaution. Grace was almost bursting with the need to vent her self-loathing.

Over the past hour, it had become obvious—Dana must have had Lucy's parents' house watched. Or maybe she'd even watched it herself? Ariana-the-spy seemed finally to have disappointed her puppet mistress; so had the various professional killers Dana had hired to silence, and then to kill Lucy. Perhaps Dana had run out of patience and decided to take matters into her own hands?

If Grace and Paolo had kept their guard up, had their wits about them, they might have seen the danger. How had they allowed themselves to feel so victorious about the simple act of getting a bottle of nail polish from Lucy's old home?

But last night, they'd been *possessed.* Grace hadn't been able to think straight. First Candace's stabbing. Then the guilt from not going straight to the police. Only the terror of her father's execution had forced her to keep it together at all.

And then there was Paolo. The prospect of a night with him had been just too much. Right until the last moment, she hadn't known for sure if she'd be able to hold back. All those months of wanting him had claimed her. She had finally faced up to it: despite all her precautions, she'd fallen for Paolo. Coherent thought had vanished somewhere around the time they'd checked into the motel. From that moment on, Grace had existed in a fog. All she could think about was Paolo.

Reluctantly, she turned to face Dana Alexander. The woman was perched on the edge of the bed now, the gun held loosely, almost carelessly, in her right hand. Even without makeup, her features still commanded attention.

A modest smile appeared at the edge of Alexander's mouth. "You're uncomfortable. My apologies for that, dear, but it can't be helped."

Grace wondered what time it was. The last time she'd looked at a clock was on her smartphone, which had been beside the bed, charging up. Alexander had interrupted them not too long after—no later than nine thirty. Based on the fact that Grace's stomach was now beginning to complain with hunger, she guessed it had to be around midday.

"How are you holding up, Grace?"

The question seemed friendly enough, but Grace

■253

couldn't bear to answer. Alexander didn't seem to expect her to. "I don't blame you one bit for being so upset. You're the innocent party here. You didn't keep a secret; you didn't spy on your friends. You didn't leave a woman for dead in the road, and you didn't steal a boyfriend from a vulnerable young woman, a poor girl with considerable mental health issues, tipping her over into another episode."

"Yoandy told Candace he wasn't dating Kay." Grace couldn't keep a tremor out of her voice. Any way you looked at this, Dana was going to shoot someone. Maybe if she kept her talking? But then again, maybe Dana was just killing time until the real killing began.

"Yoandy should have known better."

"Did he know that Kay was . . . ?" Grace tried again. "Did Yoandy . . . ?"

Dana spoke dismissively. "Did he know that Kay was unwell? No, of course not; it wasn't something we liked to broadcast. But he knew that she was sweet on him. And he'd agreed with my husband that he'd stay away from Candace for a few more months, to give Kay time to readjust."

She broke off, jabbing Paolo's thigh with the muzzle of her gun. "All right there, Paolo? You're looking a bit apprehensive. Not much longer now. Once Lucy arrives we can sort out this whole unfortunate misunderstanding."

Grace stammered out a question. "What . . . what are you going to do to Lucy?"

"Is this where I confess my plan?" Dana crossed her toned, shapely legs. Grace kept one eye on the gun. Now it was in Dana's lap. "My dear, that's not my style."

The smug grin on the woman's face, however, suggested otherwise. In fact, if there hadn't been a sharp, strident knock at the door right then, Grace was pretty sure she'd have heard the whole scenario.

Dana answered, in a tone of mild irritation. "No housekeeping, thank you."

Through the door, a man's voice answered. "This isn't housekeeping. It's the LAPD. We need to talk to a Mr. Paolo King. We've been looking for his vehicle, a Chevy Malibu. We know he's registered to this room, and he hasn't checked out."

Inside the room, there was total, stunned silence. For the first time since Grace had first set eyes on Dana Alexander, the actress seemed genuinely lost for words.

Uncertainly, the woman rose to her feet. The hand holding the gun went behind her back as she approached the door. She peered through the peephole. "Ah, officer, may I please ask what this is about?" she asked in a loud, clear voice with a bland American accent.

"We need to speak to Mr. King in conjunction with an incident in Malibu Canyon." There was a pause, and then a more committed bashing of the door. "Open up."

Dana turned her back on the door, her head turning frantically as she searched for a way out. Other than the door and a closed window, there was none. The room was on the second floor of the motel. The police were on the balcony outside, blocking the only way out of the motel.

Grace could only see two options for Dana. She could free Grace and Paolo and face the risk that they'd accuse her to the police. Or she could shoot the cops.

Behind Grace, Paolo had withdrawn his fingers from hers. His breathing sped up. Yet Dana remained frozen by the window, immobilized by indecision.

PAOLO
MOTEL 6, WEDNESDAY, JULY 8

Paolo could almost sense the instant when air stopped moving. Inside the motel room, everyone held their breath. All three jerked to attention at the sound, abrupt and harsh, of a door being kicked in. Then two men were inside the room. Behind them, the door slammed shut.

The first man was in his forties, white, clean-shaven, stocky beneath a shiny brown leather jacket, greased black hair plastered to his skull. He cracked gum noisily, pointing a pistol straight at Dana Alexander.

The second man looked younger. He had a chiseled kind of face with piercing blue eyes. Handsome. He wore black jeans and a light brown suit jacket, navy shirt open at the neck, no tie. Paolo's eyes fell on the man's shoes: soft leather, maybe calfskin, two-tone shoes in red and black. You could see it in the perfect length of his stubble and in the coif of his gelled red hair: this guy liked to look in the mirror.

There was no sign of his gun.

By the time Paolo's attention had moved away from the guy with the gun, something that might be a police badge was already being slipped back into his inside jacket pocket.

Alexander was the first to speak. Paolo couldn't see her because she was behind him, but he could guess what she was doing: holding a gun to Grace's head.

"Put the gun down or the girl dies."

There was a palpable intake of breath. Then the dark-haired man, who was edging toward Paolo's side of the room, said cautiously, "Lady, I'm gonna need you to put down the weapon and explain why you got two of your guests tied to those chairs."

"Your gun goes on the bed or a bullet goes into the girl," Alexander said icily.

Paolo caught the attention of the cop with the gun and pleaded with his eyes. There was a brief moment of acknowledgment. "Lady, I'm warning you," the cop said.

"No. I'm warning you, and this is the last time." Alexander flicked off the gun's safety.

Paolo's heart rate soared when he heard Grace beg, shakily, "No. *Please.*"

Carefully, the dark-haired man placed his sidearm on the bed. It must have been out of Alexander's reach because she didn't reach for the weapon. Instead, she ordered him to move away. When he'd joined his colleague on the other side of the room, Paolo heard her relax. He felt Alexander's fingers reaching around from behind, gripping the edge of the tape on his mouth. In one swift movement, she'd ripped it away.

"Go ahead—ask your questions," offered Alexander.

The cops looked flummoxed. They exchanged a brief glance.

"We need to take this kid down to the station," the dark-haired man said.

"Why?" Alexander fired back.

"His car was photographed at the scene of a crime. We need to interview him."

"Interview him here."

"Lady, that's not how it works."

Without further warning, Alexander fired her gun. The dark-haired cop went down instantly, crumpling backward to the floor.

Paolo and Grace both recoiled in shock. The magnolia-painted wall behind the cop was sprayed red with exploded brains and blood. The sight of it transfixed Paolo for several seconds. Then he inhaled sharply, dizzy from the lack of air. He heard Grace's panic; she was panting, gasping, terrified.

Paolo forced himself to lift his gaze. The second cop, the redhead, was staring past him, at Dana Alexander. The man's eyes narrowed briefly, evaluating the risk.

"All right, ma'am," the man said. He showed no emotion whatsoever. "How about I make you a deal? I'm going to let you leave. I'm going to let you take all the phones in the room, and I'm going to let you run. But you need to leave me here with the kids, all right? No more killing."

"First I want to hear what happened in Malibu Canyon," Alexander insisted.

"Ma'am, you've just killed a police officer. In the interest of preventing further bloodshed, I'm giving you a chance to run. I suggest you take it."

Behind him, Paolo heard Alexander hesitate. He couldn't imagine why she cared about what had happened on Malibu Canyon, or why she was sticking around with a dead cop in the room.

Unless she meant to kill the second cop, too.

"Your weapon," Alexander intoned. "I know you must have one. Take it out slowly. Hold it by the handle. Then throw it over here. One wrong move, and you're dead, too."

The second man did as she instructed. He moved slowly, with precision, dropping an automatic pistol almost within reach of Paolo's right foot. Alexander knelt forward, stretched out with her left hand, and picked up the gun.

That's when Paolo saw an opportunity. But how to convey the idea to the police officer? He began to stare hard at the man on the carpet, and then back at the redheaded cop.

Paolo could feel Grace stirring anxiously. Every few seconds, he'd catch a glimpse of Alexander's gun in the corner of his right eye.

Now the cop's cell phone was on the ground and Alexander was scooping it up. Paolo tensed, getting ready, still desperately wary of the gun that was mere inches from Grace's head. It was aimed at the cop, but that didn't make things much easier. He gazed imploringly at the cop, and

260 ■

then down at the man's fallen partner.

Please understand, please, please.

And suddenly, the cop seemed to catch on. "You want my partner's phone, too? I can get it for you. Then you got them all, and you can just leave."

"Get me the phone. Then talk about Malibu Canyon, and *then* I'll leave."

She's not going to just stroll away after you talk about Malibu Canyon, Paolo wanted to tell the cop. *Are you an idiot? She's going to kill you, and then she's going back to her first plan, which is waiting for Lucy to show up here so that she can kill her, too.*

The redheaded man nodded. "Okay, deal." As he bent low, Paolo prepared himself. This time he would rock the chair sideways, hard, land on top of Alexander, and give the cop an opening.

The cop's hand slid underneath the leather of the fallen man's jacket. Then rapid gunfire. Two shots. A gurgling sound, terrible. A faint moan. A second later, Dana Alexander slumped forward, one hand clutched to her throat. She fell on her side, facing Paolo, her head no more than six inches from his foot.

Paolo gazed at her hand. It was still moving, bathed in bright crimson blood that pumped in steady gushes from her neck. Then he was staring at the cop's shoes. Slowly, he looked up.

The cop had moved closer. Now he stood over Alexander, watching her breathe her last. Paolo's eyes met his and caught the conspiratorial wink. "What do you say, kid?"

In the man's hand was the revolver he'd taken from his partner. "Shall I put her out of her misery?"

Before Paolo had even moved his lips to respond, he lurched in surprise as another bullet tore into Alexander's head. A fresh flow of blood began almost instantly, pooling up around her head and shoulders. He became aware of Grace shuddering.

For the briefest of minutes, Paolo felt a warm flood of relief. Dana Alexander was dead. She wouldn't be able to threaten them any longer. They'd get out of this alive.

It didn't last. Despondency crushed his rising hopes. The police. Malibu Canyon—*they knew*.

The redheaded man leaned over. Nonchalantly, he picked up the gun that had fallen out of Alexander's fingers as she'd collapsed. He stretched over and picked up his own gun. Then he sat, heavily, on the bed. The partner's spare weapon went into his own holster and Dana's weapon into his jacket pocket. The partner's automatic went into his inside jacket pocket.

Paolo's eyes followed each movement as the cop scooped up all the weapons. Fresh dread surged within him. The police knew that Paolo's Chevy had been in Malibu Canyon. The only chance Paolo had was to lie, to say that the car had been stolen. Why hadn't he reported it, though? His mind flew, trying to invent an excuse.

Meanwhile, the redheaded man continued to move around the room, gathering up Grace's backpack and his own, and then the box of memorabilia that they'd taken from Lucy's. The man disappeared into the bathroom for a moment.

"Paolo, what's he doing?" Grace whispered.

There was no time to reply; the man emerged almost immediately. Paolo guessed it was because there was nothing in there.

Once everything was gathered up onto the bed, the cover of which was now spattered with Dana Alexander's blood, he sat down. Facing Paolo and Grace, he glanced across at the TV, watching as the tennis match from Wimbledon continued to play on ESPN.

"Sir, could . . . could you please untie us?" Paolo began. "We're not armed. I'll tell you whatever I know."

The cop just smiled. He closed his eyes, the first sign of any stress. He breathed in deeply, and then exhaled. "I like you just where you are, Paolo King."

Paolo shrank at the mention, once again, of his name. It was true, they knew. But how? He racked his memory, trying to think of how anyone could know. The cop had mentioned Malibu Canyon; he'd mentioned Paolo's Chevy. Was this about Meredith's death? Or about what happened on Friday? It was impossible! There'd been no witnesses to either!

The cop began to search Lucy's box. He flipped through the various snapshots, party invitations, examined a studio pass on its lanyard, and then rifled through other items, including the nail polish. All with *zero* apparent interest. He flashed Grace an easy grin, and then began to look through her backpack.

Paolo shuffled slightly. Next it would be his backpack. What the cop would find there would raise some very dangerous questions.

Sure enough, the man discarded Grace's backpack and started on Paolo's. A second later, he pulled out the two rolls of dollar bills from the stash that Paolo and John-Michael had found in the first hit man's Oldsmobile. He flipped through it, weighing one roll in his hands. "About twenty thousand; am I right?" he asked in a friendly tone. "Forty thousand in total. Maybe a tad over?"

Paolo could do nothing but nod, totally bewildered.

The man sighed and ran his hand slowly across his scalp, as if buying time to think. And then he spoke, cold and deliberate.

"Okay, Paolo King. How about you tell me—where's the rest of it, huh? Where's the rest of my money?"

GRACE

Grace was reeling. Why was this police officer asking Paolo about "his money"? Was there something Paolo hadn't told her?

"Now, I got a hunch that all this gunfire's bound to attract undue attention," the officer was telling Paolo. "So, first thing: we'll get you two somewhere we can have a nice, quiet discussion about what you did with my cash."

"You're not a cop," breathed Paolo, as exactly the same thought went through Grace's mind.

The redheaded man set about cutting her free from the chair. He pulled Grace to her feet and stuck the gun in her ribs.

"Here's what's gonna happen, Paolo. I'm going to cut you loose. Let's get you on your feet. I think we'll put you on the other side of your young lady here. You, the girl, me. A nice little sandwich. My gun's in her side. The three of us, we're heading to another room. Just three good buddies taking a walk, okay? You try to escape, you call for help, and she takes a bullet to the lungs. It will be clinical. She will be dead. And there's a good chance that the bullet will go into you, too."

Paolo caught Grace's eyes for a second as she nodded, once. He faced their captor and blinked, and then nodded.

"All righty then, shall we get started?" the man said brightly.

This was bad. It was so much worse than Grace had thought a few minutes ago. Back then, she'd worried about Paolo, about what the police might know about what he'd done, about what would happen to him if he was sent to prison. But now?

Dana was dead. *Dana Alexander was dead.*

Who would take the blame for Tyson Drew's murder? *They're going to execute my dad for something he didn't do.*

Then Grace remembered Yoandy. *Paolo and me—if we die, there's no one to speak up for him.*

The call she'd made to the police, pretending to be a neighbor: Without actual testimony in court, would it save Yoandy? Grace doubted it. What if the police believed that Yoandy had killed Kay and Candace? Was this how the nightmare ended—with another innocent man on death row?

Grace could sense Paolo's fear. The smell of Dana's blood was circulating in the air now. Like the meat counter at the market. Running on fear and adrenaline, Grace felt more grounded in her own flesh and bones than at any other point in her life.

We're animals. And this is how it feels before the slaughterhouse. You smell the blood of the ones that have gone before. You smell fear, you smell sweat—yours and everyone else's. You need to go to the bathroom. Your brain can only hang on to two things: don't wet your pants, don't let go of hope.

She had to stay alive. Her father's life depended on it. Yoandy's, too.

Once Paolo had taken up his position next to Grace, the redheaded man pushed her onto the balcony outside room 125. Then he clasped her to his left, pressing the gun tightly against her ribs. A shiver went through Grace. She leaned her head against Paolo's right shoulder and felt his arm tighten around her.

The redheaded man walked her along the open corridor of the second-floor balcony to a staircase. He stayed close to them both, one arm around her waist as they climbed the steps to the next level.

Grace risked a glance toward the parking lot below. A woman in stylish heels was click-clacking her way across the paved area, a phone in her hand. At no point did she look away from her phone.

Then they were up against a door: room 205. Their captor used his keycard to open the door, then placed a foot on the back of Paolo's calves and shoved until Paolo staggered forward into the room. He forced her to follow.

Once they were all inside a room almost identical to the one they'd just left, the redheaded man raised the gun.

"Pick up two chairs, arrange them the way you had them in your room."

When Grace hesitated, he turned the gun sideways and peered at her across the trigger. "Hey, do you really want to mess with me? I'm *so much worse* than a maid ripping off your cash stash."

A maid ripping off the cash stash? Then this guy really hadn't recognized Dana Alexander?

Grace wondered if Paolo had the same thought as her, but their captor shoved him toward the chairs. Grace followed. They both sat slowly as the man approached, holding plastic cable ties. He bound Paolo's hand to the back of one chair, and then repeated the action with her.

"Okay," began the man. "Time to talk. Anyone screams, anyone yells, and the young lady takes a bullet to the gut. I'll continue to ask questions, Paolo, until I get what I want. Meantime, your best girl is gonna be screaming and moaning and bleeding. You don't want that, do you? No? Good."

"That woman you shot, she wasn't a maid," Paolo said. His voice shook a little, but Grace saw that his words had taken effect. "That was *Dana Alexander*," he continued. "The movie star. You've heard of her, right? *She's* the one who hired your hit men."

For a moment, she saw the gun waver. With a courage that she didn't comprehend, Grace heard herself speak. "He's telling the truth."

She watched as the redheaded man smoothed down the front of his shirt. For a few seconds, he looked apprehensive. He appeared to consider his next words for a few seconds.

"Now, let's start by establishing some ground rules. I don't know anything about hit men. That's not a business I'm involved in. However, I do have some associates who might have taken a job that involved a measure of strong-arming."

"They were hit men," said Paolo. "And they came for *us*."

The redheaded man held up a hand. "Hey, you got no argument from me. I'm just pointing out that whoever arranged that was *not* me. Friday evening, I was minding my business and waiting on a delivery, is all. Now, I know your car was in Malibu Canyon on Friday night, Paolo. Piuma Road, right? An associate of mine, he went looking for my bagman, who didn't show up to our appointment. My bagman was driving an Oldsmobile. As it happens, on the occasion in question, he was carrying a half-million dollars of *my money*."

He leveled the gun at Grace's lower abdomen. "Paolo, where's my cash?"

"I don't know, man, I *swear*! We were partying on Friday night. I didn't use my car, dude!" Paolo began.

But the redheaded man shook his head. "Stop lying. It's an insult to me."

Paolo's voice faded away. Their captor moved around to face him, crouching a little.

"Don't waste my time. I *know* things, P. Bad things, about you. My associate, he's a cautious type. Calls me when he arrives in the middle of Malibu Canyon. He's looking for the bagman. At this stage, he's mildly concerned. Strange behavior. Unexpected communications. My associate has a good nose for when something's off. After that, I don't hear from my guy. So I go looking."

Grace felt Paolo shrink back in his chair. He wasn't talking now.

The man paused. "Okay, so, now I arrive at Piuma. Bagman's there. He's flat-out dead. My associate's Oldsmobile, that's there, too. But no sign of my associate. My money? No. Turns out that a bag containing half a mil in cash is *not* in the trunk of bagman's car. Now, my associate is a cautious man. I know that he has a dash cam. A habit he's been encouraging in me, which is how I know. So I take the SD card from the dash cam in the Oldsmobile. I drive home. I watch the recording. However, the audio is faint and the camera is pointed into the road. Whatever went down on Piuma, I'm still in the dark. However."

He inhaled, lowered the gun, and turned to glare at Paolo.

"Here is where it gets interesting. I'm watching the recording from Friday night. I observe that a Chevy Malibu happens along. Plates visible in the Oldsmobile's headlights. They're clear as day. *Your* Chevy Malibu, Paolo. My buddies at the DMV, they checked. It's a good thing that the cops don't have this dash cam evidence, because if they did,

270■

it wouldn't be fake cops that showed up at your door.

"Now, I don't care for cops, Paolo. I prefer to keep them at arm's length. At this point let me state that I don't intend to share that dash cam video with the cops. As a rule, I stay out of matters that don't concern me. My half million in cash, on the other hand, that *does* concern me. On that matter, all evidence points to you." He paused for a moment. "I've been frank with you, Paolo, I've explained the situation. All I want from you is the same courtesy. You tell me—where's the rest of my money? And everyone goes home to Netflix and chill."

PAOLO
MOTEL 6, WEDNESDAY, JULY 8

"I don't have the money," Paolo talked fast, afraid that Redhead's patience might dwindle. "After we found it, we drove up north. The money is still there." He stopped, licking drops of blood from the torn edge of his top lip where Alexander had ripped the gag away.

Redhead eyed him with friendly disdain. "This 'we' would be . . . ?"

"Not Grace," Paolo said, firmly. "Grace wasn't there; she doesn't know anything about it."

There was a too-long pause. Redhead looked Paolo straight in the eye. No overt threat, only a searching quality, and a level of honesty that made Paolo want to be just as candid.

"P, I know that what you just said isn't true." He sounded dispirited. "Maybe Grace wasn't with you when you took my money. But I read faces pretty well. Grace, who seems like a very nice girl, a clean girl, maybe a real *good* girl, she did not react to what you just said. She didn't seem surprised, and I think, Paolo, I'm pretty sure that a girl like that would be surprised. Disappointed, surely. Maybe even shocked. But, nothing. Which to me suggests that Grace here, she knew about the cash before we began this discussion."

He paused once again, waiting. Paolo could feel the man's breath against his cheek.

"Next time you lie to me, it will go very badly for you, Paolo King. I'm trying to help you out. Did I save you from a woman who was holding you at gunpoint? Yes. Have I hurt you? No. Have I been scrupulously honest with you about what I know, about my intentions? Yes. This is how I prefer to conduct my affairs. What I need—no, what I *demand*—from you is nothing more or less."

Paolo felt himself nodding furiously. "The money's with my friend in Napa."

Redhead sighed. His free hand appeared to reach for a necktie that wasn't there. "That's inconvenient. I'll have to make your friend bring the money. Which means coercion."

"No!" Paolo shouted.

A sideways glance silenced him. "Shhh. Quiet now. Much as I enjoy watching tennis, I'm not going to sit here eating Cheetos and watching Wimbledon while your friend drives down from Napa. Thanks to your dead, Academy Award–winning *chambermaid* downstairs, I no longer have anyone around to watch you. I'll have to force you and Grace to cooperate. Would you like to know what I do to people who refuse to cooperate with me?"

Paolo could feel ice in his fingers and toes, a numb sensation that crept through him. There was such understated menace in those words.

"Please, please don't hurt us," Grace said, her voice cracking. "We were witnesses to a murder. In Venice yesterday. There's an innocent man's life at stake. We *need* to be able to testify."

The man stood up straight. "I'll give you this much: that's not an excuse I hear every day."

"It's the truth," Paolo said.

"Is that so? Then why aren't you in Venice talking to the cops right now?"

"Because on top of all that, my dad's on death row," Grace conceded. "And we went looking for some evidence that might prove he didn't do it."

This time, their captor actually smiled. Not nastily, but in genuine amusement. "You two are either the stupidest, bravest kids I've ever met, or you're telling the truth."

A solution occurred to Paolo. "Look, sir, if for whatever reason our friend doesn't show up with the cash in a few hours, or if it comes up short, I'll pay you back every penny. I promise."

"You?" Another grin. "Are you rich?"

"I'll pay you out of my tennis earnings. Look me up. I'm a pro; I'm ranked number twenty-four in the USA. I'm getting better; in three years I'm gonna be playing the Majors. I'll pay you back. With interest."

This time, there was fascination in Redhead's voice. "With interest? You have my interest *now*. Have you spent the money? I can't think of another reason why you'd talk this way."

"I don't know what my friend is planning to do with the money," Paolo said desperately. "That's the truth." He could hear Grace stifling a gasp. Total honesty. It was terrifying, like walking out onto a wire between two skyscrapers. He'd either wind up dead or under this man's control forever. But it was worth it for a chance to free Grace.

"Gee, Paolo," the man said, his voice laden with sarcasm, "I don't know. Seems to me that if you think I'm not getting my money, I'm putting a bullet into at least one of you. So you may want to rethink your position."

"No!" yelled Paolo. "Please, sir, let Grace go. She really does need to testify. Me—I'm your collateral. If you don't get your money back, you've got me."

"You'll pay me from your earnings?"

"Every penny."

"And the vig?"

"I'm sorry, sir?"

"The interest," the redhead said patiently. "I'm not MasterCard, kid. It's twenty-five percent *a month*."

"Oh," said Paolo, faintly. "I can't win money so fast."

Redhead shook his head, as though he'd been disappointed by a favorite student. He paced over to the bed and sat down. "Paolo, Paolo. What are we gonna do?" From his jacket pocket, he took out a smartphone. "You're ranked number twenty-four, really? Let's take a look."

Paolo fell silent as their captor scrolled through pages on his phone's screen. After a few minutes, Redhead shot him a languid grin. "There may be a way."

"Yes!" Paolo cried. "Please! You got it!"

"Stop!" Grace exclaimed. "You don't even know what he's going to say."

Redhead chuckled. "Wise words, young lady. Paolo, maybe you should listen."

"Anything," said Paolo fervently. "I'll agree to anything. Just give me your word that you'll let her go free."

The gun was on the bed now, apparently forgotten. From outside, the sound of police sirens began to intensify. Redhead seemed to notice. He reached for his weapon. "Here's my offer. You have ten hours to return my money. If the debt isn't cleared by then, Paolo comes to work for me. I'll take eighty percent of your income until the debt is paid. And five games a year, you're my boy on the court."

This request took a few seconds to sink in. Paolo's breath caught as he tried to reply. "You . . . you want me to fix tennis matches for you?"

Redhead gave a dry laugh. "Quit clutching your pearls, Penelope. We both know it happens."

"For how long?" Paolo asked weakly.

The man considered. "Five years. Twenty-five games spread out, so the bookies don't notice."

Paolo felt nauseous. His whole future was going up in flames right before his eyes. Grace had gone quiet, but he could feel her wrists straining against the arms of the chairs as she struggled to make contact with him.

This was it; this was the moment of truth. Who knew what Redhead would do if John-Michael and Maya didn't show up with all the cash? "How can I trust that it'll only be five years?"

The man laid the gun across his knees, scrutinizing Paolo. "P, the way I see it, I'm holding all the cards. You kind of *have* to trust me."

Paolo exhaled. "Sir, no disrespect for how you make a living, but it's not for me."

Redhead cracked a sympathetic grin. "Relax, pal. You don't want your kids to have a crook for a daddy. Some of us didn't get that choice. But I understand."

And in that instant, Paolo knew it was the truth. After everything that had happened to him since he'd met Darius on Venice Beach, after Jimmy, and Meredith, after Malibu Canyon, and Candace's murder, Paolo knew—all he wanted was an honest life. Peace. Happiness. A family.

"All right," said Redhead. "I give you my word. That's all a man has, when everything is said and done. This is a bona fide offer, P."

It certainly was that, Paolo thought. *A bona fide deal with the devil.*

"Okay," he said, quietly. "It's a deal."

MAYA

MORGAN HILL, WEDNESDAY, JULY 8

"How much money is left?"

The phone exaggerated it, maybe, but there was a touch of hysteria in Paolo's voice. A second later, he'd calmed down. A smart move, because he'd apparently been detained by the police.

"I thought you said that the cops were fake?" Maya asked.

Painstakingly, Paolo proceeded to explain how the fake cop had left them in the room where he'd bound them back-to-back. Then the *real* cops had found him and Grace. They'd been called to the scene by hotel guests who'd heard the gunshots.

"But why are the cops holding you?" she asked him. "I mean, if they found you and Grace cuffed to some chairs, surely you're victims, too . . . ?"

"Yeah, except that they also found Dana Alexander and some random guy in our hotel room, all blood and no pulse!" Paolo hissed. "And now you're telling me that you've blown our only chance to walk away?"

So Dana Alexander was dead. Maya felt like she should care more. But all she registered was: one less thing to worry about.

More worrisome, right then, was Paolo's reaction. He couldn't say it—couldn't bring himself to say aloud how much money Maya's plan to switch into Bitcoin had cost them. Maybe someone was listening to his end of their conversation?

"We've got around three hundred twenty thousand in Bitcoin now," she said.

"Goddamnit, Maya, where's the rest?" Paolo hissed.

For a moment, all she heard was what sounded like Paolo hyperventilating. After thirty seconds, his mutters began to make a kind of sense. "You've finished me. That's what you've done. I'm totally and completely screwed."

She hesitated. The Bitcoin deal had been risky, but they'd all agreed that they needed to hide the cash. This was the only untraceable way to retain access to it from *anywhere.*

"I could try to get some of it back. Would that help?"

"Of course it would!" Paolo cried. "Get it back fast, or my life is over."

"What's happened?"

His voice dropped even lower. "I can't talk. Cops."

"All right. I'm gonna go now. Give my love to Grace."

Maya cut off the call with Paolo's curses still ringing in her ear. She reached across to the passenger seat. Inside her messenger bag, nestled next to her laptop, was the pistol they'd lifted from the kidnapper Pete Martens had taken captive. The handgun she'd used to cover the bodyguard when he'd tried to rescue Jack—a Glock.

Maya dropped out the magazine and tested its weight in her left hand. She guessed there were at least four bullets left in the mag. Easily enough for a few warning shots.

Hopefully it wouldn't come to that. She slammed the mag back into place, checked that the safety was on, and then tucked the gun into her jean shorts, right up against the small of her back. Over the gun, she pulled the edge of her fitted check blouse. She undid two more buttons at the lower end of the blouse to give her easier access. Then she picked up the messenger bag.

How the heck was she going to get out of this? What if Seneca decided to call the cops? Then Maya would be finished, just like Paolo.

She locked up the car, put the key in the front pocket of her shorts, and began to walk.

Paolo's call had come less than two minutes after she'd left Seneca's lakeside house three blocks away. But driving back would involve making a three-point turn in a narrow road, something she hated to do. It might attract attention to her ineptitude as a driver, which was all her mom's fault for insisting on teaching her, instead of getting a real instructor. The few lessons Maya had ever had wound up with them screaming at each other and her mom saying, dismissively, *You can take taxis!*

On Seneca's porch, Maya noticed a tiny security camera in the top corner of the wall. Last time, Seneca had simply shown up at the door. This time, he talked to her through an intercom.

"What's going on?"

Maya sweetly smiled at the camera. "Jeez, I'm such a dork. I got a really long drive ahead, and I could seriously use a trip to the bathroom."

There was no response. Maya could feel a blush coming on, genuine shame this time. More than anything, she wanted to turn and sprint. But she couldn't. Paolo needed her to get that cash. She's never heard him so panicked—not even with the two hit men on Friday night. He'd sounded borderline hysterical. The stash of money must belong to someone really, really scary.

"You said something about making me breakfast," Maya said. She smiled again. "Although it's more like lunch."

"Not to me. I just got out of bed."

"C'mon dude. How obvious do I have to be?"

Eww. How was she making herself go through with this?

Another moment passed. Then the door opened, and Seneca stood there, looking at her with a mixture of hope and amazement. "You want some breakfast?"

Maya smiled again, more easily this time. "You did say you 'gave great egg.'"

Seriously. He deserves what's coming just for that.

He stepped aside. "Welcome back to my humble abode,

pilgrim. I'm pretty sure we can scare up a wholesome repast before you set back onto the road."

Maya let him lead the way, smiling shyly and acting like she couldn't quite meet his eye.

Once they were in the living room, she spotted the duffel bag, now open on the coffee table where he'd evidently been counting the rolls of bills. She let her messenger bag slide to her feet, slowly, freeing up both her hands.

"Hey, is there any chance we can review that commish?" Maya asked breezily. "'Cause now that I think about it, it seems kind of steep." She turned to him with a sleepy grin and leaned against a wall. Casually, she placed her right hand close to the concealed weapon.

Seneca looked astounded. "Are you suggesting that I *shook you down*?" His nostrils flared, and points of red appeared in both cheeks like bee stings. Before the rage could hit his eyes, Maya pulled her gun.

Seneca's hands went up slowly, following Maya's gestures with the Glock. He finally managed to spit just one word. "Bitch."

"Don't call me that!"

Now he was incredulous. "You think *you're* gonna rip me off?"

She stepped backward, out of range of his hands. *Never get closer than arms' length,* her mother had often warned her. *Some people know how to disarm you when you're that close.*

Maya raised the gun boldly, directing it right into his face. "No; I'm the one that's getting ripped off, right now.

Twenty-five percent is what I call a shakedown."

"Bitch!" he repeated venomously. "You have *any* idea how much extra work I gotta do when the money is illegal? What kind of trouble I could get in?"

Maya maintained a steely tone. "Say that again, and I'll shoot off your pinky toe. Now, *five* percent is fair. And I guarantee that no one scary is gonna come looking for it, so you can stop whining."

The second she'd finished talking, her own words reverberated in her head. Some remote part of Maya still wondered how she was going through with it.

Seneca spat on the carpet.

Maya tipped her head toward the pile of cash, but kept her eyes trained on him. "Put eighty-five thousand back into the bag and bring it over here. That leaves you with what you gave me in Bitcoin plus five percent for your trouble. Four rolls and fifty hundreds."

Seneca held still for a moment. Deliberately, Maya removed the safety. "You must really hate that pinky."

"You're not going to shoot me, you dumb bitch."

Without another thought, Maya squeezed the trigger. Seneca fell to the ground, clutching his left foot and howling. When he moved his foot, the spatter pattern of blood left the clear outline of his sneaker. Curses dripped from his tongue, but at least now he didn't dare to utter the forbidden word.

"You can't even be original. Next time, listen to my warnings. It'd be *easier* to kill you," Maya remarked. "I'd take all the money and keep your lousy Bitcoin, too. I've got a gun full of bullets, a getaway car, and no one knows I'm here except you," she said.

Her tone was calm and calculated, and it was no act. Maya watched Seneca's eyes widen as he realized she was telling the truth.

She cocked the weapon upward, this time aiming for his belly. "Need any more persuasion?"

"I get the picture," he said, bitter in defeat. He winced, lifting his wounded foot. "Let me go over there and grab the bag."

Maya was just about to let him pass when a thought struck her. "No! Stay where you are." She backed toward the duffel bag, both eyes on Seneca and her finger against the trigger.

When she reached the bag, she crouched, pulled it wide open. Inside, exposed by the displaced rolls of cash, was a revolver. She raised an eyebrow. "Naughty, naughty." One by one, she tossed out the rolls of bills until only four were left inside the bag. She threw him one of the discarded rolls. "Five thousand. I want to see you count it. Put the elastic around my share, and toss it back to me."

As he complied, Seneca grimaced with pain and fury. His blood was leaking all over the wooden floor.

Maya thought: *This guy can't stand the idea that he's been beaten by a girl.*

"You're finished on the internet," he informed her. "I'm gonna find out your real name. I'm gonna blacklist you. I'm gonna get every hacker I know to hit anything you build, like *ever*, with frikkin' *thousands* of denial of service attacks."

Maya felt her face twist as she recoiled. "Aren't you forgetting something, 'Seneca'? *I know where you live.* You do *anything*, and I come back here with some *very* unpleasant friends of mine. And they go to town on you."

Seneca snapped the rubber band around a short stack of fifties. With a final, hate-filled glare, he threw it over to Maya.

Now that she was clutching the eighty-five thousand dollars she'd come for, all Maya could think about was getting out of that house. Minutes earlier, she'd seriously contemplated killing someone she barely knew for money.

For money.

How had she ended up here?

JOHN-MICHAEL

Candace was alive—just.

The news that she'd survived Kay Alexander's attack was followed by a horrible caveat: she was still in intensive care. Kay Alexander had sliced neatly into Candace's lungs and punctured a major artery. Candace had been minutes from total lung collapse when the EMTs arrived at the Venice Beach house.

Grace's mother and stepfather had flown in from San Antonio. They picked her up from the police station and took her directly to the hospital. Meanwhile, John-Michael and Lucy had gone straight to Lucy's parents' place.

Between the police station and the hospital, John-Michael hadn't even seen Grace until she'd shown up much later, at Lucy's parents' in Claremont. She'd been exhausted from her lengthy vigil at Candace's bedside.

Grace's parents had dropped her off in Claremont, but it was obvious that they were reluctant to be parted from Candace, so they'd gone back. They were staying in a hotel close to the hospital, just a few streets from the Venice Beach house.

Right now, Grace wanted to be with Lucy and John-Michael. He hoped that Grace's parents understood. It wasn't just about Candace. There was Paolo, too.

Paolo had spent the night in a Claremont jail cell. Only John-Michael knew how that felt. He'd lain awake most of the night thinking about Paolo in there, reliving the night he'd spent cooped up with thugs and drug dealers, waiting to find out: Would the axe fall today?

When it had been his turn, John-Michael had feared for his life because he knew he was guilty. It had taken him almost a year to understand, but now he did. He couldn't claim that his father had died from too much mercy or too much pity; not while a part of John-Michael had simply wanted him dead. The only way he could ever have been sure it was mercy was if he'd loved his dad. And ol' Chuck Weller had made that impossible.

Tears sprang to his eyes. Furiously, John-Michael wiped them away. *No.* His father didn't deserve his tears. He'd helped to turn his son into a killer. Tears were a waste.

Paolo, on the other hand, was not guilty. There was no way he'd intended to kill that first hit man. He'd simply struck out to defend Lucy. When it had come to a point-blank kill shot, he'd faltered. Whatever he was suffering in that jail, Paolo didn't deserve it.

Neither John-Michael nor Paolo thought of themselves

as tough guys. But John-Michael had learned the truth: however soft they looked, both had a violent core.

Maybe there really were no good people or bad people—only people who responded differently under pressure. John-Michael might be a killer. But he wasn't the type to let a friend take a punishment meant for him.

He picked up his phone and stared at the time. 5:32 a.m. Too early to disturb Grace and Lucy.

The police had released Grace almost immediately—right after questioning her about the double murder in the motel room she'd shared with Paolo. The fact that they'd been bound and gagged by both Dana Alexander and the man who'd subsequently abducted them spoke pretty strongly in their defense.

But Grace and Paolo weren't exactly free from police suspicion. A dead movie star accused of holding two teen-agers at gunpoint and shooting a criminal—that was big news. It was a scandal that would shake Hollywood even harder than the murder of Tyson Drew. Now Grace and Lucy had both supplied testimony that linked Dana Alexander to that killing, too.

Once the police had spotted Paolo's Chevy Malibu in the parking lot, their questions had shifted. *Where had Paolo been on Friday night?* More than one witness had placed a Malibu close to Piuma Road and the killings there.

Dana Alexander's deranged behavior was the only silver lining. John-Michael tried to remind himself just how huge it really was. Surely *now* there had to be enough suspicion around Alexander to undermine the conviction of Grace's dad? Paolo wasn't the only one of the group on tenterhooks today. Grace would be waiting to hear from her father or his attorney.

John-Michael wondered if she was awake, too. But the girls deserved a chance to rest, to put one of the most stressful days in their lives behind them. John-Michael's insomnia was his own problem.

His guilt at letting Paolo take the heat, plus the fear of confessing; both were consuming him. How many deaths could he even admit to? Two? Three? All four?

A good lawyer would tell him to admit to precisely *none*. His father had died from choking, and no one could prove otherwise. The first hit man had swallowed his own tongue during his post-trauma fit. John-Michael knew the others would back John-Michael if it came to lying on the stand. The second hit man was self-defense, plain and simple. Manslaughter at the very worst. And as for the guy he'd shot to death in Napa, the one who'd attacked them in the *casita*, who would ever know?

Right now, no one was accusing him of anything. The only way the accusations could come his way would be if Paolo told the cops what they'd done. And so far, Paolo had taken the fifth.

It would be up to John-Michael to confess, to put his entire future at risk. There was no way out. He couldn't leave Paolo to face an investigation and trial.

John-Michael was terrified. His hands shook so much

that it took several seconds for him to realize that his cell phone was buzzing. *Maya.*

"Dude, are you awake?"

His lips quivered. All he managed was a garbled sound.

"Sorry if I woke you," Maya said. "But I really need to know if there's any news about Candace."

"She's still in intensive care."

"Thank God she's alive, though, right?"

"Uh-huh."

"And I guess they're going to release Yoandy?"

"I guess," he said.

"They have to, don't you think?"

Now he detected a hint of anxiety. "Uh-huh," he said again.

Maya was quiet for a minute. "John-Michael, I just wanted you to know, I'm trying to fix what I did."

"What did you do?"

"Paolo didn't tell you?"

"I haven't spoken to Paolo," John-Michael said. "When he was arrested, he'd only get two calls. He probably told them *you* were his attorney."

"Oh. Jeez! Okay. Well, then, I'd better tell you. I changed most of the money into Bitcoin. We've got cash, too. When you add it all up, we still owe Declan Kreutzer about fifty thousand."

"Who's Declan Kreutzer?"

"I guess he's, like, a mob boss, or something. That bag full of money was his," Maya said. "The guy who came for

Lucy—he was carrying it for him. Kreutzer wants Paolo to pay him back any shortfall from the cash we found. But I don't think we should let Paolo pay. That debt, it's on all of us."

A wave of nausea welled up inside John-Michael. He sat up fast, afraid that he might throw up all over the Egyptian cotton sheets of Lucy's parents' guest room.

Another thing that was his fault. How clearly had Lucy warned them not to take the cash? John-Michael couldn't remember any longer whose idea it had been, but he was pretty sure he'd gone along when it had mattered—when he and Paolo had first discovered the bag of money.

"You okay, JM? You're awful quiet."

"Maya," he said, "where are you?"

"Not far from Claremont. I have a few more things to set up before I get over there."

"Other things?"

"Later," she promised. "Right now, though, I need to know—how bad d'you think it would be if I spent another twenty thousand bucks? I mean, for Paolo, with Kreutzer?"

John-Michael exhaled, shivering slightly. "Things are looking real bad for Paolo," he admitted. "Inside or outside of prison. It's no joke for a minor to get arrested for a thing like this."

"Listen to me," she said with sudden passion. "Don't be scared. I know a way to fix this."

"You?"

"Yes. Trust me?"

"You can't fix anything," John-Michael said, his voice crumbling. "Because you didn't break it. I'm the one that did that. And . . . I'll admit this to you, Maya. But not to anyone else. I'm afraid to fix it. I'm *scared.*"

LUCY
KITCHEN, LUCY'S FAMILY HOME, THURSDAY, JULY 9

Around six in the morning, Lucy heard John-Michael leaving the guest room. She rolled over, tucked the goose feather pillow under her chin, and tried to go back to sleep. After a minute or two, she tuned in to the sound of Grace's steady breathing.

She wondered how long it had been since Grace had slept so peacefully. The past few days had been the worst, Lucy was certain, as time had run out for her friend's father. Vesper's attorney had been present when Lucy, Grace, and Paolo had made their statements to the police late the previous night.

"No cast-iron guarantees," the lawyer had told Grace, "but no judge I have ever dealt with would allow Alex Vesper's conviction to stand: not after hearing what Kay and Dana Alexander have done to all of you, together with Lucy's testimony. There's no way those women are innocent of Tyson Drew's murder. That's never going to be proven. But there's enough evidence to exonerate your father."

Grace and Lucy had hugged and held on to each other afterward in the parking lot. Lucy had wanted to say she was sorry, that if she'd understood the reasons for her confusion earlier, she'd have come forward. But remembering she'd known a younger Kay Alexander had come as a huge shock to Lucy. It was like finding a black hole at the heart of the universe. Everything she'd ever mislaid or forgotten was deep inside.

"Dana wasn't the killer," Grace had told Lucy. "We think Kay did it."

"Oh, she totally did it," Lucy admitted.

"You remembered?"

"Enough."

"Why?"

"Blackmail."

Grace had nodded. "Because Kay was her daughter." Then she'd reached out tentatively to touch Lucy's arm. "It . . . it was unfair of me. To blame you for my dad. I had no idea what it's like, Lucy. To see such horrible things. On TV, it doesn't . . . you can't see. The way your whole body shakes. The way your memory clouds."

"Once in a while, you get a break," Lucy had told her. "The fog gets thin. And you get little peeks."

"I'm glad you got that break."

So was Lucy. A memory that wouldn't leave her; a reminder from somewhere deep in her subconscious, waiting to be resurrected. Waiting until Lucy grew up. That memory had worked its way into their lives, a spark that spread like wildfire. It had freed Alex Vesper, yes. And now they were standing on scorched earth.

Lucy slid out of bed and yawned. She reached for her phone on the nightstand. 6:24 a.m. On the other side of the bed, Grace stirred.

It was time to find John-Michael. He hadn't returned to his room, which meant that he'd probably gone down to the kitchen. She went downstairs bare legged and stealthy, wearing a baggy Clash T-shirt. In the kitchen, she found John-Michael opening cupboards.

"Corn-bread muffins," he said, holding up a bag of cornmeal. "Would it be too weird if I baked something? You think your mom would mind?"

"My mom?" Lucy shrugged. "She barely knows her way around the kitchen. Elena, our housekeeper, might have something to say. But she won't be here until nine thirty."

John-Michael began assembling ingredients. Lucy poured herself a tall glass of skim milk and pulled out one of the stools from under the kitchen island. She watched him work, zesting an orange, hunting through the refrigerator until he'd come up with a box of fresh blueberries from Whole Foods, and stirring melted butter, milk, and a whisked egg into a mixture of flour, cornmeal, and baking powder.

A few minutes later, a set of twelve muffins was baking

and she was watching him clean up. Like always, John-Michael was quick and efficient.

"You ever consider catering as a career?" she asked. "Or baking, pastry chef, something like that?"

John-Michael dried his hands on a tea towel. A delicious smell wafted from the oven. "It wouldn't be my first choice."

"Oh, then what?"

John-Michael looked at her for a moment. "International assassin?" he said, with a twisted grin.

Lucy managed a dry laugh. "Ha. Sure; call the CIA."

She sniffed the air, sweet and comforting. It felt good to be home again; in the kitchen where she'd eaten all the pancake breakfasts of her elementary school years. Strangely, she felt much younger. Not seventeen and emancipated, but fourteen at most, having her gay best friend over for a sleepover. Later maybe they'd go down to the basement and jam. Her thoughts were already turning to the stash of weed she'd hidden down there once, wondering if her parents had ever discovered it.

But it was just nostalgia. Those days were over, done and dusted and never to return.

She showed John-Michael the cupboard with all the jelly, honey, and syrups. He selected a grape jelly, and maple and boysenberry syrups.

"You seem happier, Luce," he said. "Is it because you're home?"

"Nah, it's 'cause I finally got to spend some quality time

with my boy without Maya-the-girl-genius on our case." She wrinkled her nose. "That makes me a bad person—right?"

He seemed dumbfounded at Lucy's admission. "That taxi ride down from Napa—*quality time*? That doesn't make you bad. Crazy? Maybe, yeah. Not *bad*."

"Say what you like, JM. But we'll always have Instagram," she said archly. To say it any more clearly might lead to emotion, which wasn't her style. Yet Lucy meant it from the bottom of her heart.

John-Michael just shook his head, bemused.

"You should call Ruben today," Lucy told him. He blinked a couple of times, and eventually shook his head. "Really?" she said, surprised. "No?"

"I can't!"

"JM, the guy has even resorted to calling *me*."

"What did you tell him?" he asked warily.

Lucy set down six small plates. "Nothing, of course. What am I gonna tell Ruben?"

John-Michael's hair fell forward, shielding his face. "It's better this way."

"Better how?"

"Better if I don't talk to him. We'd only just got together. Anyone can make a mistake."

"Gee," Lucy said with sarcasm. "I wish you'd let *me* be the one to make the mistake. Unlike you, I actually liked him."

"It wasn't *my* mistake," John-Michael exclaimed. The outburst seemed to take him by surprise. "Lucy, can't you see?" He tried to smile. "*I am the mistake*. Ruben should have never picked me." He picked up an oven mitt and turned toward the oven, pulling out a pan of perfectly baked muffins. He set them down carefully.

Lucy tried to reach for a muffin, but John-Michael brushed her hand away. "Wait a few minutes. The blueberries will burn your tongue."

Lucy began to set plates on the table. Meanwhile, John-Michael was already rifling through a bowl of Nespresso pellets beside a large coffee machine.

"The light blue ones are good," she told him. "What makes you think Ruben made a mistake?"

John-Michael slammed down a coffee cup. "What part of this are you not getting, Luce? I'm going to *prison*!" he said. His grief and rage were so palpable that she flinched. "I'm going to prison," he repeated, this time steadier. "It's the only way to be sure the cops won't go after Paolo."

She waited, holding her breath as she watched John-Michael struggle to bring himself back under control. A moment later, he picked up a knife and began to ease the corn-bread muffins out of the pan. He broke one muffin in two, put the stump and muffin top on one of the plates she'd laid out, spreading butter on both pieces. Finally, he drizzled a shot of maple syrup over the buttered muffin and passed her the plate. All in silence.

Lucy was openmouthed with admiration at the methodical nature of his mood control.

"I'm Paolo's best way out of jail," John-Michael said,

now sounding matter-of-fact. "Which is why I'm going to tell my lawyer that I'll hand myself over to the cops. I'll say I did it. Today, by three in the afternoon, I'll be inside. And Paolo will be free."

PAOLO

Grace was waiting for him. They gazed at each other from a distance, eyes locked.

It was frustrating, at first. Paolo was behind the desk, waiting for the paperwork to be rubber stamped before the cops would let him through. Once his eyes had met Grace's, though, he didn't care. He could wait another minute or two. Time to look at her a little longer. Perfect.

For the life of him, Paolo could not imagine how he'd ever found any other girl remotely as attractive. Grace wasn't just cute, she was electric. He'd spent the whole night in jail thinking about her—it was the only thing that had gotten him through.

One night curled up against her had been enough to make him realize that he'd do just about anything to repeat the experience. Even if that's all she'd ever let him do, right at that moment, Paolo could almost persuade himself that it would be enough.

Well, he thought, *not really*, but hopefully he wouldn't have to wait forever.

She was gazing back at him with an expression of hope, of sorrow, and maybe of love, too. Paolo had to believe it was love. Because only love would allow Grace to overlook the yawning chasm between them.

Grace was a good person; he wasn't. She wasn't vain; he was. She wasn't in trouble with the law. She wasn't in hock to some up-and-coming underworld Mr. Big; a guy so "new" that once Paolo's parents had managed to get in touch with their attorney, the lawyer had scrambled to talk to other, more sketchy clients and come up with absolutely *zilch* on Declan Kreutzer.

Grace was in a totally different league. The moment he'd agreed to Kreutzer's deal, Paolo had felt the connection between him and Grace stretching thin.

He smiled at her, a fragile, tentative smile. When she smiled back, affectionately, Paolo felt his eyes water.

Then, with a simple nod from the cop who was signing him out, Paolo was free.

He almost tripped over the step between the reception area and the waiting area. Grace was rushing toward him, with John-Michael right behind her. A second later, Paolo was clasping her to him, burying his face in Grace's soft hair, inhaling a sweet perfume that smelled of black tea and white flowers and a hint of candy apple. Grace kissed his neck, just under the jaw, and then tilted her chin upward until their lips met.

But the moment he felt Grace's hand on his neck, pulling him closer, he broke away, gently. "Hey, we're in the middle of a police department," he said.

Grace was breathless, her eyes blue and shiny and full to the brim with tears. "I'm happy. Let me be happy. Just for a moment?" Paolo brought a hand to brush her lips, and she kissed his fingers. Then she leaned in close. "You need to say something to John-Michael. He's going to hand himself in—they gave him until three p.m. today. That's why they've released you."

"What?" Paolo said faintly.

"Shhh. Don't argue. He's decided. Lucy and I have been talking to him all morning. He won't change his mind."

Paolo stared at John-Michael for a moment. Then he grabbed his friends and pulled them toward the door. The three of them jostled their way past a group of older teenagers entering the station.

Outside, the three housemates kept walking till they hit the sidewalk, past a line of pink oleander bushes. Paolo glanced around quickly, making sure that no one was in earshot. Only then did he turn to John-Michael. "You're doing *what*?"

John-Michael grinned. A shockingly casual gesture, given what he was about to do. "There's no other way. Look, think of it this way: I'm cute, I like dudes, and I'm a killer, not some straight, white-collar dingleberry. I'll find myself a tough Latino boyfriend inside, someone with a crew. They'll take care of me."

Paolo stared at John-Michael, totally unsure how to respond. John-Michael was acting like it was no big deal, but it was. His friend was refusing to face up to the reality of what could happen to him.

John-Michael gave one final grin, then moved to tap Paolo on the chest, as if he were a proud father. "Oh, and there's one more thing. You're not gonna pay Declan Kreutzer."

"Are you *insane*? He'll kill me."

"Relax, he'll get his money. But we'll all pay him. Not just you."

Before John-Michael could move away, Paolo grabbed ahold of his wrist and held him in place. "It's not about the money. Kreutzer wants to own me. He'll never agree."

John-Michael shrugged.

"Listen," Paolo whispered, pulling him closer. "You have to let me do this, man. You're not going to be the only one to pay for what we did. I . . . I need to do something. How else will I ever deserve Grace?"

John-Michael shook his head, carefully extricating himself from Paolo's grip. "Make him agree, Lawyer Boy; negotiate. You can't just let a guy like Kreutzer stroll into your life. Not if it's gonna be you and her."

Their conversation was cut off abruptly by Maya, who hurried toward them from the parking lot. She looked flushed, slightly pink in the cheeks. She exchanged a quick hug with Grace before moving closer to the boys.

Grace edged toward Paolo and found his hand with

hers. Paolo kissed her cheek and drew her against his side. It felt right, to have her there. She made him feel stronger, and he wanted to do the same for her.

Maya turned to John-Michael. "So, JM, you won't change your mind?" she asked quietly.

John-Michael chuckled softly. "Too late now."

Paolo had wondered vaguely why the cops at the desk hadn't reacted to the fact that John-Michael was in the building. They probably didn't know what he looked like. All they knew was that John-Michael had agreed to turn himself in, and that a lawyer had vouched for him.

Paolo saw his chance then. He pressed the others toward the parking lot across the road. "The cops don't know you're here, do they?" When John-Michael looked puzzled, Paolo continued, "You have until three to hand yourself in, right? But inside, it didn't look like they knew you were already here. And if they don't know you're here, man, you should split. I mean it. Just leave with me and Gracie and Maya, right now."

John-Michael was desolate. "It's useless. My attorney spoke to them already, he vouched for me. They agreed to that. If I don't, they'll come find me."

"It's a quarter after one," Paolo said. "If you run, you'd have some time."

"Where would I go?"

"You could hide," Paolo said urgently. "Find a fore-closed house and lie low for a few months. Then we'd get you out."

He could tell Grace felt uneasy. But surely she wouldn't want John-Michael to be punished for those deaths? He'd acted out of self-defense and to protect his friends.

Still, the "conspiracy" part would be difficult to defend. Paolo knew the cops had no inkling of the fact that the first hit man had been killed in the Venice Beach house. They'd asked only about Malibu Canyon. The police had fallen for the setup of the killing as a hit-and-run.

Once John-Michael started talking to the cops, it might lead to a charge of conspiracy to conceal the killings. A charge that would apply to Lucy and Maya as well as to John-Michael and himself.

"I can think of something better," Maya said, her eyes bright. "John-Michael, remember when we talked about getting a real Mexican passport using the birth certificate of a dead guy? Someone whose death hadn't been declared legally, maybe because he was involved in a crime?"

John-Michael was nodding, slowly, disbelief stealing over him. "But we were just kidding around. Right? I mean, you weren't serious? 'Cause that stuff is dangerous."

"I got one," Maya said triumphantly. "I got a birth certificate. A nineteen-year-old guy—well, he would be nineteen if he weren't dead. It's a new one, with the shiny metallic seal and all. His parents ordered it from the office in Mexico, last year. He was from Nogales. It's on the border with Douglas, in Arizona. The family wanted to leave; anyhow, their kid died before they left Mexico, but they kept it quiet and held on to his certificate."

"Jeez, Maya." Paolo stared. John-Michael looked dumbstruck. Against Paolo's side, Grace grew tense. "How the heck did you . . . ?"

"Markkinat," Maya declared. "It's a marketplace on the dark web. His family must have sold the papers to the dealer. You can get most anything there, if you're willing to pay."

"If you're willing to walk on the wild side," John-Michael said, sounding a little shocked. "Maya's crazy."

But Maya shook her head, eyes bright with conviction. "I paid ten thousand dollars in Bitcoin. Now John-Michael can use that birth certificate to get a legitimate Mexican passport. A whole new identity. And he can *run*."

JOHN-MICHAEL
W BONITA AVENUE, THURSDAY, JULY 9

"Well, it's finally happened. Maya's gone fully Kay Alexander," John-Michael shook his head. Maya really was clutching at straws. Yet he loved her for trying, for still wanting to plan her way out of the apocalypse.

They walked slowly, drifting away from the police station, down West Bonita Avenue and toward the parking lot where they'd parked Paolo's car.

"It's not such a *terrible* idea," Paolo said mildly. He seemed wary of Grace's reaction.

John-Michael found he was interested in her reaction, too. "Grace . . . what do you think?"

Grace frowned in concentration. "So, we're talking about John-Michael using that certificate to get a *Mexican* passport? How can he get one here in the USA? He would have needed a passport to get into the USA in the first place, right?"

"He'd have to get into Mexico to get the passport," Maya agreed. "That's a given."

"If I don't hand myself in by three p.m., I'm a wanted man," John-Michael said. "I can't just drive over the border."

"Border's not secure all the way," Maya pointed out. "And the guards are on this side."

"Right," Paolo said. "He'd have to get past a whole bunch of armed border guards."

"They wouldn't be looking out for gringo hikers. They'd be looking for Latinos."

"Latinos *and* escaped felons from *el norte*," Paolo said. "And if he runs, the sentence gets worse. Also, how would he survive? I mean, for money."

"Simple," Maya said. "We give him some of the cash. And I make another Bitcoin account for him, transfer some of the money. Enough for a couple of years."

John-Michael gawped. "I take even more of Declan Kreutzer's money? Now I know you're insane. Do you have any clue what kind of things a crime boss will do to a welcher? I know you had a plan for the endgame, Maya, but when you sacrifice the queen, you're not supposed to kill the king in the same move."

His words stung. But Maya ignored them. "You don't go now, you wait. In fact, Paolo's idea about the foreclosed home is good—we find somewhere like that to hide out."

"Why couldn't he just go back to the *casita*?" Paolo said. He paused then, waiting for Grace's response.

To John-Michael's astonishment, after a second or two, she nodded. "Maybe my dad's friend can help out again?"

"Pete Martens?" Maya pumped a fist. "Yes! Excellent suggestion!"

The change in Maya was extraordinary, John-Michael reflected. Last time he'd seen her, she'd been distraught, wrecked by the discovery of Jack Cato's murder. He hadn't even had a chance to ask her about it on the phone yesterday.

"Are you sure you're all right, Maya?" he ventured.

"I'm so sorry about Jack," Grace said. She threw her arms around Maya. The two girls hugged for a long time.

"Thank you," he heard Maya say quietly. "I'm just so glad that Candace is alive. I don't think any of us could survive this if she wasn't."

John-Michael wasn't sure that he was going to survive prison, but he thought better of saying it. They all seemed to be convinced that he should try running. Pure crazy town. John-Michael knew what it meant to run, to hide, to be homeless. The first few days were thrilling. The world seemed to be filled with possibility. Then came the loneliness, the hunger. The point at which you'd do anything for a warm bed and some food that you didn't have to eat while looking over your own shoulder. You'd even commit a crime, just to get into a safe place with food and books and company. He'd seen other homeless people do it when they were truly desperate.

John-Michael had survived almost a year of living rough. Another year, who knows? He'd have stooped to hustling. Maybe he'd have turned to petty crime. At least with Maya's plan, if he went on the run, he'd have money. It would make all the difference.

A laugh worked its way up inside him. The others looked at him at once, concern written all over their faces. This was no time to be the weirdo. John-Michael didn't relish being the house oddball. He just wanted to be like them. But he'd killed four human beings. He couldn't be like the rest of them, not ever.

That's where John-Michael was now, the country of the damned. He'd crossed over some night more than a year ago, probably hadn't even noticed the border. That's the way it was. There wasn't always a wall, a fence, or a sign-post. Some borders were invisible.

"We should go see her. Right now. Candace."

"She's in a medically induced coma," Grace explained. "They're giving her body more time to heal while she doesn't have to be in pain. My stepdad's gonna call me the minute she wakes up."

John-Michael grabbed Paolo and Maya and pulled them close. "Let's go," he whispered, almost overcome. They had to listen to him. It had to be now, or he'd lose his nerve. "Before the cops figure out that I'm not coming in. C'mon. Now!"

GRACE

They were barely inside the Chevy Malibu, both doors shut, before Grace fell on Paolo, her hands in his hair as she kissed him, hard. He held back for a second, and then gave himself to it, clasped her at the waist as he pressed her tightly against his chest.

Grace wasn't sure what possessed her, but was relieved when he didn't resist. When she released Paolo, he gasped.

He brought one hand to cradle her face, firm and confident, almost possessive. "Baby," he whispered, wonderingly. "What'd I ever do to deserve that?"

Grace smiled a secretive smile and leaned in slowly to plant another kiss, deliberate and delicate as her lips met Paolo's. This time she drew back instantly, resisted his attempt to draw her closer. For a long while they stared at each other until Grace felt that she'd explode from the desire welling up inside.

"For a little while there, I thought I might lose you." Her

admission was out there before Grace could stop herself.

Paolo took his time before answering. He kissed her temple, softly, before he did. "Never. If you're willing to stand by me, then you gotta know, Grace, it's you, babe, it's only you."

"Of course I'll stand by you."

He gazed at her anxiously. "Why?"

"You said that you wouldn't abandon me. Remember? I won't abandon you, either."

"But that was all *before* you knew about Meredith Eriksson. I . . . I can't hold you to anything we promised. Not now."

Last night, as she'd tried to sleep, Grace had brooded over Dana Alexander's salacious revelations about Paolo. After Declan Kreutzer had left them in Motel 6, Paolo had broken down and told her everything. How he'd lost money to a tennis hustler, how he'd doubled down on a money game only to discover that it was all a ruse to con a rich boy out of an expensive car. How the boy's mother, Meredith, had used that misdemeanour as leverage for blackmail.

It explained so much about Paolo's sudden shift in temperament over the past six weeks. Now she understood why he'd chosen to mark his skin. It hadn't been an attempt to impress Lucy—it had been a way to mark his own transition: from lawful to outlaw.

Grace knew Paolo thought she should love him a little less for that, for being less than the perfect all-American boy that she'd thought he was. Yet the opposite was true. She loved him more. He was vulnerable, flawed. *Flawed* she understood, she could work with. It was perfection she found unsettling.

"But Meredith blackmailed you, didn't she?"

Paolo gave an empty laugh. "Meredith, and now Declan Kreutzer. Seems I'm a sucker for it."

"But Kreutzer is going to let you go in five years."

"Assuming I don't get caught fixing tennis matches, get thrown out of the game, and go to jail."

"Kreutzer seems too smart to get caught. Anyhow, I'm sure Candace will help with the debt."

Paolo looked astonished. He shook his head firmly, lips trembling. "No. No way. Candace did nothing, *nothing.* She's not paying for this."

Grace placed a finger against his lips. "Shh. Relax. I'm sure she could loan us the cash. Her TV show is sure to be picked up after the publicity about Dana and Kay attacking us all. Just like you're going to find people interested in watching your tennis games now."

He turned red then, scowling as he pulled away. "You're right," he muttered. "That's how this is all going to play out, isn't it? I bet everyone starts watching Dana's movies again, too."

She took his hand between both of hers. "The point is that this thing with Kreutzer is temporary."

Paolo shook his head. There was sadness in his eyes.

"I can't believe I'm going to say this, Gracie, but I need to. Because I love you. And you deserve the truth."

Grace felt hot tears well up as he said this.

"The problem with blackmailers," Paolo explained, "is that they don't give up easily. Once they've had a taste of the goods, they come back for more."

"That's *Meredith*," Grace said, shaking her head as a tear fell. "Kreutzer isn't blackmailing you, not exactly. He made a business deal. Like you said yourself, it's risky to fix tennis matches. If it goes on too long, more chance of being caught. He might not even stick to the whole five years, who knows?"

Her voice was full of hope, but she knew perfectly well–Declan Kreutzer had his hooks in Paolo. He'd been delighted about the unexpected bonus, as if he'd been to the store and discovered a big, juicy bargain. Kreutzer was planning to enforce his "contract."

With his thumb, Paolo caught her tear as it rolled down her cheek. He wiped it away. "Okay, Gracie. So long as I've got you."

"Of course you have me," she said, her voice cracking. "I love you, Paolo."

They embraced then, both tearful. Grace screwed her eyes shut, trying to banish the grief. She knew Paolo was right. And when her father found out that she was in love with a boy who worked for a criminal boss, there was a good chance he'd forbid it.

The time might be coming, very soon, when she would have to choose. Paolo and a life of compromise with evil—or losing him altogether, abandoning him to his fate. Grace didn't think she could stand to lose him.

Now, clinging to him in the parked car, she wanted to fight harder for him. She resolved to stick with Paolo, whatever her father might say. She'd stood by Alex Vesper all these years, after all. Without Grace and her friends, Alex Vesper would be on his way to the execution chamber.

Her dad owed Grace his trust and understanding—even if she chose Paolo.

Grace brought her hand to Paolo's face, pressed her forehead to his. "Let's go somewhere," she whispered.

"Somewhere . . . ?"

She kissed him once, gently. "Now, Paolo. I need to *be* with you."

He looked at her, first in amazement, and then in disbelief. "What about going to see Candace?"

"You're right." She groaned softly in disappointment. "We're supposed to meet up with my parents. They've been at the hospital all day, sitting with Candace. I should be there, too."

Paolo kissed her again, took his time about it. They broke apart reluctantly.

"I love that you want to do it, though," he marveled, eyes sparkling with wicked intent. "But we should arrange something special. A whole weekend, just you and me, somewhere really great. Like Santa Catalina. A nice romantic hotel, a boat trip, snorkeling."

She gasped. "That sounds wonderful."

"You deserve 'wonderful,'" Paolo said. "Wonderful, and a lot more."

MAYA

Maya settled into the passenger seat of the VW Golf she'd bought from Seneca. Having John-Michael in the driver's seat was a huge relief. Her solo drive down from San Jose had been sheer, protracted tension. She hadn't let her concentration lapse for a second, watching for police cars, sweating it out each time one of them lingered in her vicinity.

When she mentioned her relief to John-Michael, he laughed sarcastically. "Oh, sure—a wanted felon is just the right driver for someone who's trying to stay out of trouble." His defeatist tone plunged them both into silence for a few minutes. "You seem different, Maya."

Maya withdrew a brown paper envelope from her messenger bag. She took out a thick sheet of pink paper decorated with a fancy red border and embossed with a foil seal.

"Here it is," she said. "*El mero-mero*—a genuine Mexican birth certificate. The guy's baptism certificate was part of the bundle, too. From now on you are José Antonio Rodiles Trujillo. *Tony Trujillo.* How'd you like that?"

John-Michael didn't reply.

"All you gotta do now is lie low for a while," Maya went on. "Pete Martens should be able to find you someplace to hide. And then, a few months from now, you sneak across the border. Get a radical haircut. Get a spray tan, some brown contacts. Throw out the plaid shirts and maybe don't shave for a few weeks. Easy on the guyliner, get rid of the nail polish."

"Should I stop being gay?" he asked, a tad belligerent.

"Your call, man. It's just a disguise. Get a job in Mexico, stay out of trouble. Practice your Spanish."

He regarded her quietly. "Maya, hey."

"With your English you could work in tourism. Cancún. The Mayan Riviera. Sell time-shares or something. Tony Trujillo. Kinda has a ring to it, no?" Maya went on.

"Maya," he repeated, firmly. "Enough about me. Can we talk about you? You seem weird."

"Weird how?"

"Last time I saw you, you were crying on Lucy's shoulder about Jack. And you haven't said anything to the others about your real name being Julia—have you? 'Cause I've been waiting for one of them to mention it, and nada."

"Oh, that," Maya said, unsure how to continue. Mainly, she was keeping going by not looking back. Talking about any of it could threaten that stability.

"You wanna talk about it?"

She really didn't. "Those things happened," she said. "But life goes on."

"For you, for *Julia.*"

"Not Julia. Maya," she snapped. She could sense a deep well of anger inside. Better to slam a lid on all of that. "I didn't know Jack all that well."

"You're gonna forget him?" he asked. "Is that the plan?"

"You're going to forget Ruben," she countered. John-Michael wanted the honesty to get brutal: well, all right. "Life is tough that way."

"I won't forget Ruben," he replied mildly. "I won't forget anyone; I wouldn't know how."

Maya flushed. "Then you'd better start learning. I've been researching how to stay off the grid–apparently that's the main way that cops catch people who jump bail. You'll reach out to someone and then bam, you're caught."

"Not if we keep using burner phones," he said. "That means I can stay in contact with you, Paolo, and Lucy."

"Sounds risky."

He glanced sideways at her. "And you're saying . . . what? I shouldn't?"

Maya shrugged. "I can't read the future. Who knows what the cops have on any of us, or what they'll have in the future? One of us might crack, use information about you as a bargaining chip."

John-Michael was quiet for a long time after that. "You've really thought about this," he said at last.

"I think about *everything.*"

He gave a quick nod. "Yup. Guess you do."

Frowning, she slotted the birth certificate back into the envelope and dropped it onto his lap. "No need to thank me."

He braked slowly for a red light and turned to her. "Thank you, Maya."

Maya mumbled something noncommittal. She was getting a strangely judgmental vibe from John-Michael. It was a little annoying. Both had done bad stuff, him more than any of the housemates. What was the point of wallowing? *Of course* she missed Jack. Of course the memory of his death was like a raw, open wound. Of course her heart ached every time she allowed herself to think about what Jack must have gone through in his final hours.

Which was exactly why she didn't. It made no sense, thinking about things that were done and dusted. They might as well be behind the sun, for all Maya could do about them now. The best—the *only*—thing was to keep looking forward.

"Maya, what's going to happen with your investor?"

"I've thought about that," she began. "I'm going back to the *casita*. The cops have no idea that anything happened there. Paolo took the fifth, so he's given them nothing. I'll clean up before the police investigate where we've been. If anyone asks, we stayed in Napa and drove down after Candace left."

"Everything goes back the way it was?" John-Michael said skeptically. "'Cause I got a feeling the cops are going to have a lot of questions for all of you if I'm not in the picture."

Her eyes were cold as she turned to him. "I'm not stupid, John-Michael. Jack's death is gonna be linked to Dana Alexander's. It'll be all over the news. Yeah–I'm probably toast with Alexa Nyborg. But I can do what needs to be done to keep her name out of our mess."

"You had other investors interested, though, right?"

"None that are likely to show up, after this," Maya said gloomily. She glanced at John-Michael's hands on the steering wheel. He really was pale–even whiter than Paolo. No one was going to believe he was from the Mexican border town of Nogales. It was practically in the desert.

"You should keep the car," she told him. "Papers are in the glove compartment. I'll sign it over to Tony Trujillo."

"José Antonio Rodiles Trujillo," he corrected. "Use my full name, dude."

Finally, they shared a smile.

"So, the car–it really is legal. You bought it fair and square?"

"Cash on the table," she confirmed. "Although I did kinda shoot the previous owner in the foot a few minutes afterward. On account of his misogynist douchery."

John-Michael burst out laughing. After a moment, Maya did, too.

"Maya, I swear," he mused, shaking his head as he calmed down. "It's too bad we can't run away together. We'd make a good team."

She smiled at him, fondly. Somewhere toward the back of her mind a series of images flashed: John-Michael wandering the beaches of Yucatán, tanned and shorn of his long, floppy black hair. Alone, and always looking over his shoulder. Would he be happy? Maya couldn't imagine how. John-Michael wasn't a loner—he was a homebody.

"Yeah," she said, softly, as unexpected tears prickled the corners of her eyes. "Partners in crime, right? I'd have liked that."

LUCY

"Señora, está aquí alguien para la señorita Lucy."

Lucy's family housekeeper, Elena, was trying discreetly to catch her mother's eye. But Professor Anne-Marie Jordan was entertaining her guests, the Deering girls' anxious parents. Too busy pouring tea and handing out slices of angel food cake. So Lucy slunk out of the room and followed Elena to the front door.

She was astonished to find Pete Martens standing on the porch. His graying hair was neatly combed now, his chin smooth as a baby's. He wore a navy blue sport jacket and tan chinos, as respectable as a Dockers commercial. The look wiped around ten years off his age.

Martens brought his gaze slowly to meet Lucy's. "Hello, Lucy. Is Grace with you?"

Lucy closed the front door behind her and folded her arms across her chest. She gave a low whistle of appreciation, looking him up and down. "Dude, are you here to protect my girl or to marry her? 'Cause if you're looking to protect her, then, man, are you way off base. Someone already tried to kill her, and some other dude already saved her ass."

Martens tilted his head for a moment, as if to say he expected better from Lucy. "You're awful sure of yourself, Lucy. I think I'd prefer to hear it from Grace."

"You ever hear of a guy named Declan Kreutzer?"

At this, Martens pursed his lips. It might have been disapproval, or maybe he was just taking his time, rolling it over and over in his mind. Lucy didn't know. She didn't care much, either.

"Point is, someone already got to Grace. Lucky for us all, he didn't kill her. You should give us our money back."

"If it turns out that any apologies are necessary, I'll direct them to Grace and her father," Martens said tightly.

"We paid you twenty thousand. You didn't rescue Maya's buddy, either."

A thin smile spread over his features. "Miss, you seem displeased. I guess I won't expect a recommendation."

"You'd *better* not."

He gave a considered nod. "Although you might want to revisit what happened. I doubt you'd be alive right now if not for me."

"Grace isn't here," Lucy said, scowling. "She'll be back in a little while."

From his inside jacket pocket Martens took out a blank card and a ballpoint pen. He jotted down a number and handed the card to Lucy. "It's for Grace. Her father told me to give it to her. He wants her to check in with me today."

Lucy took the card. "She's okay, you know that, right?"

Martens nodded. "You give that to Grace, all right, Lucy? And give my regards to Maya."

"Oh, you're so sure that *she's* alive?" Lucy called out after the bodyguard, but he only lifted a hand as he walked away, waving it once.

Lucy pocketed the card with Martens's phone number and went back inside. Elena was dusting the ornaments on a nearby mantel, very obviously hovering in earshot.

"*Está bien*, Elena," Lucy said, wearily. "Everything's okay."

In English, Elena said, "You come back home now?" Hope filled her light brown eyes.

Lucy smiled and cast her gaze down. "*No lo creo*, Elena. I don't think so. But thanks."

Lucy headed upstairs for her room. She'd already smiled demurely for almost an hour, feigning meekness as her mother hosted Grace's mother and Candace's father. All of this without any of the other housemates to help her out.

It could have been worse, Lucy thought. Candace's mother, Katelyn, was on her way back from New York City. At least she was going directly to the hospital.

Fraught, anxious parents, looking for someone to blame. Everything that Lucy had tried to escape in becoming emancipated. No, she was not "coming home"! But if Elena thought that was a possibility, then for sure, Lucy's mother had mentioned it.

Lucy closed the bedroom door and sat down beside the acoustic guitar she'd left lying on its back. It was a Spanish guitar, bought for her when her parents were trying to persuade her to take up flamenco (it hadn't worked). She sighed, moving the guitar carefully to the other side of her bed. On top of everything else, was she now going to have to fight each battle all over again?

Then she remembered. The emancipation was done; it was signed and sealed, legal as a divorce. She'd never stop being the daughter of Anne-Marie Jordan and Robert Long. That was forever. But as a person in her own standing, Lucy had achieved independence. It hadn't been an easy ride. There was no way she was going to turn the clock back.

She lay across the pillows, reaching with her left hand for the guitar. With genuine fondness now, Lucy looked around at her room. Her parents had preserved it as some kind of museum to Lucy's past. But that was all right, she realized. It was their past, too; her mom's and her dad's. It didn't need to be erased.

Did all the housemates have a room like this somewhere? Lucy wondered. A room crammed with everything but the son or daughter who'd flown the nest? A room of waiting, of hoping for a return? Or perhaps just a place where they could feel safe again in times of trouble?

They all did, probably. All of them except John-Michael. His father had ejected him, rejected his only child.

Lucy went over and over the events of Friday night, trying to remember if she'd left anything unsaid, if anything she might have done differently would have changed the outcome. And she couldn't think of one—except the scenario in which they'd have gone directly to the police.

Would Maya's Jack still be alive, if they'd done that? *Probably*, thought Lucy. On the other hand, Grace and Candace might not be, if the second hit man had lived long enough to find them.

She clutched the acoustic guitar and drew it against her, held it as though right then, it was the best friend she had in the world.

Prison had been in the cards from early on for at least one of the boys. Perhaps John-Michael was right—the way things were now was the least-worst option.

But it was still a disaster.

Softly, her fingers began to strum the introductory chords of Rancid's "Fall Back Down."

"Don't worry about me, I'm gonna make it alright."

CANDACE

She heard his voice first. She'd just been thinking about him—well, dreaming probably, since her eyes had just opened. They'd been walking along the boardwalk. A hip-hop artist jamming on the beach asked Yoandy to join in, so he did. A crowd had built up swiftly around them.

"Candace?"

Candace tried to speak, but was suddenly conscious of a raging sore throat. "Water," she managed. It was barely a croak. A hand lifted a paper cup to her lips, and she sipped. Chips of ice bumped against her lips, and cool water soothed her.

She opened her eyes a little wider. It was definitely Yoandy. He was gazing at her with those deep brown eyes. She felt his fingers circling her wrist, carefully navigating the intravenous drip in her hand.

The rest of the room took shape before her. A small hospital room with a pink-tinted window overlooking the marina. Candace lay in the only bed. Behind Yoandy was a small table that held a huge arrangement of sunflowers and birds-of-paradise, a halo of yellow and gold.

Images of the stabbing came back to her for a moment, but her mind shut them down as soon as they appeared. Candace stared at Yoandy in wonder, trying to feel the shape of her memories. It was like trying to grasp water. She could remember almost nothing, even though she tried. Kay with a knife, Kay screaming at her. And nothing else.

"Kay?" she asked, and her voice was barely more than a croak.

Yoandy shook his head, solemnly. He brought a juice box to her lips, and she drank.

She could see him watching her, raising her fingers to his lips and kissing them, his eyes still locked with hers. Forming words seemed to hurt rather a lot, so she waited for him to explain. But he didn't.

Kay is dead, then, Candace thought. That was a very bad thing. Or maybe it was good? She couldn't remember.

"Are you in pain?"

Candace shifted experimentally. Her ribs ached, but the pain felt distant and somewhat irrelevant. So she shook her head.

"You're still on a lot of medication."

"Cooool." Candace took another sip of water. "Do the others know?"

Yoandy nodded. "Lucy will be here soon."

"Lucy," Candace said. "Did she talk to the cops?" It had been very important; Candace could remember that, but not why.

"*Chula*, don't worry. Everything is okay now."

Somewhere to her left, Candace heard a knock. She turned to see Lucy standing beside the open door, leaning shyly against the doorjamb and smiling with a tenderness that she couldn't remember ever seeing on her friend's face.

"Jeez, I'm not a baby," Candace groaned. "But I hope you brought candy anyway."

Lucy approached, leaning in carefully to kiss Candace on the cheek. "Sugar, you've looked better."

"I don't know if y'all heard," Candace said, "but a reality TV star up'n stabbed me."

Lucy drew back and smiled. "Yeah, I heard that."

"Joke's on her," Candace said, and began to cough. "Takes more'n a knife in the chest to kill me."

There was an intake of breath from Lucy, and then a wry grin. "You are one lucky, skinny-ass white girl."

"Yeah, lucky . . . is what I am."

Yoandy's eyes caught Candace's. Evidently he didn't approve of the gallows humor. "Yoandy, honey? Something to eat? So hungry."

He rose to his feet, a little reluctant. "Maybe some soup? Or some rice noodles?"

"Yummy," Candace whispered, crooking her fingers into a wave.

When he'd left, she turned to Lucy. The calm facade

she'd tried to project in front of Yoandy dropped away, and she fell back into the pillow, eyes closing.

Lucy said nothing for a moment, but Candace could feel her friend's hand firmly on her own. "What happened?" Candace said. "Don't leave anything out."

"Kay stabbed you," Lucy said softly. "Then she cut her own throat. While she was bleeding to death, Yoandy went for help. They got to you in time to save you. She missed your heart, but she cut a vein in your chest, and it got bad."

"She went crazy," Candace croaked.

"She's had serious psychiatric problems since she was a kid," Lucy said. "But Dana kept it real quiet. She told me it was Kay that I saw, down by the pool, not Dana. Which I guess, means that *Kay* murdered Tyson Drew. I was always confused about that, because I remembered seeing a woman drowning him. But everything got mixed up. Kay was kind of a friend when I was a kid. I forgot that; I forgot that we used to hang out. If Kay did kill Tyson Drew, she did it while she was wearing Dana's clothes. And Dana covered for her."

Candace tried to nod. "For her sister."

"For her *daughter*," explained Lucy. "That's the other thing that came out. Kay wasn't Dana's sister—she was her kid. We're pretty certain that Drew knew and that he was blackmailing Dana."

"Her daughter!" The medication pump had just injected a fresh pulse of painkiller, and Candace's head was beginning to cloud. "Continue."

"Dana came after Grace and Paolo. She was watching my parent's house, waiting for a chance to get the nail polish, I guess, the one with her fingerprints. It turns out that the cops held back some forensic evidence. It was never connected to the murder, so it wasn't admitted. But they found a broken nail near the edge of the pool, and they never found out who it belonged to. I guess that once Dana knew I remembered about the nail polish, she had to get to it first. It was the only hard evidence that could connect her. The nail, the bottle of polish, and me."

"Did they beat her to it?"

Lucy seemed reluctant to go on. "Grace and Paolo, they're both okay," she said. "But Dana came after them with a gun. Dana's dead now—some cop took her out. Well, a gangster impersonating a cop."

Candace didn't want to talk any longer. She could hardly take it all in. It felt as though she'd downed four of Yoandy's mojitos in ten seconds, and the effect was gradually tipping her back into unconsciousness.

She was about to close her eyes when the room filled up. Paolo was there, and John-Michael, and Maya. And at her side, hugging her gently, was Grace. They were all around her, smiling down at her. Surrounded by her friends—her *family*—Candace felt her pulse throbbing, a pleasant state of calm.

"Hey, you," she said, smiling weakly at Grace. "I dreamed about you and me."

Affectionately, Grace squeezed her forearm. "Was Toto there, too?"

Candace tried to find the strength to hug her little sister. Somewhere in what Lucy had said, Candace remembered hearing Dana had threatened Grace with a gun. Dana Alexander, the person who should be in prison instead of Grace's father. But a stab of anxiety finally snapped her wide awake. "Gracie! Your dad! Did Lucy tell the cops? About Dana, did they . . . ?"

Grace shushed her. "Everything's okay, sweetie. My dad's lawyer called a little while ago. He's already lined up another appeal hearing, tomorrow. He's already struck a deal. They're going to overturn my dad's conviction."

A hopeful grin spread across Candace's face, and she let her eyes close. "Everyone's okay?"

A phone buzzed loudly. Candace tried to open her eyes again. "Who's that?"

Grace stroked her hair, tenderly. "Don't worry. It's just Lucy's phone. Everything's going to be absolutely fine."

GRACE

Lucy took out her phone. "Oh. It's not my mom—it's an email. From John-Michael." She looked around. "An email, that's weird. Why not just a text? Where'd that boy get to? I swear he was here just a minute ago."

Paolo clapped a hand to his jeans pocket. Grace felt something, too; her phone was vibrating.

"I got an email, too," Maya said. "Same email. From John-Michael."

One by one they took out their phones and stared at the screens.

When Grace read the first line, she bolted for the door. Lucy was right on her heels.

Grace flung the door wide and leapt into the corridor, frantically looking both ways. When she didn't see John-Michael, she started toward the elevator.

Lucy grabbed her hand and held her back. Her eyes were brimming with sorrow. "Grace, I think John-Michael has gone."

"Gone where?" Grace cried. "I didn't even notice him leave!"

Paolo stepped out of Candace's room. He reached for Grace, folding her up in his arms. "Don't," he said. "Come back inside. Candace is getting upset."

Grace felt herself go numb as they filed back into the room. Her eyes fell somewhat guiltily on Candace. Paolo was right—her sister looked pale and drawn, intensely vulnerable. That old Candace bravado was still there somewhere, but it would take a lot of healing to restore it to full intensity.

"Guys," Maya advised. "You need to read John-Michael's email."

Grace huddled closer to Paolo. "Read it out loud."

After Candace had nodded her approval, Maya started to read.

I don't cry easily. Where I'm headed, that's a good thing. Today, I gave myself a pass. The occasion called for it— leastways, that's how I saw the situation. You guys were the cause, just so you know—all of you.
I'm sorry that I didn't stick around to say good-bye. I wanted to stay with you, but when I saw you all there together, it was too much. Not too long ago, it would've felt like a moment I could be a part of. But now we're a band of outsiders, me most of all. Maya once told me that only a very strong person can live apart. If I leave, the rest of you might be able to return to the flock.

I kind of want to say "I'm disgusted with life." Another part
of me wants to see where this road leads. To keep going
until I'm running on fumes.

Living with you guys was the best thing that happened
to me since I was a little kid. I think you can still have all
that, I really believe it. We were more than the sum of our
parts, and anyhow, five is a stronger unit. You see five
everywhere in nature. You don't see a whole lot of six.
It's like in that song by Florence + The Machine—"you've
got the love I need to see me through." Take care of each
other, stay out of trouble, you know the drill. Next time
you hear from me, I'll be a long way from Venice Beach.
Salud, amor, y pesetas,
JM

Lucy began to cry. Grace went straight to her side and
hugged her. Before she knew it, Maya was sliding an arm
around Lucy, too, and Candace was reaching out, pulling
Grace to the bed.

Paolo was the last to join them. Lucy's sobs grew heavier
as grief tore through her. Grace felt her own cheeks damp
with tears, but when she looked at her sister, the feeling of
love and relief helped her hold despair at bay.

She looked over the bed at Paolo. He was struggling
not to cry.

"It's a message," Maya declared. "In code. John-Michael
is going to Costa Rica." She sounded resigned, accepting.

But Costa Rica wasn't even a little bit obvious, not to

Grace. "How'd you figure that?"

"A conversation we had the other day," Maya said. "John-Michael told me that if he ran, it'd be to Costa Rica. That's what made me think of the Mexican passport. Plus, the way he signs off, *Salud, amor, y pesetas*. It's a traditional Spanish toast. 'Health, love, and money.'"

"Also, 'we're a band of outsiders,'" Candace said faintly. "Remember, he made us do that dance, at the house? From the French movie? Maya, I can't believe you forgot that; you told us you saw that movie."

"Omigod, yes," Maya said, perking up. "*Band of Outsiders*! With the couple who run away to South America!"

"How is John-Michael ever gonna pass for Mexican?" Paolo said. "He's got blue eyes and skin like warm milk, and he speaks Spanish with an accent."

"Blue eyes aren't unheard of, but yeah, it might be an idea to change his appearance," Maya admitted. "I did mention it to him. The Spanish—well, he speaks the language at least. He can pick up the accent."

"Maya," Paolo said, shaking his head, "he's gonna look and sound like a norteamericano."

"You're *all* wrong," Lucy said. She broke away from both Grace and Maya and plucked a Kleenex from a box on Candace's nightstand. "John-Michael is going to turn himself in. He's going to *prison*. That's why he says that where he's going it's important not to cry easily." She wiped her damp eyes.

Everyone dismissed this idea, even Candace. Yet the

moment Lucy said the words, they resonated with Grace. No one knew John-Michael as well as Lucy. A life on the run would be too much like what he'd lived through in his year of being homeless.

"Nope—he's definitely heading for Costa Rica," Maya said. "He's got the Mexican birth certificate. He's going to call Pete Martens and ask the guy to hide him for a little while. Martens owes him—John-Michael saved his life in Napa, when those goons came looking for Lucy."

"Did John-Michael tell you all that?" Paolo asked.

Maya shook her head, but lost none of her certainty. "But he left without letting me set him up with a Bitcoin account. That's going to make things tricky. I'm guessing the cops will be looking at all our emails and his. Plus texts."

Paolo wanted them to send money to John-Michael. He was pretty adamant on the subject. He argued about it with Maya and Lucy. But the housemates were adamant, too. They didn't want Paolo to be solely responsible for the debt to Declan Kreutzer. That burden belonged to the whole group.

Grace was silent. Her eyes caught Paolo's; a shared moment. Long enough for Grace to see that they were thinking along the same lines.

After a few minutes, Grace stopped listening to their argument. She turned to Candace. There was an air of such fragility to her stepsister now, as though she were held together with gossamer and hope. She watched as Candace's fingers reached for the arrangement of sunflowers and birds-of-paradise, tracing the tips of firm yellow petals.

"Yoandy left them for me," Candace murmured. "Yellow and gold, like the necklace he gave me. For the patron saint of Cuba."

For a moment, Grace was seized by fierce protectiveness. *Take care of each other,* John-Michael had written. They hadn't before—not nearly enough. But he was right. That would change. Nothing else would.

They'd go back to their lives together. Maybe not in the same house as before—Grace wasn't sure that she could deal with the memories from the house in Venice. Somewhere else, though; someplace they'd be together and take care of each other and grow up together. In a place that faced the setting sun.

One day they'd welcome John-Michael back. He'd call to them, and they'd answer. They'd embrace him, and they'd sit together on a terrace somewhere, enjoying the warm air of a California evening. And all the intervening years, the lost years, would vanish like smoke.

ACKNOWLEDGMENTS

Wow, what a ride Emancipated has been! Back in 2013, fellow young adult and kids' author Michael Grant and I mused about what kind of intense, twisty, crime-y story I could tell about a collection of "typical" Californian teenagers. How many characters could we implicate and involve in the same murder mystery? Could we manage as many as four? How about five? Nah, we thought. We can manage it with six.

The flair and imagination of editors Elizabeth Law and Maria Barbo has been an enormous help and inspiration. Team Emancipated's assistant editor, Beth Dunfey, kept all the continuity on the straight and narrow for *Vindicated*–a crucial aspect of juggling six characters with secrets, not to mention a whole mess of crimes. Thanks also to Rebecca Schwarz and to the whole team at Katherine Tegen Books for cheerleading and marketing support.

Finally, I always like to thank my agent, Robert Kirby

of United Agents, London; my husband, David; my gorgeous daughter, Josie; and adorable son, Junior. God bless you all. Now, bring me a doughnut while I write my next book, please and thank you.

READ THEM ALL!

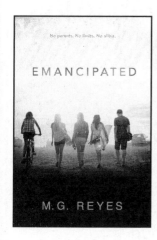

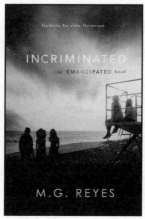

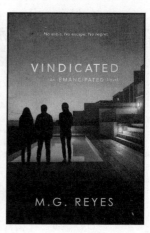

No limits. No alibis. No escape.

JOIN THE

Epic Reads
COMMUNITY

THE ULTIMATE YA DESTINATION

◄ **DISCOVER** ►
your next favorite read

◄ **MEET** ►
new authors to love

◄ **WIN** ►
free books

◄ **SHARE** ►
infographics, playlists, quizzes, and more

◄ **WATCH** ►
the latest videos